Praise for  T. C. I

"Nick and Nora are a winning team"
—Rebecca Hale, *New York Times* Bestselling author

"A fast-paced cozy mystery spiced with a dash of romance and topped with a big slice of 'cat-titude.'"
—Ali Brandon, *New York Times* Bestselling author

"Nick and Nora are the purr-fect sleuth duo!"
—Victoria Laurie, *New York Times* Bestselling author

"A page-turner with an endearing heroine."
—*Richmond Times Dispatch*

"Excellently plotted and executed—five paws and a tail up for this tale."
—*Open Book Society*

"Nick brims with street smarts and feline charisma, you'd think he was human . . . an exciting new series."
—Carole Nelson Douglas, *New York Times* notable author of the Midnight Louie mysteries

"I love this series and each new story quickly becomes my favorite. Cannot wait for the next!"
—*Escape With Dollycas Into a Good Book*

"I totally loved this lighthearted and engagingly entertaining whodunit featuring new amateur sleuth Nora Charles and Nick, her feline companion."
—*Dru's Cozy Report*

Books by T. C. LoTempio

Nick and Nora Mysteries

Meow If It's Murder
Claws for Alarm
Crime and Catnip
Hiss H for Homicide

Urban Tails Pet Shop Mysteries

The Time for Murder Is Meow
Killers of a Feather (coming soon!)

Cat Rescue Mysteries

Purr M for Murder
Death by a Whisker

The Time for Murder Is Meow

Is Meow

Urban Tails Pet Shop Mysteries

T. C. LoTempio

BEYOND THE PAGE
PUBLISHING

The Time for Murder Is Meow
T. C. LoTempio
The is a fully revised edition of a book originally published as *The Time for Murder Is Meow, Purr N' Bark Mystery #1*, copyright © 2019 by T. C. LoTempio.
Cover design and illustration by Dar Albert, Wicked Smart Designs

Beyond the Page Books
are published by
Beyond the Page Publishing
www.beyondthepagepub.com

ISBN: 978-1-954717-19-0

One

"Excuse me. Do you have any Tomkins Hairball Remedy?"

I glanced up from the pile of catnip balls I'd been sorting and smiled at the short gray-haired woman who stood uncertainly at my counter. She reminded me of my late aunt—iron gray hair done into a severe bun at the nape of her neck, a smooth, unlined face, and sharp blue eyes that peered at me over the rims of her tortoiseshell glasses.

I smiled at her. "I'm sorry, we're not open for business yet."

Her penciled brows drew together and the corners of her lips drooped down. "Oh? I saw the lights on, and the door wasn't locked."

"My bad. I forgot to lock it after me, I'm afraid." I pushed a stray curl out of my eyes. "I am planning on reopening the store, but I only came into town a few days ago. As for your question, I really don't know what we have. I was just taking an inventory, trying to determine what stock I need to order."

"Oh." She adjusted her glasses on her nose and peered at me more closely. "You're Tillie's niece." It wasn't a question.

"Yes." I wiped my hand on the side of my jeans and extended it to her. "Crishell McMillan."

"Grace Poole." She took my hand, shook it briefly, then released it and leaned against the counter. Her head cocked to one side. "You're the actress." Once again, not a question. Although the way Grace Poole said it, it sounded more like a death sentence.

"Right again," I said, "although I guess you could say I'm an ex-actress. I've retired."

Grace Poole stared at me. "Retired? But you're so young! You can't be more than twenty-five!"

"You're very kind. I'm thirty-eight." Unlike most actresses, I'd never been shy about revealing my real age. "Still young, true, only trust me, not by Hollywood standards."

Up until two months ago I was better known as Shell Marlowe, one of the stars of a popular cable TV show, *Spy Anyone*. My character, Hermione DuVal, had been a large part of my life for ten years, yet that role seemed a

1

lifetime ago. I'd gotten word the series had been canceled two days before receiving a telegram from my mother informing me of my Aunt Tillie's passing. Out of the two events, my aunt's passing was the more traumatic to me. When I'd found out she'd left me not only her Victorian mansion in Fox Hollow, Connecticut, with all its contents, but also a healthy assortment of stocks and bonds and the Urban Tails Pet Shop, I'd felt as if a huge weight had been lifted from my shoulders. I'd grown sick and tired of the phony Hollywood scene. I jumped at the chance to make a fresh start three thousand miles away.

Besides, I'd always harbored a secret desire to be a veterinarian. Managing a pet store seemed like the next best thing.

The woman looked so forlorn that I held up one finger. "Just a minute, Ms. Poole. I thought I saw something here before . . ." I ran my finger along the boxes that graced the shelf in back of me, grabbed one, and held it out to her. "It's not the Tomkins brand, but I have used this on my own cat. It's pretty good."

Grace Poole's eyes brightened as she snatched the box from my outstretched hand. "Jordan's. I've heard of it. This'll do." She started to reach inside her purse. "How much?"

I waved my hand. "Consider it a free sample. And I do hope you'll come back and visit once we're officially open for business."

"Oh, you can bet on that." Grace stuffed the box into the voluminous floral tote slung over one arm. "We've been hoping and praying that the business would continue. Fox Hollow needs their pet store. The others on the highway are so . . . impersonal." She paused. "Not to mention a pain in the you know where to get to. Do you have an opening date in mind?"

"There's a lot of straightening up I need to do first, but I'm hoping by the end of the month."

"Wonderful. I'll tell my friends. They were all worried too." She turned, paused, and looked at me over her shoulder. "Nice to meet you, Crishell."

"Call me Shell."

Grace tossed me a wave and bustled out the door. I uncrossed my legs and stood up with a groan. "Boy, not going to the gym every day sure takes a toll on your muscles," I observed.

"Ow-orrr!"

I glanced down and saw a sleek brown form wriggle out from underneath the counter. My coffee-colored seal point Siamese had been a birthday gift from my mother two years ago, after I'd hinted at adopting a shelter cat. "No daughter of mine is going to have a mutt animal," she'd hissed as she'd pressed the basket into my arms. Actually, the name on the cat's papers is Her Royal Highness Tao T'Sung, but there was no way I was going to call a cat Your Royal Highness, so instead I'd started searching the internet for suitable names. The problem was solved the next morning when I found her curled up in my liquor cabinet, her paws wrapped around a bottle of Kahlua, my favorite liqueur.

I reached down and gave Kahlua a scratch behind her ear. She jumped up on the counter and licked my hand with her rough tongue. I picked her up and cuddled her against my chest. "What do you think, Kahlua?" I whispered. "We've got our work cut out for us, but I can just visualize the finished product. We'll make Aunt Tillie proud yet."

Kahlua head-butted my chin. "Merow."

I chuckled. "I'm glad you agree."

My pants pocket started to vibrate. I set Kahlua back on the floor and fished out my iPhone. I took a look at the Caller ID and stifled a groan. I was so tempted to let it go to voicemail, but he'd only keep calling. This was his fiftieth call in two days. I squared my shoulders and hit the Answer button. "Yes, Max?"

"Oh my God. Did I finally get you and not a recording? I thought you'd have come to your senses by now. What's gotten into you? Why have you thrown away a promising career to tend to the needs of cats and dogs? Why? Tell me why!"

My agent Max Molenaro's nasally whine reminded me just why I'd been avoiding taking his calls. I'd started to forget just how pitchy his voice could get when he didn't get his way. "I guess it all depends on your definition of a promising career," I said.

"Your aunt didn't say you had to run that business personally, did she?" Max snapped. "I'm sure you could find someone capable to run it, and you could fly in once or twice a month to check up on things. I know you, Shell. You're used to bustle and bright lights. Small-town living isn't for you."

I exhaled a long breath. "This has nothing to do with small-town living, as you put it, does it, Max? This is about the *Spy Anyone* cable reboot, isn't it?"

The silence stretched on for so long that I thought we'd somehow gotten disconnected (which wouldn't have bothered me in the least, by the way) and then Max spoke up. "The cable reboot could be your door, Shell, not that pet store. Aw, Shell, you weren't cut out to sell dog food and kitty litter. You were born to act."

I stifled a laugh. "I think you have me confused with my mother." My mother, Clarissa McMillan, was a classically trained actress who'd enjoyed a long career on the Broadway stage. She'd always had opinions about my career and had never approved of my role choices. She'd always had something derogatory to say about the cable show, calling it "a cheap James Bond ripoff." I had no doubt she'd be even less thrilled about my selling dog food and kitty litter, which was one reason why I hadn't told her about my decision yet. "No doubt she would agree with you, but my answer is still the same. No."

A few more seconds of silence and then Max blurted out, "Tell me the truth, Shell. Is Gary the reason you don't want to do the new series? Because if it is, we . . . we can do something about him."

I switched the phone to my other ear. "Do something about him? That sounds ominous." Not that I hadn't been tempted to do away with Gary Presser many times myself. He could be a sweetheart, but he could also be a royal pain in the you know where. "Relax. My decision has nothing to do with Gary, Max. I just want to do something different with my life. I want to be my own boss for a change."

"I can understand that. But does it have to be running a pet store?"

"The people of Fox Hollow have always been big animal lovers. They cherish their pets, and my aunt knew that. Max, you should see this place! It's got every type of pet need one could ever imagine!" As I spoke, my eyes roamed over the store's vast shelves, stocked to the brim with toys for cats and dogs, beds, litter pails, and the like. My aunt hadn't catered solely to cats or dogs, either. There was a section for parakeets and parrots, some fish tanks, and cages where hamsters, guinea pigs, and even rats had been kept. They were all empty right now, but I was hopeful to have them refilled within the next few weeks. I'd also planned to contact several local shelters to see if we could arrange to hold Adopt A Pet Saturdays once a month. "You know I've always loved animals. Besides becoming a veterinarian, this is the next best thing." I snapped my fingers. "Which reminds me: I have to put an ad in the paper for an assistant. Know anyone in Connecticut who'd be interested in giving dogs a bath and clipping cats' claws?"

"Not off the top of my head," he said dryly. He hesitated briefly and then said, "Would this life-altering decision of yours have anything to do with Patrick?"

My throat constricted and my heart skipped a beat at the mention of my former director slash fiancé. I swallowed over the lump and replied, "I won't deny that putting distance between me and Patrick Hanratty held a certain amount of appeal, but it wasn't the only deciding factor."

I could hear Max snicker, although he tried to hide it. "I'll bet you my next commission you'll be on a plane to LA within a month."

I laughed. "I hate to take your money, Max. You work so hard for it."

"So your mind is made up? There's nothing I can do to change it?"

"Nope."

Another long sigh. "Well, then, I wish you luck, Shell, although . . . I've got to warn you, Gary probably won't be thrilled by this news."

My nose wrinkled. I could well imagine my former costar's reaction, which was one of the reasons I hadn't told him I was moving either. Don't get me wrong, Gary and I had always gotten along. He'd been a good friend over the years, and a confidant when my relationship with Patrick started to blow up. But he also has a very intense personality and an ego the size of Texas, which can get a bit crazy at times. And right now, crazy was the last thing I needed. Aloud I said, "Gary will be fine. He's like a cat. He always lands on his feet. Trust me, he'll be thrilled. Now he can convince the new producers to hire a young chippie as his new sidekick."

"It's not that easy." He hesitated and then said, "I might as well tell you the truth. You were the one the producers really wanted. Without you, I doubt there'll be much interest in the new series. But that's not your problem. Take care, Shell—oh, wait! Are guest roles totally off the table?"

Click.

• • •

After I hung up with Max I flopped down in the worn chair behind the register and leaned back, my hands laced behind my neck. Max's words bothered me more than I cared to admit, and a twinge of guilt arrowed through me at the thought I might possibly cost Gary this job. Kahlua hopped up on my lap and swatted my chin with her paw. "You're right, Kahlua," I said. "Max might have been exaggerating, hoping to play on my sympathy. Gary's a big boy and a good actor. He might balk a bit at first, but he'll understand . . . eventually. He'll push through no matter what the role."

I needed to think about what was best for me for a change. As Aunt Tillie used to say, "If you don't put yourself first, it's a sure bet no one else will." Well, it was high time I did that. I'd put everyone else's needs above mine, far too often, most recently with disastrous results. I glanced at my hand—the empty third finger of my left hand, specifically—and a small sigh escaped my lips.

Everything happens for a reason.

A mental picture of Patrick rose in my mind's eye, and I resolutely pushed it away. I'd been so certain he was the one. I'd spend hours in my trailer between scenes, fantasizing about the perfect life we'd have together and then, in one afternoon, it had all come crashing down. I'd flung my four-carat diamond ring at Patrick and the script girl he was in bed with, stormed out of the apartment, and never looked back. A month later the show was canceled, and three weeks after that I was on a plane to Fox Hollow for a funeral. And now here I sat, sorting through boxes of catnip balls and doggie chew toys. Go figure.

The bell above the shop door tinkled, jostling me out of my reverie and reminding me once again I'd forgotten to lock the door. "I'm sorry, we're not open for business yet," I began and then stopped short.

Three people stood grouped in the doorway, two women and a man. One woman was short and stout. She had flame-colored hair (think Lucille Ball, only *redder*) teased up off her head and anchored with what had to be at least a pound of hairspray. She wore an aqua and orange flowered caftan a size too small, which served to accentuate her generous frame instead of hiding it. Her age was hard to judge, but I placed her as approximately ten years older than myself, late forties to mid-fifties.

The man was around the same age. He had a brown beard shot with streaks of gray, and kind eyes behind large tortoiseshell glasses. His jeans were neat and pressed, and held up by multicolored suspenders with a thread of glitter running through them.

The other girl was a good bit younger than either of her companions. I placed her in her late twenties, early thirties tops. She had long, luxurious dark brown hair, almost black, that flowed across her shoulders like a waterfall. I couldn't see her eyes behind the massive Jackie O sunglasses she wore, but I was betting they were the same color as the hair. Her slender frame was accentuated by skintight capri jeans and tank top. Toenails painted a bright blue peeped out from flip-flops of the same color. The girl carried a massive basket wrapped in yellow cellophane.

"Welcome to Fox Hollow," they chorused, almost as if they'd either rehearsed it or else done it a million times before. It was hard to tell which. "We know you're not open yet," the redhead added. "But we saw the light on, so we figured maybe this was as good a time as any." She held out her hand. "Rita Sakowski. I run the coffee shop up the block, Sweet Perks."

"Oh, yes." I gave an enthusiastic nod. "I did notice your shop. I'm rather a coffee nut. Sorry I haven't had time to stop in yet, but I've been busy."

"Oh, we know," Rita gushed. "You're Crishell Marlowe, the actress, Tillie's niece. I've always loved that name. It's so unusual. How did you think of it, or did some Hollywood bigwig do it for you?"

"Nope. If anyone's to blame, it's my parents." I took the hand she shoved in front of me and let her pump it up and down. "They couldn't decide between Shelley and Christine, so they invented Crishell. It's kind of a mouthful for most people, though, so I go by my nickname, Shell." I paused. "I should also mention I'm using my real last name now, McMillan."

"Oh." Rita dropped my hand abruptly. Her smile faltered just a bit and then it was back in place. "Well, I have to tell you everyone in Fox Hollow is just thrilled you've decided to keep Tillie's legacy alive."

I smiled back. "It's my pleasure." I waved a hand around the store. "I've been taking inventory. I wanted to open next week, but I doubt I'll be ready much before the end of the month. As you can see, there's still a lot of work to be done. I have to restock a lot of items, and, of course, get some pets in here."

Rita nodded. "Of course. Tillie did let things slack off a bit those last few months. I guess we should have been quicker to take that as a sign something was wrong. Your aunt never slacked off. Never."

We were all silent for a few seconds, and then the man reached out and took my hand. "Well, I'm pleased to meet you, Shell McMillan. I'm Ron

Webb. Webb's Florists. My store is right next door to Rita's." He grinned. "Sure comes in handy during the slow hours when I need a cup of java or a fresh-baked scone to pick me up."

The brunette reached up to brush a strand of hair from her glasses. I noted the blue polish on her fingernails had added glitter. "And I'm Olivia Niven," she said. "My claim to fame is running the dance academy on Main Street." She wrinkled her nose at me and looked pointedly at my feet. "Do you dance, Shell?"

"Not very well. I turned down *Dancing on Air* because I have two left feet. My costar, Gary Presser, was on last season though. He came in second."

"I know. I voted for him. He got robbed." Olivia looked me up and down. "I bet I could make a passable dancer out of you." She laughed and flicked her hand dismissively. "If I can train the Boswell twins to win last year's annual competition, I can train anyone."

"That's true." Rita's red hair swayed to and fro as she nodded. "Talk about left feet, those girls had 'em, and now, well, you should see them foxtrot."

Olivia shot me a mischievous grin. "Come by the studio. My girls will be thrilled to meet you. The boys even more so. They were all big *Spy Anyone* fans." She shifted the basket to her other hand and whipped off her sunglasses, and I saw her eyes were indeed the same color as her hair, maybe even a shade darker. "So." She reached out to tap the top of the basket. "We just came over to give you this small token to welcome you to the shop community, and to offer any help you might need."

Rita gave Olivia a small nudge, and the younger woman held out the basket to me. Through the cellophane I saw cookies, cakes, an assortment of gourmet teas and coffees, and a small plant.

"Some treats Rita, Ron, and I put together," Olivia said with a sidelong glance at her companions. "To be honest, it was mostly Rita. Enjoy."

"Thanks." I had to grip the basket hard. It was really loaded down. "This was very nice of you."

Rita waved her hand carelessly. "Oh, don't mention it, sweetie. We all loved your aunt, and this store is one of the most popular in Fox Hollow. When the tour buses come through, they always make a stop here. Nothing people like better than to take a little souvenir home to their pets. Oh, and you might want to give Kathleen Power a call. She knits the most darling doggie and kitty sweaters and booties. Your aunt used to sell them for her all the time, on consignment."

"Thanks, I'll do that." I smiled. "I hope I can live up to my aunt's reputation."

"I'm sure you will, dear." Rita hesitated and then added, "I have to say, we were all surprised when we heard that you would be moving here and taking over the store."

"Oh, don't be so coy, Rita," Olivia cut in. She turned to me. "We were shocked. After all, Fox Hollow's no Hollywood."

I nodded. "Thank God for that."

Now that her arms were free, Olivia crossed them over her well-endowed chest. "So, you're really planning on staying and making a go of this? Or is this just a pit stop before your next series?"

It seemed Olivia wasn't the type to pull any punches. Personally, I found that refreshing after living in the phony Hollywood community for so long. "I assure you, I'm here to stay. I've retired from show business."

Olivia's perfectly arched eyebrow skyrocketed. "Retired? Really? I would think that would be hard. Isn't it in your blood? I mean, your mother's an actress too, right?"

I shot her a wry smile. "If that's true, then I want a transfusion."

"I was sad to hear about your series," Rita cut in. "I always watched *Spy Anyone*. It was one of my favorite shows."

"Mine too," said Ron, and Olivia nodded.

"I watched it for your costar," Olivia said with a shrug. "I hope he's not retiring from show business too."

"Gary? I doubt it. He's too much of a ham."

Olivia leaned one arm on the counter. "Frankly, I'm disappointed. I thought your moving here had something to do with that breakup of yours, you know with that director—*ow!*" She rubbed at her side and glared at Rita.

"No sense in rehashing things I'm sure Shell must be sick of hearing, right?" Rita said smoothly.

"Oh, for pity's sakes, the woman lived in Hollywood, the gossip capital of the world. She's used to it, aren't you, Shell?" Olivia demanded.

"Now now, Olivia, don't put her on the spot," chided Ron. "She might not want to talk about it."

"Oh, don't be silly. Shell's a public figure. Her life's been an open book for years," snapped Olivia. "Besides, I'm curious about this retirement. What made you decide to give up the bright lights to follow in your aunt's footsteps?"

"Those bright lights aren't all they're cracked up to be," I said. "When you're on a hit show, your life isn't your own. As for taking over Aunt Tillie's business, well, I've always loved animals. I think if I hadn't been pushed into going into acting, I probably would have gone for a career in veterinary medicine. And I feel I owe it to my aunt. She was always there for me when I was growing up. One of my biggest regrets is not having had much contact with her before she passed. No one in our family even knew she was ill."

Rita made a sympathetic noise. "Don't beat yourself up over that, dear. No one did. Tillie could be quite closemouthed when it came to certain things, and her health was one of them. I doubted she'd have told you anything anyway, even if you talked twice a week. Tillie never liked folks worrying or fussing over her."

"But she did enjoy fussing over others," Olivia put in. "Take her roommate, for example."

My head swiveled in Olivia's direction and I let out an astonished gasp. "Roommate? I've been staying at the house all by myself since the funeral. And my aunt's lawyer didn't mention anything about her having a roommate." It was true I hadn't really searched Tillie's decidedly large house, but all the things there seemed to be hers. Maybe this roommate only used one room, like a renter?

"No?" Olivia shrugged. "Maybe it slipped his mind."

"Kind of an important detail to slip up on, don't you think?" I placed my hands on my hips. "Are you sure about this? I mean, I find it a bit hard to believe my aunt would take in a boarder. She didn't need the money, and as you've already pointed out, she valued her privacy."

Olivia chuckled. "That's because you never saw the two of them together. He doted on your aunt, and she was a sucker for him."

He. A male boarder. A sudden thought occurred to me. "Were my aunt and this boarder involved?"

"Oh, absolutely!" Olivia nodded. "There was nothing Tillie wouldn't do for him. He had her wrapped around his little finger. Or maybe I should say paw."

"Paw?"

Eyes twinkling, Olivia reached toward the basket I'd set on the counter, undid the cellophane, and crinkled some of it between her fingers. "That should bring him running. See! There he is now."

I turned and caught a blur of white out of the corner of my eye. The next instant, the blur streaked past me and with one graceful leap landed on all fours right in the center of the counter.

"Oh my God," I cried. "What is that?"

"Merow," said the blur. "Owww."

The others started to laugh. "That," choked out Olivia, "is the store mascot and your aunt's roomie. Shell, meet Purrday."

Two

For a second I was speechless. The cat and I just stared at each other, which was a little off-putting, because I saw at once he only had one eye: one large, brilliant blue one that seemed to pierce right through me. He had the typical flat nose and face one associates with a Persian cat; a thick, luxurious coat of shiny, snow white hair; plus plenty of good old-fashioned cattitude. He pranced regally across the table and arranged himself right next to the basket, tail wrapped around his forepaws, and studied me with what I imagined my aunt would have referred to as catly disdain.

"Purrday?" I said at last. "That's an odd name."

"It was your aunt's homage to her very favorite Cary Grant movie," said Rita.

I frowned, and then my expression cleared. "Friday. Purrday. Got it." I looked at all of them. "You said he was the store mascot?"

"Yes," Olivia said, inclining her head slightly. "Tillie always had him here in the store. Never saw a mouse anywhere around, either."

"Oh." I let out a relieved sigh. "Then he wasn't her house cat?"

Olivia placed her hands on her hips and wiggled her eyebrows at me. "What part of roommate didn't you get? Of course she had him in her house. Purrday was her pet."

"He hasn't been back to the house, though, since she passed," Rita cut in. "We all have been taking turns looking after him, feeding him. We figured he'd be lonely in that big rambling house, and no one knew how long you'd be here or if you even liked cats. He has everything he needs in the store. Besides, he's more useful here right now, keeping the mice at bay."

At the word *mice*, Purrday lifted his head. "Ffft," he said.

They all laughed. "He takes his job seriously," said Ron. "Not that there are many mice about, but one never knows," he added quickly.

Rita reached out and stroked the cat's back. He let out a loud rumble. "Don't let his appearance fool you. He might look like he's been through the war, but he's a pedigreed Persian. Got papers and everything."

A Persian named Purrday? Oy. I pushed a hand through my hair. I didn't even want to think how my pedigreed Siamese would react to the news that she now had a brother. Come to think of it, where was my Siamese? Either in hiding or planning a rear flank attack on the newcomer, most likely.

"What's wrong?" Olivia's sharp voice intruded on my thoughts. "Why are you looking around? Did you lose something?"

Only my mind. "I'm just wondering how all this came about. Is Purrday a rescue cat?"

"In a way," chuckled Rita. "You could say he rescued old women from being lonely."

Olivia reached toward the cat and held out her hand. Purrday leaned toward her, sniffed her fingers, then gave them a quick lick and sat back. "He belonged to Mrs. Trimble. When she died suddenly last year, no one in her family wanted him. They were going to bring him to a shelter over in Newton."

"Unfortunately, that shelter is a kill shelter, which means if the cat wasn't adopted within a certain amount of time, he'd be put to sleep. Tillie just wouldn't hear of that, so she took him in and renamed him," Rita finished with a flourish.

I regarded the cat dubiously. He was pretty much ignoring me, his full attention now devoted to washing his long bristling tail. "Wouldn't it have been simpler to just find a no-kill shelter?"

"Probably," Olivia said cheerily, "but as we said, your aunt was a sucker for Purrday. She always used to bring him treats when she visited Mrs. Trimble."

"Yep," Ron said with a laugh. "She loved him even back when his name was Creampuff."

"Creampuff, eh?" I looked at the cat, who let out a soft *grr*. I chuckled. "I think I can guess how he lost the eye."

"I don't know for sure, but rumor has it he got into it with an old tom a few years ago," Olivia said. "Believe it or not, the tom got the worst of it. Purrday might look like that pampered Persian on those cat food commercials, but deep down he's a fighter at heart."

Purrday had apparently decided his tail was well groomed enough, and he stretched out on the counter, his eye fixed firmly on me. "He looks like he's studying me," I said.

"He probably is. He's a very discerning cat." Olivia smiled at me. "Since you're staying for good, you're going to keep him, right?"

"I-I don't know." I hesitated and then blurted, "I already have a cat."

"Oh." The three of them looked at each other and then Olivia said brightly, "Well, that shouldn't be a problem. Purrday gets along with other cats. Usually."

"Your aunt loved that cat like he was a human," Rita put in. "I'm sure she would want you to take care of him."

Purrday rose from his supine position, stretched, then ambled over and gave my elbow a soft butt with his head. When I showed no reaction, he butted me again, but gentler this time, almost like a caress. He jumped down from the counter and started winding around my ankles, around and around, making slow figure eights.

"See." Olivia's tone held a note of triumph. "He likes you. And he's lonely now. He misses your aunt."

I worried my bottom lip; then I sank into a crouching position and reached out my hand. Slowly, tentatively, I let my fingers glide over his silky white fur. I trailed them down his back and then rubbed the top of his head. He angled his face so that my fingers slid under his chin.

"Like that, do you?" I asked.

His response was a deep, rumbling purr.

I laughed. "Wow, that's loud! He sounds like a B-52 coming in for a landing. I totally get the name." I looked at each of them in turn. "Are you sure one of you wouldn't like to keep him?" I asked.

Three heads shook emphatically in unison. "I love cats," Rita said quickly, "but my husband is very allergic. I would have taken Purrday in a heartbeat if not for that."

Ron held up both hands. "My two Great Danes would no doubt find Purrday fun, but I doubt the feeling would be mutual."

I looked at Olivia as if to say *And what's your excuse?* I noticed she studiously avoided my gaze as she shrugged and answered, "I have a parrot."

I'll bet.

Sensing my attention to him was waning, Purrday butted my hand with his head. I scratched his chin with one hand while I ran my other down his long back. The purr came from deep within him. It was oddly . . . comforting.

He raised his head and fixed me with his piercing one-eyed stare. I lifted my hands away and rose.

The purring abruptly stopped. Purrday struggled to a sitting position and sat looking at me, tail wrapped around his forepaws. His look plainly said, *Oh, come on, Missy. What have you got to lose? And I've been around here longer than you have, anyway.*

"Okay," I said. "It's up to Kahlua."

"Huh?" Olivia said. "Whether or not you keep Purrday is up to a liqueur?"

"No, to my Siamese." I started to walk around the room. "Kahlua, where are you? There's someone I want you to meet."

The cat in question emerged slowly from behind a large box in the far corner of the store. Very slowly, Kahlua made her way toward us. She stopped a few feet away and her big blue eyes widened as she caught sight of Purrday. She moved forward, putting one paw in front of the other, until she was about a foot away from him. Then she peeled back her lips and let out the loudest hiss I'd ever heard.

"Oh, isn't that sweet," cried Rita.

I whirled on her. "Sweet? That sounded terrible. Kahlua doesn't like him."

Olivia shook her head. "Cats are the most territorial creatures around. Of course they won't like each other at the beginning. But they'll get used to each other. And Tillie's house is huge. The two of them could go for days, even weeks, without running into each other."

The part about Tillie's house being huge was true. At one point I'd even toyed with the idea of turning it into a bed-and-breakfast, but getting rid of all the collectibles my aunt had scattered around the mansion in order to do that would have been an insurmountable task. I chewed at my bottom lip. "Kahlua, we really have no choice. Purrday was Aunt Tillie's baby, just like you are mine."

Kahlua shot me a look that plainly said, *Well, I don't have to like it now, do I?* She lay down, head on paws, her eyes fixed on the Persian.

Purrday, for his part, seemed unfazed by the Siamese's reaction to him. He rose, stretched, and inched toward her, sniffing. When he got within a few inches, Kahlua raised her paw and smacked him straight across the nose. Purrday looked dazed for a minute, then turned, tail swishing, and hopped back up on the counter.

"See that," Rita cried triumphantly. "They'll get along just fine."

I shot both cats a dubious look. "We'll see," I said at last. "I guess I owe it to Aunt Tillie to try, anyway."

"See, that's the spirit." Olivia nodded approvingly. "Trust me, the three

15

of you will be fast friends in no time."

Kahlua removed herself to a far corner of the store and Purrday lifted his head and let out a soft meow. "He might be hungry," ventured Rita. "We've been keeping food and water for him in the back. Come, I'll show you."

I followed Rita into the back storage area. I put the overhead light on, and it was then I noticed the cutout in the back door. A cat door, no doubt. Rita saw me eyeing it and grinned. "Your aunt did that so Purrday could wander out. He likes to sun himself on the back stoop and watch the birds in that old elm tree."

I nodded. It seemed as if Purrday was pretty much at home in the store. Worst-case scenario, I could always leave him here. If my aunt's ghost didn't haunt me.

Rita dug out a bag of dry cat food and filled the white ceramic bowl, then pulled out a jug of water and topped off the blue bowl that sat beside it. A minute later Purrday's contented crunching was all we heard. We left the cat to chow down and returned to the main showroom.

"So have you decided what you're going to do with all of your aunt's collections?" Olivia asked. "Tillie had enough collectibles to fill a dozen museums. Surely you're not planning on keeping all of them."

"Truthfully? I haven't decided yet. I'll need to go through them, but it will take a while. Take her doll collection, for instance. I imagine there are quite a few very valuable ones that an avid collector would love to have. I just hate the thought of splitting everything up."

"True, especially when you think of all the time and energy that went into collecting them," agreed Rita. "Does she still have that room on the third floor with all her movie memorabilia?"

"Oh, yes." I nodded. "I was in there the other day. That one life-sized cutout of Cary Grant looked so real I started talking to it."

"Oh, I know the one. I think it's from *His Girl Friday*," squealed Rita. "Your aunt had a lot of memorabilia from that movie alone."

"It was her favorite. She always said she could identify with the Rosalind Russell character," I agreed. "She's got lobby cards from that movie signed by Grant. Those are—were—the pride and joy of her collection."

"The Ridgefield Playhouse is having a Cary Grant retrospective in a few weeks," Ron put in. "If I'm not mistaken, *His Girl Friday* is the centerpiece movie."

"I know," I said. "As a matter of fact, I'm supposed to meet with a representative from the Fox Hollow Museum about putting Aunt Tillie's collection on display there to coincide with that event. Mazie Madison assured me—goodness, is something wrong?"

The moment I'd mentioned Mazie Madison's name, the smiles had disappeared from all three faces, replaced by furrowed brows. Olivia cleared her throat. "What makes you think something's wrong?"

"The three of you look like you all just bit into sour lemons," I answered. "Is there something about this Mazie Madison I should know?"

They all exchanged a quick glance, and then Rita said, "Why, nothing, dear. Mazie is a lovely woman."

"Yes," Olivia added pointedly, "she can be."

There was another few moments of uncomfortable silence, during which the three of them exchanged covert glances. I spread my hands across the countertop and leaned forward. "I'm pretty good at reading people, and right now I can tell you all are keeping something from me, so I'll ask again: Is there something about Mazie Madison I should know?"

"Oh, no," Ron and Rita both chorused. "She's a dear," Rita added. "Very easygoing."

"Too easygoing," sniffed Olivia. "Those vultures take advantage of her. She's like a coiled spring. You mark my words, one day she'll unwind."

I looked from one to the other. "What vultures are you talking about?"

Rita let out a long-drawn-out sigh. "The museum board," she said. "They have the final say on all the big decisions."

I nodded. "Yes, she did mention having to speak with the board in the message she left me. She didn't indicate it would be a problem."

"Really?" Rita shrugged. "Well, then let us know when to bring over the champagne to celebrate."

They all headed for the door and I followed. "Thank you all for coming, and for the lovely basket," I said. "I'll let you all know once I decide on a definite date for the reopening."

"Good!" Rita clapped her hands. "I'll be glad to supply the treats and coffee, free of charge."

"And I'll be glad to donate a floral arrangement," Ron said with a wink. "I can't be outdone by Rita, here."

"I can get my girls to give a little show, if you want," Olivia offered.

"That would be wonderful. Maybe something from *Singin' in the Rain?* That movie had such wonderful numbers."

Olivia grimaced. "With my troupe, *Flashdance* or *Footloose* are probably more logical choices. Anyway, don't hesitate if you need any help with anything. Dissecting your new neighbors, or town gossip." She winked and took my hand. I felt something small and hard press into my palm.

Olivia hurried after the others, and I closed—and this time made sure to lock—the door. I looked at what Olivia had pressed into my palm: a pink and gray business card with tap shoes in one corner, ballet slippers in the other. *Niven School of Dance, 86 Banta Place, Fox Hollow 555-8675.* On the reverse was another phone number in pen, which I assumed was Olivia's cell. I slid it into the pocket of my jeans, and as I did so, Purrday leapt up on the counter and stretched his kingly body out, watching me.

"So, Purrday," I said, "I have the feeling they were holding something back from me. What do you think?"

Purrday blinked his good eye twice, then rolled over on his side. From the far corner I heard a loud yowl. I walked over and found Kahlua curled up in a tight ball behind a box of litter mats. I picked up the Siamese and cuddled her to my chest.

"You know that you are my baby," I whispered. "But Purrday here has suffered a loss. He's lost Aunt Tillie, the same as I have. Let's cut him a break, shall we?"

Kahlua looked at me, then over at Purrday. Her lips peeled back in a sharp hiss and she wriggled free of my grasp, dropped to the floor, and scurried underneath the counter.

I sighed. So much for cat camaraderie. This wasn't going to be easy. Then again, what in life was? I whipped out my cell, tapped it against my chin. "Maybe I should give Mazie Madison a call?"

Purrday lifted his head and gave a sharp meow. From beneath the far counter, I heard another faint meow. I laughed. "Okay then. But first, let's go home. If I'm ever to reopen this store, I need to get my stuff unpacked."

Purrday let out a rumble of assent and hopped down from the counter. Kahlua crawled out from her hiding place and minced over to where I stood hunched behind the register. She planted herself right at my feet and glared at the other cat. I shook my head and rummaged through the drawers for a piece of paper. I found one and a black magic marker. I wrote out a sign,

Reopening Soon, tacked it on the front door, and then drove my convertible back the short distance to Aunt Tillie's house, my house now. I expected a bit more of a struggle from my feline companions, but to my surprise Kahlua curled up in the passenger seat and dozed and Purrday did likewise, stretched full-length across the backseat. Once we went inside, Kahlua headed straight for her food bowl in the kitchen while Purrday immediately started sniffing all the boxes that lined the hallway and parlor.

"I know, I know, it's a mess. But trust me, it won't take long to put everything to rights. After all, my stuff only got here four days ago."

Purrday gave me a look that said he clearly didn't believe me. I, however, knew better. After taking one look around Aunt Tillie's house, I'd decided against moving my furniture. It had been secondhand anyway, and my aunt's antique sets were in far superior shape.

Purrday rubbed against my ankles. I figured he might be thirsty, so I went into the kitchen and took a small bowl out of one of the cupboards, filled it with water, and after a moment's hesitation set it down on the opposite side of the kitchen from where Kahlua's bowl resided. If Purrday had bowls already set up in the house, I'd yet to see them. I left the cats happily slurping, shrugged out of my light jacket, and headed up to the room I'd already branded as my office. My aunt had used it for a second-floor den, and it was cozy, with its floor-to-ceiling bookshelves, a large picture window, and another built-in fireplace. An antique bureau desk was right in front of the picture window, and one of the movers had been kind enough to set up my computer on it. I hurried over, started it up, and found the contact info for Mazie Madison. I dialed the number, but it went straight into voicemail. I left a message and then, figuring I'd done just about all I could do, decided that unpacking more boxes would take my mind off things.

For the next two hours I busied myself unpacking the few belongings I'd brought with me from LA. The first item to be unpacked was a large twelve-by-fourteen framed poster depicting myself and Gary Presser, standing back to back holding guns. The caption above us read *Who Says Spying is a Lonely Profession?* Right below our figures in bright red letters was the show's title, *Spy Anyone*. And underneath that our names, followed by *Tuesdays, WPIX, 8:00*. I looked at it, then turned it facedown and slid it underneath the couch. I'd figure out where to hang it later—if I hung it at all. That part of my life was over and done with.

19

The last box held my own book collection. I didn't have many books, but I loved them, most of them having been birthday gifts from my aunt through the years. I set the entire original Nancy Drew hardback series proudly on the top shelf. My first editions of *And Then There Were None* and *Murder on the Orient Express* went on the second, along with leather-bound editions of *Gone with the Wind* and *Little Women*. I had a few Ian Fleming novels, most sent to me by fans (obviously because I played a spy on TV, they thought I was a fan of the genre). The complete set of Perry Mason novels followed, along with a complete set of J. D. Robb novels. I'd just slid the most recent one into place when the doorbell rang. I hurried down the stairs, pausing for a moment to shoot Purrday a look as he lounged full-length across the bottom stair step.

"We're certainly busy today," I murmured. "What do you think? More people with welcome baskets? More people wanting to know how I could have the audacity to ditch Hollywood for Fox Hollow? Or curious as to why an ex-actress wants to run a pet shop?"

He folded his paws, rested his head on them, and closed his eye.

I chuckled. "You're right, Purrday. It's none of their business, and I shall tell them that. Tactfully, of course."

I flung open the door, startling the woman who stood on my stoop, hand poised over the doorbell. She wore a simple tailored shirtdress, the lines of which accentuated her trim figure. The dress's color matched her eyes, a vivid shade of blue that practically screamed *tinted contacts*. Her hair was cut short and framed her heart-shaped face in gentle waves, although I suspected its soft, ash-blonde color was courtesy of Lady Clairol. I put her age at somewhere in the mid-fifties, but she could have been either older or younger. "Crishell McMillan?" Her voice was soft, well-modulated. "I'm Mazie Madison."

"Ms. Madison, how nice. Did you get my message?"

She looked puzzled. "You left me a message? I'm sorry, I've been having problems with my phone."

"It's all right. You're here now." I swung the door wide. "Won't you please come in?"

She hesitated, then gave her head a brisk shake. "No. I'll just say what I came to say. The board voted on displaying your aunt's collection of Cary Grant posters last night."

"Last night?" I frowned. "I thought you said it wouldn't be voted on until their regular meeting next week?"

Mazie twisted her hands nervously in front of her. "They called a special meeting to discuss it. The vote was three to four."

"Oh. Well, I was planning on giving you some photographs of the collection to show the board, but since they've already voted in favor, I guess that won't be necessary," I said.

Mazie Madison let out a deep breath. "I'm sorry, dear, I should have been more clear. The vote was three to four *against*. We won't be displaying your aunt's collection. I'm sorry."

Three

"I don't understand," I said. I pushed a stray curl out of my eyes with the heel of my hand. "When we spoke last week, you seemed very positive about everything. What changed?"

"That's hard to say." Mazie shifted her weight from one foot to the other. "The majority just didn't feel the exhibit would be beneficial to the museum."

"That's ridiculous," I sputtered. "My aunt has one of the best and most extensive Cary Grant poster collections around! Besides being the perfect complement to the retrospective, I'm sure it would attract lots of people to your museum." I cocked my head at her. "You did mention that it was Matilda Washburn's collection, right? And that several of the posters were actually signed by Cary Grant?"

Mazie's eyes darted nervously around. "I really can't stay," she murmured. "I just felt that you deserved to hear the news in person, from me, rather than a phone call or a letter." She gripped my hand, squeezed it hard. "Please, dear. If it makes you feel any better, I'm as disappointed as you are. I was looking forward to working with you and displaying your aunt's collection. And now I really must go." She turned and started to walk down the steps.

"Perhaps I should speak with the board members," I called after her.

Mazie whirled around, her blue eyes so big and wide I thought they might bug out of her head. Her hand shot to her throat. "Oh, no, dear. That would end up doing more harm than good. Trust me, it's best for you to leave this alone and move on. Perhaps you can find another venue to display the collection, or better yet, a buyer for it. Besides, I'm sure you must be busy, what with getting your aunt's pet store ready to reopen and all."

She clattered down the rest of the steps as quickly as she dared in her high heels and walked swiftly down the block. I watched her for a few moments, then shut the door and walked slowly into the parlor, sank into the high-backed Queen Anne chair in front of the fireplace. Purrday waddled over and leapt into my lap, purr going full throttle. He butted the tip of my chin with his head, turned around twice, then wiggled himself into a comfortable position across my thighs, his head on his paws.

"Do you believe that?" I whispered into the cat's soft fur. "Why on earth wouldn't they want to display Aunt Tillie's collection?"

Purrday burrowed his head into the crook of my elbow and I leaned back in the chair. Mazie had never answered me when I'd asked if she'd told the board it had been Matilda Washburn's collection. Could the fact that it was have something to do with their rejection? And if so, why?

"Don't tell me Aunt Matilda's the reason I got rejected," I cried, digging my fingers into Purrday's ruff. I must have dug a little harder than I intended, because he raised his head and looked at me.

"Merow."

I patted his head. "Sorry, boy. You probably think I'm overreacting, but that collection is amazing. Aunt Tillie practically dedicated her life to it. For all the good works she did for this town, I just feel that the least they can do for her is have her memory be recognized and remembered through this display. Over-the-top or not, it's important to me."

Purrday looked at me for a moment, then butted his head against my hand. I smiled. "I knew you'd understand. So . . . Mazie said the vote went against displaying the collection four to three. I've got to find out who those four people are, and why they voted against it."

Purrday let out a loud yowl. He jumped off my lap and padded over to the far corner of the room, arranged himself comfortably against the wall, and started licking his chest. I reached into my pocket and pulled out the card Olivia had given me with her private cell number on the back.

She answered on the first ring. "Taking me up on my offer so soon?" she asked.

"Yes, as a matter of fact, I am. I just had a visit from Mazie Madison. What can you tell me about the museum board members?"

Olivia laughed. "How much time do you have?"

I glanced around the room at the boxes in their various stages of disarray. "I can make as much time as you need."

"Sure, I'll tell you what I know. I don't have another dance class till four thirty. How about a coffee? Can you meet me at Rita's shop in twenty minutes?"

I looked down at my grubby sweat suit. After unpacking for two hours, I needed a shower.

"Make it forty," I said, and hung up.

23

• • •

I took a refreshing shower and changed into a clean navy sweatshirt and matching yoga pants. I swept my blonde curls back into a loose-hanging ponytail and after a short debate, added a swipe of blusher across my high cheekbones and a light pink gloss on my lips. I'd been trained to always look my best no matter where I went, whether it was to a black-tie premiere or just a run to the supermarket. One never knew when the paparazzi would pop up, cameras in hand. And while I was certain none of them had tracked me to Fox Hollow yet, I didn't want to take a chance and run around the streets of the town looking like I'd been digging ditches (which I hadn't) or unpacking boxes (which I had). With my luck, someone from a rag like *Insider Tidbits* was probably lurking in the town square, waiting to snap a candid photo and run it on the cover with the caption: *Look who we caught in her new home trying to fit in with the natives, sans makeup: Shell Marlowe!* That wouldn't help my new business.

I was just about to leave when I remembered something. I hurried back into the den and rummaged quickly through the top drawer. I found what I was looking for and tucked it into the pocket of my sweatshirt. I found Purrday lounging on the chair and Kahlua stretched out across the back of the sofa. Well, at least they weren't killing each other. With a quick goodbye to both I hurried out the door.

Aunt Tillie's house was only a stone's throw from the center of town, so I decided to walk rather than take my convertible. I glanced at my watch. Fifteen minutes to go. If I cut through the park, I'd just be on time.

The path was wide enough for two people to pass comfortably. It was a beautiful day, the sky was clear and blue, and the sun was shining. There were a lot of people out on the path, either jogging, power-walking, or just meandering about. I saw an elderly man walking his basset hound, and twin girls whiz by on roller skates. A double stroller passed me, a tiny woman wearing earbuds behind it. I rounded a bend and saw two figures up on the grassy knoll. Two women. One was short, with shiny brown hair cut in a chin-length bob that swung around her face. She had on a bright pink track suit that matched the large glasses perched on the bridge of her nose. The other woman had long white hair that streamed across broad shoulders. She was tall and rangily built, almost like a linebacker. Her face was thin and pinched, and a mental image of Margaret Hamilton in *The Wizard of Oz* flashed through my mind. They looked to be in the middle of an argument. The shorter one started to turn away, but the white-haired woman put her hands on her shoulders and spun her around. She towered over her, her finger jabbing right under the shorter woman's nose. I was too far away to hear what was being said, but from their stances I could tell that it wasn't good.

Suddenly the white-haired woman turned and her gaze fixed right on me. I gasped. The gaze was filled with such hatred that I instinctively glanced over my shoulder, but there was no one else on the trail at that moment. That look had obviously been aimed at me, but why? I'd never seen either woman before in my life. I started to move away when I heard a sharp "Rocco! No!" behind me. The next instant an enormous dog bounded into my path. I started to swerve, but the dog leapt toward me. He jumped up and put his front paws on my shoulders. I staggered slightly but managed to retain my balance. Then I felt a wet tongue caress my cheek.

"Rocco! Down!"

A man jogged across the grass. He wore a Giants cap backward over longish, coal black hair, and a dark green T-shirt, stretched taut against what appeared to be a muscular body. His skin was tanned and a dark stubble was visible on a strong jawline. The dark glasses he wore hid his eyes, but from what I could see, he was cute . . . no, scratch that. *Very* cute.

He approached, panting slightly, and grabbed the dog's collar to force him into a sitting position. "Bad dog, Rocco. You don't do that to strangers." He pulled the glasses down on the bump on the bridge of his nose, and now I could see that his eyes were hazel, with little flecks of gold and green. "I'm very sorry, miss. Are you all right?"

"I'm fine." I reached up to adjust my ponytail. "Rocco didn't hurt me." I gave the dog a once-over. "He looks like a mix." I studied the face. "Pit bull?"

"Yep." The stranger nodded. "Pit bull and golden retriever. I know, I know. Unusual, right?" He ran his hand over Rocco's thick, mottled brown coat. "He's got retriever personality and pit bull coloring. Granted, the pit bull face scares a lot of people off, but he's basically harmless—unless you count maybe getting licked to death."

"Yes, he certainly seems friendly—oh!" I gasped as Rocco pounced on me again, and this time I did lose my balance. I would have fallen right on my derriere on the grass if the stranger hadn't grabbed my arm and pulled me against his chest to steady me. His rock-hard chest.

His head swiveled in the dog's direction. "That's enough, Rocco," he said in a commanding tone. "Sit! Now! Or no treats for you."

Apparently, the dog understood the meaning of *treats*, because he sat back on his haunches, tongue lolling. The stranger rolled his eyes and turned to me. "I apologize again. I can only say in my defense that Rocco's not my dog."

I looked at the dog, who now had stretched his long body out across the grass and was lying on his side. "He's not?"

He shook his head. "No, he's my sister's pride and joy. She got called to work unexpectedly, so I'm dog sitting." He laughed. "She always calls me as a last resort. I'm Josh, by the way."

He still held my arm. I directed a pointed look at his hand, and he let it go with a grin.

"Hi, Josh. I'm Shell."

The grin turned into a frown. "Shell? That's an unusual name."

"It's a nickname," I said. I didn't elaborate further, and there followed a brief, awkward pause. "Well, it was nice running into you," I said. I glanced at the dog. "And you too, Rocco." I turned and started down the trail, and a moment later, Josh fell into step beside me, Rocco trotting along obediently at his side.

"Are you from around here, Shell? Or just visiting?"

I gave him a sidelong glance. "I just moved here this week," I said.

"You did? Odd. Usually people move *out* of Fox Hollow, not into it."

I laughed. "That's not a very good advertisement for the town."

His fingers reached up to rub casually at the nape of his neck. "No, I guess it isn't, is it?" He chuckled. "I hope Rocco here didn't leave you with an unfavorable impression of our little town."

I laughed. "Hardly. I think Rocco is rather . . . sweet." I swiped at the wet streak on my cheek. "He's certainly enthusiastic."

Josh chuckled. "Wait till you get to know him better, and then we'll see what you have to say."

The way he said that gave me a warm feeling in my belly. I paused, floundering for something witty to say, but he spoke again. "I've got to get going. It was nice to meet you . . . Shell."

"You too," I said. I liked the way he'd lingered over saying my name, sort of like a caress. I hesitated and then blurted, "Maybe we'll run into each other again."

His lips split in a wide smile, revealing white, even teeth. "Maybe we will," he said, and then he tugged at the dog's leash, pulling him in the opposite direction. I glanced at my watch and groaned as I realized I had exactly three minutes to get to Sweet Perks.

As I rounded the bend, I cast a quick glance in the direction of the grassy knoll. It was deserted. The women had vanished.

• • •

It wasn't too hard to find Rita's shop. The coral-and-white-striped sign that read *Sweet Perks* was by far the biggest and most colorful on the block. The large front window offered a tantalizing glimpse of the baked goods within. A bell tinkled a greeting as I pushed the door open and I stood on the threshold for a moment, drinking in the delectable scents of baked goods and fresh brewed coffee, feeling like I'd died and gone to heaven. There were a few customers scattered at the small tables, eating muffins and slurping down coffee or coffee drinks. A few looked at me curiously as I made my way to the register.

There was a woman standing there, her back to me. As I approached, she turned and I saw that it was Olivia. She glanced at her watch and grinned. "You're punctual, I see. Find us a table," she said. "I'll get us something to drink. My treat. What'll you have?"

The blueberry muffins looked tempting, but I patted my stomach. "Just coffee," I said. At Olivia's puzzled look, I added, "It's hard to break years of watching your weight."

Olivia gave me a once-over and sighed. "You're not on camera anymore, sweetie, but I know what you mean. How about a double mocha latte with skim milk? That won't expand your waistline *too* much," she added with a wink.

I wandered over to a café table all the way in the back, sandwiched in between a shelf filled with brightly colored mugs and another display case filled with necklaces, earrings, and bracelets, many of intricate design.

Olivia appeared a few minutes later and set a tall, frothy glass in front of me. She slid into the seat opposite mine and raised her glass. "Here's to—what?"

"How about success? That's always good." I took a long sip of the latte, sighed contentedly, and settled back in my chair. I glanced around the quaint store. "Where's Rita?"

"She always takes Saturday afternoon off. Drives her husband for his arthritis treatment in Boyne. Poor guy, he's got it bad, especially in the hands." She curled her own fingers into a clawed fist. "He used to be an accountant. He must have gotten his condition from punching all those adding machine keys. Her niece usually watches the store for her." She inclined her head toward the apple-cheeked girl behind the register.

I nodded toward the display case. "And she sells jewelry too?"

Olivia glanced at the case. "Yep. Some she makes, some she picks up at estate sales and resells. Jewelry's always been a hobby with her." She leaned forward. "So, now, let's get to it. Just what did old Mazie say, exactly?"

I leaned back in my chair, wrapping my hands around my drink. "The board didn't approve showcasing Aunt Tillie's Cary Grant poster collection. They voted four to three against."

"Hm." Olivia gave a small sigh. "That sounds about right."

"What do you mean?"

She glanced quickly around the shop, then leaned midway across the table and said in a whisper, "It sounds as if a certain board member is up to her old tricks again; the one who possesses the superpower of being able to sway votes." Her tongue clicked against the roof of her mouth. "The wicked witch of Fox Hollow herself: Amelia Witherspoon. Very few people in this town—or on earth, for that matter—get along with her." Olivia stretched her long legs out in front of her and cradled her cup in her hands. "If she knows the posters belonged to Tillie Washburn, that could have something to do with it. As the gossip goes, she and your aunt had a falling out some years ago. Over what, I'm not sure. But whatever it was, it must have been a doozy. The two of 'em always went out of their way to avoid each other."

"You're kidding! She'd turn down something that would only benefit the museum in the long run over an ancient feud?"

Olivia nodded. "It'd be just like her to do something like that, out of spite."

Great. In some ways, Fox Hollow seemed just as political as Hollywood.

"Do you know the names of the board members who would have voted with Amelia?"

"Sure. Lawrence Peabody, Ginnifer Rubin, and Andy McHardy. It's sickening, really. Everyone thinks that Amelia must have something on them. They always side with her." Olivia shot me a sympathetic look. "Not a great start to your first week in Fox Hollow, is it?"

"It sure isn't." Abruptly I straightened up. "I can't just take this lying down, Olivia. I have to do something."

"And by 'do something' I'm guessing you mean talk to Amelia." As I nodded, Olivia shook her head. "That's like chasing unicorns, sweetie. Once that old bat makes up her mind about something, it takes practically an act of God to change it."

"Yeah, well, I've run up against some pretty tough producers with the same attitude in my day." I puffed my chest out. "Not to brag, but trust me, I can handle it."

"You think so?" Olivia glanced significantly out the large picture window. "Okay, then, there's your chance." She made a jerking motion with her thumb. "See the white-haired crone standing on the corner, talking to the short, stout guy? That's Amelia."

I peered out the window and almost fell off my chair.

Amelia Witherspoon was the white-haired woman I'd seen earlier in the park. The one who'd given me the dagger eyes. Lovely.

Four

Olivia reached over and tapped my shoulder. "Everything okay, sweetie? You look a little pale."

I pointed out the window. "I saw her when I was on my way here. She was in the park, arguing with another woman with short dark hair. And from the looks of things, Amelia was winning."

Olivia tapped at her chin. "Short dark hair, you said? It couldn't be Ginnifer. Her hair is almost as red as Rita's." She stared off into space for a few minutes. "It could have been Londra Lewis. She's the museum administrator, Mazie's right hand. She's wanted a docent position for a long time, but whenever one becomes available, Amelia just happens to have a better candidate. Plus, it really irks Amelia how loyal Londra is to Mazie."

I fiddled with the edge of my napkin. "I couldn't hear anything, but it certainly seemed more serious than some disagreement over a job. Amelia was really in the other woman's face."

"Who knows?" Olivia spread her hands. "Arguing is what Amelia does best. If you don't believe me, take another look outside."

I did. Amelia was now bent over the shorter man, her fingers curled into a fist. She was waving the fist in front of the man's face. To his credit, though, he didn't shrink back. He held his ground, and I could tell from the set of his jaw and the way he held his shoulders that he was probably just as angry, if not angrier.

"Who's the man?" I asked. "Lawrence Peabody or Andy McHardy?"

"Neither. That's Garrett Knute. He's on the board too." Olivia squinted out the window. "I wonder what that's all about. Garrett's face looks like a thundercloud, and he's usually pretty easygoing."

"He might welcome an interruption, then." I pushed back my chair and stood up. "Wish me luck."

Olivia gave me a careless wave. "That's a given. You'll need it."

I took a last large gulp of my latte concoction, set it back on the table, and made my way to the front door. As I stepped out onto the sidewalk, I noticed that Amelia and Garrett had taken their battle to the street corner diagonally across from Sweet Perks. The argument was still in full force, as evidenced by the raised voices that floated across the street toward me.

I crossed the street and quickened my steps. As I drew closer I saw a large manila envelope clutched tightly in Amelia's right hand. Garrett reached out to snatch it, but Amelia slapped his hand away and then started to laugh. The other man's face twisted into an expression of fury, and he gestured again toward the envelope.

"Over my dead body. Or yours," he hissed, and then he glanced up. Our eyes locked for the briefest of instants and then he clamped both lips together, turned on his heel, and stormed off in the other direction without so much as a backward glance. Amelia's thin lips twisted in a triumphant expression that vanished almost immediately as she caught sight of me. She thrust the envelope into the plaid tote she carried and I fully expected her to storm off as well; instead she advanced toward me, hand out, finger pointing, eyes blazing with the same naked fury I'd seen earlier in the park.

"What are you, spying on me?"

The accusation was so sudden that all I could do was gape. Amelia took my hesitation as assent and plunged ahead with both barrels.

"Don't try to deny it. I saw you in the park, watching me. Who put you up to it? Wait, don't tell me, let me guess. You're one of Watson's interns, right?"

She moved closer, her hands raised threateningly. I took a step backward and found my voice. "I have no idea what you're talking about, and the only Watson I know is in Sir Arthur Conan Doyle novels. I just wanted to talk to you for a minute. You are Amelia Witherspoon, right?"

She stopped, her eyes narrowed. "Yes," she said slowly, a note of suspicion evident in her tone. "I am. And who, might I ask, are you?"

I started to extend my hand, thought better of the gesture, and let my arm fall limply to my side. "My name is Crishell McMillan."

Her thin lips quivered slightly. "And that's supposed to mean something to me?"

"It should," I snapped, "since I understand you voted against displaying my aunt's collection of Cary Grant posters."

She stared at me and then suddenly flung her head back and laughed. "Oh, my stars! You're Tillie Washburn's niece!"

I thrust my shoulders back and lifted my chin. "Yes, I am. And I'd like to know why you voted against displaying the collection."

She raked me with her gaze again. "Simple. Every museum within a twenty-five-mile radius will be displaying some sort of Cary Grant memorabilia during that week. We want Fox Hollow to stand out from the crowd."

"That might be true, but I greatly doubt they'll be displaying a collection like my aunt's. She has posters from every one of Grant's seventy-plus films, and there are even stills from some of the older ones that would complement the posters nicely. Plus, I understand the kickoff movie is *His Girl Friday*, and there's a lobby poster autographed by Grant that would certainly be a stand-out piece." My hand flew to my pocket, and I pulled out a photograph I'd gotten from the den and handed it to her. "This is a photograph of the *His Girl Friday* posters. You can see Grant's signature on the bottom on the center one, right there."

Amelia stared at the photo, her brows drawn together. "Is that authentic?" she said at last.

"With papers to prove it," I responded with a curl of my lip. Amelia made a motion to give the photo back, but I held up my hand. "Keep it," I said.

Amelia Witherspoon frowned, then slid the photo into her jacket pocket. She shifted her weight from one foot to the other. "A collection like that no doubt would require a lot of special handling and upkeep. To be frank, we have other issues that money would be better spent on."

"That doesn't make any sense," I cried. "The publicity and the increased traffic to your museum alone would more than compensate you."

"Where I come from, a no is a no and that's that. Or maybe that's not how they do things in Hollywood." She opened the voluminous tote bag she carried and dropped the photo inside. "You're a stubborn girl, just like your aunt."

"Yes, I am. Look, all I'm asking for is a chance to talk to the board—convince you all that you're making a mistake."

Amelia clutched the black jacket she wore tightly around her body. "The board has already voted."

"Yes, but surely another meeting could be called, another vote taken."

"It could," she said slowly. "But it's a moot point. The vote won't change."

"How can you know that for sure?" When Amelia said nothing, I added,

"It would be unfair of you to deny me an opportunity because of some grudge you harbor against my aunt."

Amelia's jaw dropped and her eyes widened. She took a step backward. "You're a very impertinent girl," she snapped. "Any history your aunt and I shared had nothing to do with my decision. Who's spreading that lie anyway? Watson? Or Mazie Madison?"

"I told you I don't know anyone named Watson. And I didn't hear it from Mazie," I answered.

Amelia waved her hand in a dismissive gesture. "It doesn't matter, anyway. I've fed the gossip mill in Fox Hollow for years and I expect that will continue till the day I die. The matter's closed. There's nothing you can say to me that will change my mind. The decision's been made. Period. End of story."

She turned on her heel and started to walk away but I cried out, "I-I'll file a formal protest. It wasn't a fair vote, not when you somehow bullied other board members into siding with you."

Amelia stopped dead in her tracks. Slowly, very slowly, she turned around. Her mouth was slashed into a thin red line, and her eyes glittered with barely repressed fury. I instinctively took a step backward, positive she intended to strike me.

But she didn't. Instead she leaned over until her lips were scant inches from my ear and hissed, "If I were you, I'd stick to your plan to reopen the pet shop and keep out of things that don't concern you."

Despite the sudden chill that swept over me, I managed to maintain my composure. I looked her right in the eye and said, "But this does concern me. Perhaps I can convince one of those other members you're wrong. It only takes one more vote to tip the scales in my favor, right?"

She stared at me long and hard. "You think you can do that? Be my guest," she snapped, and then with one last withering glance at me, she turned on her heel and lumbered up the sidewalk.

"You'll see," I shouted after her retreating form. Like all the Washburn women, I needed to have the last word. "You're the one who'll be sorry, Amelia. Very sorry."

I turned to retrace my steps to Sweet Perks and caught a flash of green out of the corner of my eye. I turned my head just in time to see the cute guy from the park, Josh, staring at me from the doorway of a shop called Secondhand Sue's.

Judging from the expression on his face, he'd most likely caught the tail end of my conversation with Amelia.

And he didn't look happy. Not at all. As a matter of fact, he looked upset, and I had to wonder why.

Five

Olivia was waiting for me with a fresh mocha latte when I trudged back into Sweet Perks. I pooled into the chair opposite her and leaned my chin dejectedly in my palm. "You were right. She is a beast. I had visions of her pulling a poisoned apple out of her bag and force-feeding it to me."

Olivia made a clicking noise with her tongue. "That bad, huh? Were you right? Was it because of your aunt?"

"She says her relationship with my aunt doesn't figure into it. She said it's because every other museum will be displaying Grant items that week and they want Fox Hollow to be different."

Olivia let out a snort. "Well, that's a load of bull. No one else's display could even come close to Tillie's. Did you believe her?"

"Hell, no." I grabbed the latte and took a long sip. "I think she just voted it down out of spite. I could tell I got under her skin, though, when I suggested that she'd bullied the other members into going along with her. I even said I'd file a formal complaint, but it didn't faze her. She says the matter's closed."

"Sounds about par for the course."

"Well, she did keep the photo I showed her of the autographed *His Girl Friday* poster. Maybe that means something."

"Yeah. It means she wants to keep a trophy of her triumph."

I grimaced. "She said something odd, though. She asked if I was one of Watson's interns."

Olivia's brows knit together, and then her expression cleared. "Oh, she must mean Quentin Watson. He's the editor of the *Fox Hollow Gazette*. He can be persistent when he's after a story, although why he'd be pestering Amelia is anyone's guess. Unless he's doing a feature on 101 Ways to Irritate People." She chuckled as she wrapped her hands around her coffee cup. "What are you going to do now?"

I plucked a napkin from the container on the table and started to fiddle with the edges. "There seems to be only one course of action left. I've got to try and convince at least one of those other board members to reopen the matter and vote against Amelia."

Olivia rolled her eyes. "Talk about Mission Impossible! Honey, no offense, but you've got about as much chance of doing that as Hugh Jackman coming to Fox Hollow to shoot a movie."

"Now that's an interesting analogy." I pushed the napkin away. "You're probably right, but I've got to give it a try. I just need to sway one over from the Dark Side. Any ideas on where I should begin?"

Olivia's gaze was fixed at a point just beyond my left shoulder. "Yes. Ginnifer Rubin." She gestured toward the register. "She just stopped in for a cup of coffee. That's her standing right over there."

I turned and studied the lone woman waiting at the counter. Ginnifer Rubin was slight of build and walked with her shoulders slightly hunched over. Her face was tanned and lined with a web of fine wrinkles that were particularly visible around the eyes. Her short hair was red, but not a brassy red like Rita's. Her age was hard to guess; I placed her in her mid-sixties. She wore knit pants and a red-and-black-checked shirt that seemed to be about a size too big for her. Everything about her seemed to reek of insecurity.

I waited until she'd taken her coffee and muffin to a table near the back of the store, then I picked up my own cup and wended my way through the maze of tables over to her. She glanced up as I approached, and her eyes widened slightly as she saw me, but her expression was neutral.

"Hello," I said brightly. "Ginnifer Rubin?"

She took a quick sip of her coffee and then leaned over to peer at me more closely. "I'm sorry, do I know you?"

"No, I'm sorry. I'm new in town. Please allow me to introduce myself. I'm Crishell McMillan." I looked pointedly at the empty chair. "I was wondering if I might have a few moments of your time?"

Ginnifer looked as if she really wanted to refuse but couldn't think of a good enough reason. At last she gave a curt nod and gestured toward the chair. "Please, by all means. Sit down."

I slid into the seat, wrapped my hands around my now cold coffee cup. I figured some warming up was in order. After all, I just couldn't jump right in to plead my case. "I believe you might have been acquainted with my aunt, Matilda Washburn?"

Her eyes widened slightly. "Tillie was your aunt?" At my nod she continued, "We weren't particularly good friends, but she was a charming woman and a tireless champion of causes. She'll be missed." Almost as an afterthought she added, "And I'm sorry for your loss." She lifted the muffin to her lips, took a bite, then picked up her napkin and swiped delicately at her lips. "Tillie often spoke of her successful actress niece. I take it that's you?"

"I was very fortunate. I was discovered doing the lead in a play in college that I wasn't even supposed to be in. I was the understudy, and the girl who had the lead took ill on opening night. A talent scout happened to be in the audience and the rest, as they say, is history."

"Yes, I used to watch *All My Tomorrows*. I was sad when it was canceled. And of course, I've seen *Spy Anyone*." Ginnifer's index finger tapped against the handle of her cup. "You're here because it was canceled, right?"

"Partially. My aunt left me her house and her business. Urban Tails."

Ginnifer clapped her hands. "Oh, the pet shop. We all wondered what was going to happen to it. It's quite a tourist attraction. You'd be surprised at how many people want to get a little something for their pets. I've missed it as well." She let out a sigh. "My Chihuahua Charlie likes those Bradley liver treats, and Urban Tails is the only store around that stocked them."

"I'll definitely look into that. My aunt let everything deplete during her illness, so I've been busy trying to get everything back up to speed. But the store will reopen, never fear."

"That's good to know."

I leaned forward. "I'm sure you're also aware that my aunt was an avid collector of movie memorabilia."

Ginnifer smiled thinly. "Yes, I had heard she had quite an extensive collection."

"Which brings me to the reason I wanted to speak with you. I offered to loan my aunt's Cary Grant poster collection to the museum, but Mazie Madison told me the board voted it down." I looked her straight in the eye. "Would you mind telling me why?"

She shifted a bit uncomfortably in her chair. "Nothing against you personally, dear, but . . . ah, we just felt that we didn't want to jump on the bandwagon and do what everyone else would be doing that week. We want to be . . . different."

"I see. And in what way do you want the museum to be different?"

She hesitated and then said, "Well, we haven't figured that part out quite yet."

"I see." I let out a breath. "And is this desire to be different a consensus, Ms. Rubin, or just one person's opinion?"

Her eyes darkened. "Just what are you implying, Ms. McMillan?"

"I'm not implying anything. But Mazie Madison informed me the vote against my proposal was four to three, so obviously, some members of the board feel otherwise."

"I can't speak for everyone else. I can only tell you how *I* feel."

I decided to take a gamble and looked Ginnifer straight in the eye. "Do you know anything about a feud between Ms. Witherspoon and my aunt?"

Ginnifer looked away and studied the checked tablecloth as if the pattern had suddenly become the most interesting thing in the room. "Nothing other than they had a falling out over something years ago, and neither one had much use for the other after that. Why do you ask?"

I leaned forward and said in a conspiratorial tone, "Because I think Amelia Witherspoon is still holding a grudge. I think the reason she voted against displaying the collection has nothing to do with your museum being unique, but is just a continuation of an old feud, and I for one think it's grossly unfair."

Ginnifer looked decidedly uncomfortable now. "Amelia is intensely committed to certain things, and the museum is one of them. She's only doing what she feels is right. Unfortunately, doing the right thing isn't always easy."

She was silent for several seconds, her face a study in mixed emotion, almost as if she were waging a silent battle. Finally she said, "I'll mention what you told me to the other board members. But I can't promise anything."

"Oh, thank you." I reached over and impulsively grabbed her hand. "That's all I ask. And thank you for your time."

I scraped my chair back and with a curt nod, made my way back to where Olivia was sitting. I slid back into my chair and said, "Well, she was a bit reluctant at first, but she said she'd speak to them." I tapped my chin with the edge of my nail. "She said Amelia didn't influence her, but I'm not so sure. She certainly seems to be afraid of her. It wouldn't surprise me in the least if Amelia does have some sort of dirt on those three and holds it over their heads to get what she wants."

Olivia chuckled. "You're not in LA anymore, sweetie. Fox Hollow's a small town. Everyone has skeletons in the closet."

"Yes, and it seems Amelia knows which ones to rattle."

Olivia glanced at her watch and stood up. "Goodness, look at the time. I've got to get to the studio and get ready for class." She leaned over and squeezed my arm. "Listen, if you want to talk to Lawrence Peabody and Andy McHardy, I'd suggest the Captain's Club. It's an upscale pub on North Street. They usually head over there around four for a midafternoon brew and the special of the day." She gave my outfit a once-over. "I'd dress it up a bit, though. Show some cleavage."

"Why, Olivia," I said and laughed. "Are you telling me those two are dirty old men?"

"I'm not *telling* you anything." She closed one eye in a broad wink. "Trust me, strutting your stuff can't hurt. Especially if you're looking to pry information out of them they might not be willing to share."

Six

"So, what do you think, kids? The black or the red?"

After Olivia had gone back to the studio, I'd ordered another skim mocha latte to go and brought it back to the house with me, then devoted the rest of the afternoon to unpacking my boxes and setting my new house to rights. I stopped at three, took another shower, dried my hair, and arranged it in soft curls around my face. I added blush, eyeliner, and lip gloss, and now all that was left was my wardrobe choice.

Purrday was sprawled full-length across my cream comforter, blinking his good eye sleepily. I gave a mental note of thanks for deciding on a neutral color, since my new roomie tended to shed, as evidenced by all the long white hairs now deposited on the furniture. Kahlua was across the room, perched on top of the highboy. She watched, head cocked, as I held the two dresses up before the full-length mirror. The red had a scoop neckline and a princess skirt that came to just below my knees. The black was a form-fitting sheath, with a low neckline and cap sleeves. I'd worn both to premieres in Hollywood before, and they'd both received flattering reviews from the Fashion Police. Now that was about as high a praise in Hollywood as a dress can get.

Purrday stretched out his paw, and he seemed to be pointing toward the black one. I held it up and Kahlua inclined her head and let out a sharp yowl as only a Siamese can. I nodded and slipped it off the hanger. "That's what I thought, too," I said. "It might be a little much for a late-afternoon drink in Fox Hollow, but Olivia did say to show some cleavage."

I glanced over at Purrday. His eye was closed. When I looked over at the highboy, Kahlua had done a disappearing act. No matter. She wasn't that up on fashion anyway.

I slipped the dress on over my head, gave my hair a quick brush, slid into high-heeled black pumps, and then surveyed myself in the mirror.

"Not bad if I do say so myself. What do you think, Purrday? Purrday?"

I heard a low buzzing noise coming from the direction of the comforter. Purrday had rolled over on his back and lay there, all four paws in the air. He was snoring.

"Sorry to bore you, pal. If you're awake when I get back, I'll fill you in." I snatched up my purse and cell, which immediately started to buzz. I glanced at the name on the incoming call.

Gary Presser. Uh-oh. Max must have told him I'd turned down the series. No doubt he was going to try and talk me into it. I sighed. While I was fond of Gary, there was no way in hell I was taking this call now. I stuffed the phone in my purse. I'd have to deal with him at some point, but right now later was better than sooner.

• • •

I took the convertible downtown in deference to my heels. It was a lovely afternoon, with a clear cloudless sky and a soft, gentle breeze. I tied a scarf around my hair and drove the short distance with the top down, taking in the country ambiance of my new home. I drove past Urban Tails and for a moment I was tempted to forget about confrontation, pull over, and go inside the store. That temptation lasted only a moment. If I were to make any kind of a life for myself here in Fox Hollow, I had to get this other matter resolved. I wasn't going to be able to form friendships or drum up customers if I had an ongoing feud from the get-go.

I found North Street without much trouble and there was a parking spot right on the corner, lucky me! Luckier still, it was right in front of the pub. The building stood on the corner's edge and was totally black, save for the battered stone front flanking heavy oaken doors with lights on either side. A wooden plaque right above the doors read in large block letters *Captain's Club*, and the name was repeated in gold raised lettering on the large picture window that took up almost all of the building's right side. I stepped inside and stood for a moment on the threshold, letting my eyes adjust to the dim lighting.

A young girl wearing a trim black skirt and white blouse appeared almost instantly, a menu in her hand. The brass name tag pinned to her blouse said her name was Mollie. "Hello, there," she said. "Table for one?"

I glanced around at the tables. There was a guy in a beat-up jacket seated at one, busy devouring what looked to be a corned beef sandwich, a frosty mug of beer pushed off to one side. A middle-aged woman sat alone at a table near the sign marked *Restroom*, and she seemed to be more interested in what was on her tablet than the salad in front of her. No one was seated at the bar.

I turned my attention back to Mollie. "Yes, that would be fine."

She showed me to a small table off to the left of the bar and placed a leather-covered book the size of *War and Peace* in front of me. "Your server is Gretchen," she said. "She'll be with you shortly." As she started to move off, I touched her arm.

"Excuse me. Do you know if Lawrence Peabody and Andy McHardy have been in here yet?"

"Larry and Andy? They usually get here just after four." She gave me a curious look. "Why?"

I flushed a bit under her scrutinizing look. "I have some business I need to discuss with them."

"Oh. Well, they should be here soon. I'll point them out to you, if you want."

"That would be great, thanks." As Mollie moved away, I heard the dulcet tones of my iPhone inside my bag. I pulled it out. Gary. Again.

"God, Gary, give it up," I grumbled, shoving the phone rather unceremoniously back into my bag. Behind me someone cleared their throat loudly.

"Wow! You really didn't want to take that call, did you?"

I whipped my head around to gaze at the speaker. Josh stood behind me, his lips twisted into a rueful grin. If I'd thought he looked fabulous earlier in his beat-up clothes, he looked a hundred times more so now. He had on pressed chinos and a topaz-colored collared shirt that brought out the gold flecks in his hazel eyes. The shirt stretched taut against his muscular frame, and I noted again that he was in great shape. I mean Great. Shape.

"Yeah, well, I get a bit cranky when I'm hungry." I tore my gaze away from him with an effort and tapped at the menu. "I didn't get to the supermarket yet, and someone told me the food here was good."

"Oh, it is. The drinks are even better." He paused. "So, how do you like Fox Hollow so far?"

I picked up my glass of water and took a sip. "Very much, at least so far."

He gave me a long, searching look. "Getting along with the natives? Some of 'em can be rather difficult."

He was subtly referring, no doubt, to my earlier altercation with Amelia, and I recalled again the distressed look I'd seen on his face. I was debating how to answer when Mollie sidled up, a wide smile on her face. She laid her hand on Josh's arm. "Hey, Joshy! Michelle's in the back. She'll be right out."

Joshy!

He smiled. "Thanks, Moll." He nodded in my direction. "I've got to go. It was nice to see you again." He waggled his fingers at me. "You behave yourself, now."

I watched out of the corner of my eye as Josh went over to the bar and slid onto a stool. A few minutes later, a pretty brunette wearing a black shirt and matching slacks came out of the back. Her dark eyes lit up when she saw Josh and she ran over, leaned across the counter to give him a buss on the cheek.

"Hey, stranger! About time you showed up," she said.

He laughed and then the two of them moved off to the side of the bar, talking in low tones. I found myself wondering just what their connection was. Casual acquaintance, or boyfriend-girlfriend maybe?

I sniffed. *You behave yourself too, Joshy.*

I was spared further speculation as Mollie came back and touched my shoulder. "You wanted to know when Larry and Andy came in?" She nodded toward the front of the bar. "They're here."

She moved off, menus in hand, and I glanced casually in the direction of the foyer. Two men stood there, and for a fleeting moment I had the impression of the old comedy team of Abbott and Costello. One man was older, tall and thin, with a thick head of gray hair that looked to be professionally styled. His close-clipped mustache matched the color of his hair, and he wore a blue plaid sport coat over a sky-blue shirt and navy trousers. The color of the shirt matched exactly the color of his eyes, which were large and very, very round. They almost reminded me of a frog's eyes.

The other man was short and squat, and his tan chinos looked to be about two sizes too small for his rotund frame. He had what my aunt would have called soft features. Dull brown eyes set deep in a face with doughy cheeks and thick, bulbous lips. He too had a thick head of hair, which he wore slicked back from a high forehead, and thick sideburns, Elvis Presley style. The hair might have been dyed, I couldn't be sure.

They both greeted the hostess effusively. "Give us a table in the back today, Mollie," said the shorter man. He reached up to clap the tall man on the back. "Larry and I have some private business to discuss."

I watched as Mollie led them to a small table over in the far corner of the room. She deposited menus in front of them and then moved past my table, pausing to give me a discreet nod. I rose, mouthed a thank-you, and made my way slowly over to their table, pausing once to glance casually at the bar, but Josh and Michelle were nowhere to be seen. I turned and made my way over to where tall Lawrence Peabody and short Andy McHardy were seated. As I drew closer, I paused. It was evident they were in the middle of an argument. Andy was frowning, his finger tapping impatiently against the tabletop, and I could see a vein bulge slightly in his forehead.

"Even you must admit something's got to be done," I heard him say. "We can't go on like this, with her expecting us to jump every time she snaps her fingers."

Larry shook his head vehemently. "I disagree. I . . ." He turned his head slightly and apparently caught sight of me, standing awkwardly not two feet away. He nudged his companion, who let out a sharp "Ow, what the heck . . .," and then he stopped speaking as he, too, saw me. Well, if I'd learned nothing else in Hollywood, it was that the best defense is usually a good offense. I squared my shoulders, stepped right up to the table, and smiled.

"Mr. Peabody and Mr. McHardy, I presume?"

Larry rose and held out his hand. "I'm Lawrence Peabody, and he"—he swept his arm wide to encompass his companion—"is Andrew McHardy. How may we be of service?"

I took Larry's hand, released it, then smiled at the two of them. "I'd like a few moments of your time, if I may."

"Of course." Larry grabbed a chair from a nearby table and pushed it over. His big froggy eyes rested for a moment on my V neckline and the swell of my breasts, and then he quickly raised his gaze to meet mine. "Please, sit down. What can we do for you?"

"Yes." Andy nodded. His thick, dark hair bobbed in time with his head, and I found myself thinking *hairpiece, definitely*. "We're at a loss here, I'm afraid," he continued. "It's not often a pretty girl seeks us out. We've never met before." His gaze traveled to my cleavage, then he quickly averted his gaze. "I'd have remembered."

I settled into my seat and offered them my most dazzling smile. "We haven't met, gentlemen, but I understand the two of you are on the board of the Fox Hollow Museum?"

They exchanged a glance, and then Larry leaned forward. "The museum, eh? Well, yes, as a matter of fact we are. Why? Are you a patron of the arts?"

"In a way. I understand you voted down my offer to display my aunt's poster collection. I'm Crishell McMillan."

They looked at each other, and then Larry gave me another once-over. "You're the niece, eh? Why do you want to speak with us? I was under the impression Mazie was going to talk to you."

"She did. However, I have some concerns."

"Concerns?" Larry made an impatient gesture with his hand. "What sort of concerns?"

"I'd like to be sure I was turned down for the right reasons."

They exchanged a look, and Andy fidgeted uncomfortably in his chair. "I'm not sure I understand what you're getting at. We considered your offer carefully, pros and cons, and we voted. You lost, four to three."

"Might I ask the reason the two of you voted against me?"

"Oh, for pity's sakes," sputtered Larry. "We didn't vote against *you*, we voted against displaying the collection. We didn't want to be like every other Tom, Dick, and Harry around.."

I leaned forward, smile still in place. "Trust me, this collection isn't like any other around. I'm sure no other museum will be offering a display of posters of all of Grant's movies, some of them signed, no less."

Larry frowned, reached up a hand to curl one corner of his mustache. "There is such a thing as overkill, you know."

"Perhaps." I exhaled a breath, trying to figure out the most diplomatic way to get my point across. "I don't mean to upset you gentlemen. I just wanted to be sure that you all sincerely felt that way, and weren't . . . unduly influenced."

Andy picked up his napkin, twining it between his stubby fingers. "Unduly influenced? By whom?"

I paused, coughed lightly. "Well . . . I've heard that Amelia Witherspoon and my aunt had a long-running feud. And that Ms. Witherspoon is a major force on the board."

Both men started. They looked quickly at each other and then Andy said, "We're not familiar with any story about a feud, but your aunt was a fine woman, Ms. McMillan."

"Yes," Larry said with a nod. "And while it's true Amelia Witherspoon is a major force on our board, you may be assured that neither she nor anyone else exerts any undue influence on us."

"I see," I said, although I wasn't quite sure I believed him. His voice seemed to crack a bit when he mentioned Amelia's name. I waited a few minutes and then added, "Ginnifer Rubin mentioned she's willing to give my offer further consideration. I wondered if perhaps you might be willing to do the same?"

They exchanged a quick look and then Larry said, "I don't believe it's necessary, Ms. McMillan. We've voted and that's that. As far as we're concerned, the matter is resolved."

I could see that further argument wouldn't get me anywhere. It appeared they were all a united front on this point. Best to back away, try a different tack. I shrugged. "I guess we have nothing further to talk about, then."

Larry's big eyes looked about ready to pop out of his head, and the little vein in his neck was throbbing. "No, we don't. Frankly, if I were you, Ms. McMillan, I'd stick to reopening your aunt's pet shop. The community has a need for such a store." He rose, giving his jacket a sharp tug. "Come on, Andy. I think I've lost my appetite for today."

Andy nodded and rose. As he passed me he whispered, "Larry's right. You should concentrate on reopening your aunt's store. Some things are best left . . . alone." Then he turned and followed the other man out of the pub.

I returned to my table and sat for a moment, my thoughts whirling. It was painfully obvious I wasn't going to get anywhere with them. The person I had to convince was Amelia. I needed to find out what that feud was all about, and right now there was only one person I could think of who might be able to shed some light.

Much as I disliked the idea, I was going to have to poke the bear.

I whipped out my cell phone and scrolled down the list of contacts until I found the one marked *Mother*. I hit the button to dial and waited, mentally reviewing how to broach the subject of Aunt Tillie's past. She and my mother had never really gotten along—the adage that opposites attract didn't apply in this case. As it turned out, I didn't have to worry. My call went straight to voicemail. *"You've reached the voicemail of Clarissa McMillan. I'm not available right now. Please leave a detailed message and I shall return your call as soon as my schedule allows."*

I bit back a grimace. "Hello, Mother. This is your daughter. Could you give me a call when your sch—when you have time? I've got some questions I need to ask you."

I dropped the phone back into my purse and looked around. The waitress hadn't come by yet, and I suddenly found the heavy menu just too much to navigate. I was about to get up to leave when a shadow fell across the table. I glanced up and saw a man I could best describe as strange-looking standing there, staring at me. He wore a long peacoat buttoned all the way up, even though the temperature was a pleasant seventy-four degrees. Ratty-looking jeans peeped out from the bottom of the coat, and he wore sandals on his feet. He had a full head of thick, gold-red hair and large tortoiseshell glasses perched on the bridge of a beak-shaped nose. He held a notebook and pen in one hand. "Don't tell me. Crishell McMillan?"

I looked at him. "Yes. Who are you?"

He bared his teeth in what I assumed was supposed to be a smile, but looked more like a leer. "Quentin Watson, editor in chief of the *Fox Hollow Gazette*. I understand you've just moved to our little burg?"

Ah, so he was the Watson Amelia'd accused me of working for. I forced a smile to my lips and said, "I have. Just this week, as a matter of fact. Are you here to welcome me to town too?"

"Too?" He looked puzzled and then his expression cleared. "Oh, yes, Rita and her welcome wagon." He made a face, as if he thought the idea silly. "Well, welcome, of course, but what I'm really after is an interview. You're the first celebrity to set down roots here in a long time. No, scratch that. *Ever.*" He flipped open the notebook and tapped at its edge with his pen. "It's quite newsworthy."

"I'm sure it is," I said carefully. "And I would love to accommodate you, Mr. Watson, however, I still have a lot of unpacking to do, and I'm really not settled in yet. I don't even have groceries in my house yet. It's really not a convenient time."

"Of course, of course," he murmured, pen still poised. "Perhaps just a quick quote then, on how you like the town so far, are you finding the people friendly . . . I heard you intend to reopen your aunt's store. Do you have a date on that?"

"No firm one. Very soon, I hope."

"I see, I see." He scribbled something down. "Any comment on the rumor that the museum board turned down displaying your aunt's poster collection?"

"No comment." Quentin Watson was sending off a vibe I didn't like. "I'm sorry, I've always made it a point that any interview must be cleared with my agent, Max Molenaro, first."

"Molenaro?" He scribbled in his notebook, closed it, and capped his pen. "How long does that usually take? I was hoping to feature you in next Sunday's edition, if not tomorrow's."

"I'll let you know," I said, in a firm enough tone to let him know that any further argument or wheedling would be pointless. I rose, clutching my purse. "And I really have to get back. I've a lot to do."

His lips quirked downward and I caught a flash of annoyance cross his face, but it was gone in an instant and he offered me a wide smile. "Of course, of course. Thank you for your time and . . . welcome to Fox Hollow." He turned on his heel and was gone.

I waited a few minutes, hoping Josh and the brunette bartender would reappear, but they didn't, so I picked up my purse and started toward the door. As I passed the hostess station, I glanced up and noticed a man sitting alone at a table on the side, busily engaged in slapping mustard on what looked to be a huge pastrami sandwich. I recognized the suspenders immediately. It was Ron Webb. He glanced up and our eyes met. He lifted his shoulders in a shrug and shot me a sympathetic look before he turned back to his sandwich. Whether he was sympathizing with me over my argument with the board members or the newspaper editor or both, I couldn't say.

Out on the street, I shut my eyes and tried to will all the pent-up frustration inside of me to vanish. My first week in Fox Hollow certainly hadn't started out as I'd planned. For the first time since I'd decided to move, I wondered if I had, indeed, done the right thing.

Seven

I slept on and off, my dreams plagued by visions of a white-haired woman in a witch's hat, standing over a simmering cauldron. I ran this way and that, trying to get away, and everywhere I went, she popped up, pointing a long-nailed crooked finger at me and cackling. She plopped herself on my chest, leaned over and ran her tongue over my chin. I woke up sputtering to find not a wicked witch but Purrday sprawled comfortably there, his tongue grazing my cheek. When he saw me looking at him, he reached out one paw and gave my cheek a pat. I gave his fur one in return.

"Thanks for the wake-up kiss," I told him. "After yesterday I sure need some lovin'." I sighed. "I used to be so good at catching the bad guys on TV, Purrday. But in real life all I seem to do is make a mess of things."

His response was to lean closer and meow loudly in my ear. Then he blinked his good eye.

I laughed. "Yes, yes, I know. You've been waiting patiently for breakfast."

I felt another thump and the next second Kahlua's head popped up. She saw the Persian cuddled close to me and her lips peeled back. She let out a loud hiss. Then she moved forward, paw upraised, and swatted Purrday right across his nose. The Persian let out a groan and leapt from the bed. Her work completed, Kahlua snuggled up close to me and brushed my chin with her tongue.

I sat up so I could look the cat straight in the eye. "You do know that you have no reason to be jealous of Purrday, right? I told you, you are my baby. Purrday was Aunt Tillie's baby. He's mourning her just like I am."

Kahlua looked as if she might be considering what I said, then rolled over and started to lick her front paws. I sighed. So much for communication.

My iPhone started to buzz. I snatched it up from the nightstand and groaned when I saw the number. "Speaking of witches," I grumbled with a sidelong glance at Purrday, then I hit the Answer button. "Hello, Mother, thank you for calling back." I was tempted to add *so promptly* but thought better of it. No doubt my mother considered returning a call the next day quite prompt indeed.

"No need to thank me, dear. Why wouldn't I call my favorite daughter back?"

"I'm your only daughter, Mother."

"Oh, Crishell. Why must you always split hairs?"

I sighed. I knew that tone well. It was her *you've hurt my delicate feelings, so now what are you going to do about it?* tone. How my dad put up with that for nearly thirty years was beyond me—I'd escaped as soon as I turned eighteen, three thousand miles away to college. And even though I was thirty-eight years old, my mother always succeeded in making me feel like I was ten again.

My mother rushed on without waiting for me to answer. "You said you had some questions? Funny thing, I've got some for you, too."

Uh-oh. "You do?"

"Yes. Like why you turned down a six-figure deal to star in a reboot of that series. Offers like that don't grow on trees, you know."

"First off, the offer was not six figures. Oh, wait, maybe it is if you count the cents. Secondly, I don't have to take on just anything anymore. I can afford to be selective now."

"Ah." There was a moment of silence and then, "I wonder if Matilda would have left you her entire fortune if she'd realized it would be the ruination of your acting career. She was very proud of you."

I wondered if my mother would share that opinion if she knew I intended to reopen Urban Tails. Obviously that tidbit of news wasn't on her radar . . . yet. I gritted my teeth and silently counted to ten before I answered. "I know she was. Which brings me to the question I had for you—" I began, but she cut me off again.

"I think you should reconsider that series. It seems like a wonderful opportunity and"—she lowered her voice—"it's a good role for a woman, and they're hard to come by these days. You're not getting any younger, you know."

I let out a huge sigh. "Let it go, Mother. There are other things I can do besides acting, you know."

This time the sigh was dramatic. "Such as running that smelly pet shop of Matilda's? Oh, yes, I know, Crishell. People tell me things."

"I'm sure they do." *Thank you, Max,* I fumed silently. If he weren't three thousand miles away, I'd hunt him down and throttle him.

"Please tell me you're not going to do that."

"I can't, because that's exactly what I am going to do. Very shortly, too."

"Oh, for God's sakes, Crishell! You've too much talent to waste slaving away catering to the needs of cats and dogs."

I scrubbed one hand across my eyes. "You wouldn't understand, Mother, and I didn't call you to discuss my career choice. I need your help."

"Really? My help?" The tone turned wary. "With what?"

"Did Aunt Matilda have any enemies?"

Dead silence, and then my mother burst into laughter. "You're still an actress at heart, dear. So melodramatic! What makes you think Matilda had enemies?"

"Because . . ." I hesitated, then plunged ahead. "Because the museum turned down displaying Aunt Tillie's Cary Grant poster collection, and I have the feeling it's got something to do with some sort of feud she had with one of the museum board members."

"Well, goodness, why didn't you say that? A feud's different than having enemies."

I rolled my eyes and mentally counted to ten before continuing. "Did you ever hear anything about Aunt Matilda *feuding* with anyone?"

My mother cleared her throat loudly. "I do seem to recall something about her and a woman in the town. She always referred to her as 'the wicked witch.'"

Well, that sure sounded like Amelia. "She never mentioned a name?"

"Well, she might have. Truthfully, I don't really remember. I wasn't all that interested."

Of course, I should have known. If Clarissa McMillan wasn't the main topic of conversation, then the topic wasn't worth squat. "You don't know what the feud was about, then?"

"Oh, of course I do. It was over a man. What else?" She let out a long sigh. "I know she talked to your father about it. I suppose you could call him."

I ignored the frosty tone in her voice. It was par for the course whenever the topic of my father came up, the miscreant who'd dumped her after she'd given him the best years of her life. "I would, but he's on that photo shoot in Africa."

"Africa, huh? Did he take Darlene with him?"

"I don't know, Mother." Did I mention that a week after the divorce my dad had hightailed it off to Vegas with Darlene Rule, my mom's best friend, and they were married in one of those all-night chapels? My mother has refused to set foot in Las Vegas ever since.

"No matter. So, now that I've answered your questions, quid pro quo, Crishell. Are you even remotely considering that reboot?"

"No, Mother, I told you . . ."

"Patrick isn't going to direct."

I almost lost my grip on my phone. "What?"

"Patrick isn't going to be the director. They hired someone else. Wait. You didn't know?"

"Know my ex-fiancé was on tap to direct that series? Hell, no."

"Oh, goodness." Did I imagine it or did she sound contrite? "I thought for sure that was the real reason you turned it down . . ."

Uh-huh. One thing I can say about my mother, she's a firm believer in misery loves company. Thankfully, my call waiting buzzed at that moment. I frowned at the unfamiliar number. Usually I let them go to voicemail, but right now . . . any port in a storm. "Oops, sorry, Mom. I've got another call. I've got to take this, but thanks for your help. We'll talk soon."

"Crishell, we haven't finished—"

I cut her off mid-sentence, aware that I'd pay for that at some point, and took the other call. "Crishell McMillan."

"Hi, it's Rita Sakowski."

"Oh, yes, hi, Rita. I stopped by Sweet Perks yesterday. Fabulous coffee."

I could hear the pleasure in the woman's voice as she responded, "Yes, Olivia told me. I'm sorry I couldn't join you." She hesitated and then said, "I heard you had an . . . unfortunate encounter with some of the museum board?"

Oh my God! Gossip certainly did travel at the speed of light in Fox Hollow. "Do you mean Lawrence Peabody and Andy McHardy? Where did you hear that?"

A much longer pause, and then . . . "Well, I guess you didn't see the *Fox Hollow Gazette*, then?"

"The town newspaper?" I recalled my brief encounter with Quentin Watson. He must have witnessed the whole thing, and he hadn't looked happy when I'd put him off for an interview. "Oh, no," I whispered.

"Oh, yes. It should be outside on your stoop. Newbies always get a complimentary Sunday copy. Page six."

"Thanks. I'll talk to you later." *After I kill Quentin Watson,* I thought grimly. I chucked the phone onto the couch and raced outside. Sure enough, a fat paper lay on my steps. I snatched it up, set the pile of advertisements and circulars to one side, and riffled the pages to six. There it was, in bold, right at the top of the page.

Frenemies, Anyone?

What new resident of Fox Hollow is making "frenemies" of the members of our museum board before she logs twenty-four hours into our little town? Said resident was spotted at the Captain's Club yesterday getting two of FH's finest, Lawrence Peabody and Andy McHardy, hot under the collar and was spotted earlier in a heated altercation with one of our more prominent citizens, initials AW. Who might this rabble-rouser be, you ask? Far be it from us to name names, but hint: Our new resident has graced the small screen for years, and recently was laid off from her hit series. Rumor also has it she's planning to reopen one of Fox Hollow's most popular shops. Tip for the Newbie: Don't take out your frustration over a failed career out on the natives. Your energies would be better concentrated on reopening a beloved store that has been regarded as a landmark here for years.

"Great," I muttered. "Fricking great." I grabbed my phone and eyed Purrday, who was lounging across the brocaded love seat, busily washing his tail. "I've got to be able to sue. This . . . this is libel. Failed career, my a—"

"Merow," said Purrday.

"He doesn't mention me by name, but come on! Graced the small screen for years, recently laid off from her hit series? And the part about concentrating my energy on reopening a beloved store? Who else could it be?"

Purrday's response was to flick his tail, hop off the love seat, and stalk off toward the kitchen in search of his food bowl.

"Okay, you're right. It kinda did happen, so it's not libel. So, what? Invasion of privacy?"

I sighed. Probably no more an invasion than my listening in on their conversation, although that had been an accident. Another pitfall of fame: your life was an open book and you pretty much walked around with a target on your back.

My iPhone rang again and I snatched it up and tapped the screen without even looking at the number. "Yes," I growled. "If this is about that article . . ."

"Hardly that," a harsh voice snapped, "although I did find it amusing."

I blinked as I recognized the growly tone on the other end. "Ms. Witherspoon? How did you get my cell number?"

"I can usually get pretty much anything I set my mind to. Plus, it was in your file at the museum." There was a pause and then Amelia cleared her throat. "I'm calling you because I think it's time the two of us discussed . . . a certain matter. I think you know to what I'm referring."

I almost dropped the phone. Purrday had come back into the room and now he rubbed impatiently against my black pants leg, leaving a smattering of fine white hairs. "Owrrr," he said.

"Yes, yes." I waved my hand at him. "I'll fill your bowl in a minute," I said.

Something else butted against my other leg. I looked down and saw Kahlua squatted there. "Ma-row!" she trilled.

"Yes, I'll feed you too," I hissed.

"Pardon?" Amelia asked.

"Sorry, I was talking to the cats. So, Ms. Rubin spoke to you then?"

"Ginnifer?"

"Yes. I spoke with her and she said she would try and talk to you."

"I know nothing about that," Amelia snapped. "This matter has nothing to do with your aunt's collection, as you well know. I'm offering to clarify certain things for you, so you don't end up making a fool of yourself and drag me down along with you."

I frowned. None of what Amelia had just said made the slightest bit of sense. "I'm sorry, I have no idea what you're talking about. If it's not about the display . . ."

"Good God, stop sounding like a broken record," Amelia spat. "You needn't play dumb with me, young lady," Amelia snapped. "What I want to know is just how you became aware of these erroneous facts. Who you've been talking to."

This conversation was getting worse by the minute. I felt like Alice, just dropped through the rabbit hole, and I pushed my hair out of my eyes with the heel of my hand. "I'm sorry. I haven't the vaguest . . ."

"Oh, save it. Just meet me at the museum in an hour. I'll leave the side door open for you. I'm sure we can come to an amicable agreement."

"What sort of agreement? I don't—"

I was talking to air. Amelia had hung up. I heard a plaintive *merow* and I looked down at Purrday, who stood glaring up at me, his majestic plume of a tail waving to and fro. "Owrr," he said again.

I bent down to stroke his head absently. "Yes, yes, I know. You're hungry. I have no idea what that woman was talking about. Come to an agreement over what?"

Kahlua appeared and meowed loudly, so I headed for the kitchen, both cats close behind. "Okay, okay," I said as I opened the cupboard door. "Your food's coming." I filled both bowls with kibble and set them down next to each other. Both cats regarded each other warily for a second, then hunger won out and they hunkered down in front of the bowls. A minute later the only sound was their contented slurping. My job done, I dialed Mazie Madison's number. The call went straight to voicemail. I hung up without leaving a message and dialed Ginnifer Rubin's number. That too went to voicemail.

"Well," I said, tapping my iPhone against my palm, "I guess there's only one way to get to the bottom of this. Confront the witch in her lair." I glanced over at the cats. They'd finished eating and were now stretched out on the floor, not close but not far away from each other either. Purrday was lying on his side and Kahlua was washing her paws. "Wish me luck, guys," I called.

Both cats lifted their heads, and then two paws went up in the air. "Er-Owl!" said Purrday.

"Thanks," I said. "I'll need it."

• • •

Exactly fifty-five minutes later I parked my car in the lot of the Fox Hollow Museum. I climbed out, locked it, and took a quick look around. There was a big black Caddy parked at the far end of the lot, and I figured that must be Amelia's car. There were no others around that I could see.

The museum was a handsome, L-shaped brick building that took up most of the block. I walked around to the side door and pulled on it. Locked. I frowned. Amelia had distinctly said she'd leave it open, hadn't she? Or maybe I'd misunderstood, and she'd said the back door? I walked around the building and over to a brown door marked *Service*. I pulled on the door handle and it swung out on squeaky hinges.

In between my two television series, I'd done a low-budget horror film called *Night of the Stalker*. In it, an axe murderer targeted a group of teens who'd violated what he considered his home, a shack in the woods. I'd played the gang leader's girlfriend, and I'd had exactly twenty minutes onscreen, fifteen of them trying to avoid being axed in a deserted building. As I stood uncertainly in the museum hallway, I was reminded of that movie. And how I'd screamed when I'd found the body of Jasmine, my BFF, right before the axe landed in my back. I shivered.

"Amelia," I called, my voice just a shade above a whisper. "It's Crishell McMillan. I'm here for our meeting, as you requested."

I glanced at my watch. Of course, it was possible the Caddy wasn't her car, and she wasn't here yet, but . . . Amelia somehow didn't strike me as the tardy type. I moved cautiously down the long hallway, peering this way and that, looking for some sign of life. I rounded a corner and saw a door straight ahead, slightly ajar. I bit back a sigh and quickened my steps. The placard on the door read *Library*. I gave the door a push and it swung gently inward. I stood for a minute, letting my eyes adjust to the dim lighting. I had an impression of floor-to-ceiling bookshelves in front of me, and some low-slung display cases off to my right. The room appeared deserted, and I started to turn away when I caught a glimpse of something out of the corner of my eye.

An arm. A very still arm. And a hand that clutched what looked like a photograph.

For the next few seconds, I couldn't think, couldn't breathe. The room spun before my eyes, and when it stopped I opened my mouth and let out a long, bloodcurdling scream that movie director would have been proud of.

Amelia Witherspoon lay on her back in the far corner of the room, in front of a large bust of William Shakespeare. Her eyes were wide open, her white hair fanned out like a flag around her head and shoulders, and her thick lips formed a perfect O of surprise. Judging from the red stain that spread halfway across the front of her white shirt, she was also quite, quite dead.

Eight

"I've told you twice, Amelia Witherspoon called me and asked me to meet her in the museum office. We had an appointment."

Once I'd screamed myself hoarse, I'd managed to pull myself together to whip out my cell to dial 911. The policeman who'd shown up ten minutes later, Officer Riley, looked as if he'd just graduated from the police academy. Sandy hair with a stubborn cowlick, slightly mottled skin that spoke of a bout with acne, and a firm, prominent jaw. It wasn't so much his looks, though, that bespoke his youth and inexperience, but rather his take-no-prisoners attitude. His clear blue eyes widened, though, at the sharpness in my tone, and when he spoke again he managed to sound very apologetic indeed.

"I'm sorry about all the repetition, ma'am. It's just I've only been on the force two weeks and this"—he scratched at his sideburn with the tip of his pen—"is my first dead body." From the pained expression on his face, I had a feeling he also hoped it would be his last.

I barked out a short laugh. "Mine too," I said. "At least, it's my first real one." At his puzzled look I added, "I, ah, used to be an actress on a spy series. Over the years my character stumbled across tons of dead bodies. At the end of the day, though, they get up and walk away."

He cast a glance over at Amelia's white-sheeted body. The paramedics had arrived right after him, and now they were just waiting for the coroner's wagon "She's not going to do that," he said. "Anyway, this is my first homicide, and I want to have all the facts straight for Detective Bloodgood. I've never worked with him before, but I hear he's a stickler for detail."

Bloodgood, huh? It sounded like a perfect name for a homicide detective. I pictured a gray-haired guy with a close-clipped mustache, a bit of a paunch, and an even worse attitude than Officer Riley. "So, is this Bloodgood guy in charge of Homicide?"

"You could say that." The officer's lips twisted into a wry half grin. "He's the *only* detective assigned to Homicide. We share him with the other county towns. Don't get very many murders in this neck of the woods." He flipped a page in his notebook. "You knew the deceased?"

"Not really. We only met once."

He scribbled something down. "Over museum business?"

"Yes."

"And that's why you were meeting her here this morning as well?"

"She requested we meet," I said carefully. "She didn't say as to the meeting's nature." Or at least she hadn't said anything that made sense.

He frowned, looked at his notes. "O-kay." Then he scribbled something else down.

I glanced out the window at movement and saw a dark sedan pull up, followed closely by a black SUV with *Coroner* printed in gold letters on the side. Two men got out of the SUV, pulling on disposable gloves. I couldn't see the occupant of the sedan yet, but I figured that must be Detective Bloodgood. The sedan door opened and I caught a glimpse of a man's leg, and then I jumped a mile high as Officer Riley's hand clamped down on my shoulder. I spun around, gasping for breath.

"Good Lord, don't *do* that."

"Sorry. Will you come with me, please?"

I stole a quick glance out the window, but both the sedan and SUV now appeared to be deserted, the occupants having gone around the building to the main door. I followed Riley down the hall, past the partially closed office door, and into a smaller cubbyhole with a desk, filing cabinet, and a small printer set up on a low table. A Keurig coffee maker was on top of the filing cabinet, and there were some napkins, paper cups, a bottle of Cremora beside it. There were two chairs, one behind the desk, one in front. Riley motioned me to the one in front. "Detective Bloodgood will be in shortly," he said. "Help yourself to some coffee, if you want. I think Londra keeps it in the top drawer."

Londra had to be Londra Lewis, the woman I'd seen arguing with Amelia yesterday in the park. I leaned back and shifted my position in the chair. God, had that only been yesterday? It seemed a lifetime ago. I got up, walked over to the file cabinet, pulled open the top drawer. Sure enough, there were a half dozen boxes of different Keurig coffees neatly stacked there. I plucked a Dark Magic pod out of the mix and was just about to put it in the coffee maker when I heard the creak of the door behind me.

"Crishell McMillan?"

Something about his voice struck me as familiar. Oh, no, it couldn't be, could it? I turned around, very slowly, to gaze at the other occupant of the room. Yep, the same dark wavy hair, tanned skin. Only now he wore black slacks and a black shirt under a black and tan jacket that molded to his muscular frame and fit him like a second skin. "You-*you're* Detective Bloodgood?" I eked out.

Josh started at seeing me, and then he did something totally unexpected: he smiled. "And *you're* Crishell McMillan? Some detective I am, huh? I should have suspected you were Tillie's niece when you said your nickname was Shell." He swiped at his forehead with the back of his hand. "Don't take this the wrong way, but I never pegged you for an actress."

"Don't feel bad." I offered him a lopsided smile. "I'd never have figured you for a homicide detective and yet you are."

"You certainly have had an exciting first few days in Fox Hollow, haven't you?" The smile vanished, the eyes narrowed, the conversational tone of a few seconds before replaced by one that was cool, impersonal. I recognized the signs, even though my prior experience with it had been on a soundstage. Josh Bloodgood had morphed into cop mode. "So, you found the body?"

"That's right."

He reached into his jacket pocket and pulled out a small notebook that looked almost identical to the one Riley had. Standard cop issue, perhaps? He pooled his tall frame into the chair behind the desk and leaned both his elbows on the desk, pen poised over the notebook. "Tell me exactly what happened."

"Okay, well, as I told Officer Riley, Amelia Witherspoon called and asked me to meet her at the museum in an hour. She—"

"And what time was that?"

"Around ten." When he remained silent I went on, "She said that she'd leave the side door open for me. I arrived here at precisely eleven ten—I know because I checked my watch against the dashboard clock—and saw a black Cadillac that I assume was hers parked at the other end of the lot." I let out a deep breath. "I went to the side entrance but it was locked, so I went around to the service entrance. That door was open, so I came in. I called out her name but she didn't answer, so I walked down the hallway and saw a light in the room at the end of the hall. I went in and found her, lying there . . . dead."

"Did you touch the body?"

I stared at him, wide-eyed. "Good Lord, no. I could see she was dead. There was nothing I could do for her."

"Touch anything in the room?"

I scrunched up my lips as I thought. "The door was ajar, and I pushed on it so I could enter. I saw the body almost immediately, so, no. I didn't touch anything else."

He scribbled quickly in the book. "Why did Amelia want to meet with you?"

I hesitated. "I can't say for certain."

He looked up. One eyebrow winged skyward. "Pardon? She asked you to meet her here but didn't tell you why?"

"Oh, she told me why. It's just, it didn't make any sense." He continued to stare at me, so I went on, "I offered to loan the museum my aunt's Cary Grant poster collection to showcase here in a few weeks."

Bloodgood's hand paused in midair. "There was a photograph of a Cary Grant poster in her hand," he said.

"That must be the one I gave her. I thought maybe it might convince her she was making a mistake."

"Mistake?"

"The museum board voted against displaying my aunt's collection. I had a feeling that Amelia might have been behind it."

"That was the reason she called you and asked to meet? To straighten all that out?"

I flexed my fingers. "As I said, I'm not sure. Her reasons for meeting me seemed vague." Suddenly I felt cold, and I folded my arms across my chest. I could just imagine what my mother would say if she could see me now: *Don't say anything without a lawyer!* Which might not be bad advice. I was just about to ask Josh if I needed one when Officer Riley stuck his head in the door. "Detective Bloodgood? The coroner would like to see you. He found—"

"Tell him I'll be right there." Josh cut the officer off, pushed back his chair and stood up, jamming his notebook into his jacket pocket as he did so. "You can go, Sh—Ms. McMillan." He caught himself and then paused, stared intently at me. "I might have some more questions for you later, though. You'll be available?"

I nodded. "Yes. I've no plans to leave town. After all, I only just got here."

He looked at me and didn't say a word. So much for my little attempt at humor. I felt myself flush, and then Josh made a dismissive motion with his hand. "Thanks for your cooperation."

I nodded curtly and had to force myself to walk, not run, down the hall. When I passed the library, I noticed the door was wide open, and I couldn't resist taking a sidelong glance.

I saw the edge of a white sheet on the floor, and my stomach roiled again.

• • •

Purrday lay sprawled across the rug by the love seat and Kahlua was sprawled across its back when I got home. He was chewing on something, and as I entered the room he looked up with a *Home so soon?* expression on his flat, furry face.

I set my bag down and crossed the room to kneel beside him. "What do you have there, Purrday?" I asked. In answer, he put both his paws on top of whatever it was he'd been feasting on and blinked his good eye at me. I shook my head and gave him my sternest expression. "Let me see."

He dropped his head and lifted one paw. Kahlua leaned forward, watching with interest, probably rejoicing in the fact her new brother was getting a scolding. I could see a rounded edge peeping out from under the other paw. We stared at each other for a few moments, and then he lifted that one too. Purrday's prize was a round piece of wood. I snatched it up for a better look, and he let out a plaintive meow. The object in question was a button. The edges appeared to be well-chewed—thanks to Purrday, no doubt—and there was a carved initial in the center that could have been either an M or a W. It was faded, so it was hard to tell. I looked at the cat again. "Did you find this in the house somewhere?"

He leaned forward and gave me a head butt. I took that as a yes.

"Where?" I asked and then stopped, realizing that I was, indeed, sitting here talking to a cat, and worse yet, expecting him to somehow answer me. Purrday lumbered to his feet and set off at a brisk canter down the long hallway. Kahlua was up like a shot, racing after him. I followed the cats into the kitchen. Both walked right over to the spot under the picture window where I'd set a place mat with food and water bowls for both of them, now that they were mostly getting along. Purrday tapped at the empty one twice with his paw, hesitated, then tapped at Kahlua's as well. Both cats shot me a reproachful look designed to shame me for not tending to their needs above all else.

"Yes, I know. Time for a refill." I slid the button into my pocket and reached underneath the sink to pull out the sack of kibble. No doubt the button had belonged to my aunt, but how had Purrday gotten his paws on it? He'd shared the house with Aunt Tillie. No doubt he knew many nooks and crannies where things might be secreted. Then again, how did cats get their paws on anything? It had probably popped off one of her dresses or coats, and the cat had claimed it as a toy. Purrday bumped my hand as I finished filling the bowl. "What else of Aunt Matilda's have you got stashed around here?" I asked him.

He ignored me and stuck his head in the bowl. I gave myself a mental slap. Had I really thought the cat could understand me and would answer?

Umm . . . yeah.

Once both cats had their noses happily buried in their bowls, I walked up to the third floor and opened the door to the room that held my aunt's private collection. I had to admit she'd done a beautiful job in here. The walls were painted a soft green, a contrast to the mauve rug that covered the floor. There were two glass cases that stretched the length of the room, and they contained what a collector would regard as unique items: an ashtray that had been used by Vivien Leigh, a handkerchief that had belonged to Lawrence Olivier. There were movie scripts autographed by famous actors, among them Jimmy Stewart, Kirk Douglas, Douglas Fairbanks, and of course Cary Grant. Some of my aunt's extensive collection of movie posters and lobby cards were framed and graced the walls, while the rest were in shallow bins along the back of the room. I walked over to the large framed poster of *His Girl Friday* and looked at it, pausing to run my finger over Cary's scrawled signature in the corner.

A rumbling purr at my feet made me look down. Purrday squatted beside me, his head cocked, his good eye fastened right on the *Friday* poster. He raised a paw and pointed at the poster, letting out another rumbling purr.

I couldn't help but laugh. "You know you were named after that movie, right?" I said.

"Merow."

I bent down and gave him a scratch under his chin. Purrday rumbled his thanks, and I picked him up and cradled him against my chest. "I imagine you and Aunt Tillie spent a lot of quality time here, huh? I hope to as well, once things get settled down. They must," I said with determination. "It would be a shame not to be able to share any of these pieces with the world." I sighed softly. "I'd planned on going to the pet store tomorrow, looking through the stock, start getting things set up for reopening, but right now . . . I hate to say it, but my heart's just not in it."

Purrday snuggled in more comfortably, almost as if to say, *Who could blame you?* I took another long look at the room, sighed, then closed the door and, still holding Purrday, retraced my steps into the parlor and dropped down onto the sofa. The afternoon's events had been puzzling, to say the least. Bloodgood had said Matilda had been holding the photograph I'd given her. Had that been the reason for her call? I dismissed that thought as quickly as it entered my mind. She'd said what she wanted to discuss had nothing to do with the collection, but then why had she been holding that photo?

My iPhone buzzed and I picked it up. It was a number I didn't recognize. I hesitated, intending to let it go to voicemail, but then figured that with my luck it might be Bloodgood, so I'd better answer. I tapped the Answer button. "Hello?"

"Crishell McMillan! Or should I say Shell Marlowe? Quentin Watson here."

Oh, great. Time to get an unlisted number. "Mr. Watson," I said through clenched teeth. "What can I do for you?"

"I understand there was some excitement down at the museum today, and you were right in the thick of it."

Good God, was the man a stalker? How did he know my every move? "That's correct," I said.

"Can you share some details?" He paused. "Or do I have to clear *that* through your agent, too?"

It took all my willpower not to go off on the man. "I'm sorry," I said, "but I really think you should contact the police department if you want details."

"I understand Amelia Witherspoon was murdered, and you found the body?"

OMG! News traveled that fast? "I'm not at liberty to say."

He paused. "Well, then, could you tell me why you were at the museum on a day when it's closed to the public?"

"I'm sorry, Mr. Watson, but I don't have authorization to release any details. Those have to come from the detective in charge."

Another brief silence, and then, "Well, then, can you verify that you accused Amelia Witherspoon of influencing the board members to vote against displaying your aunt's poster collection?"

Good God, how had he found that out? "I—no, I can't."

"Then it's not true?"

I took a deep breath, slowly exhaled. "You really should contact Detective Bloodgood if you want details. I'm not at liberty to say."

"Detective Bloodgood will know the details of you accusing Ms. Witherspoon of influencing the board?"

No wonder people thought this guy was annoying. He certainly was tenacious, I had to give him that. "I have no idea what Detective Bloodgood knows or doesn't know," I snapped.

"I see. Then perhaps you'd care to comment on why the deceased was found holding a photograph of one of the posters in your aunt's private collection?"

I bit down hard on my lower lip. "No comment. And that will be my answer to all your questions, so you needn't bother asking any more."

"Fine." His tone was decidedly frosty. "Thanks so much for your . . . cooperation."

"Don't mention it," I grumbled, tossing my iPhone next to me on the sofa. I glanced over at Purrday, who'd hopped up on the sofa beside me. "Yes, yes, I know. Max would have told me to bite my tongue and be chillingly polite. Now I suppose Quentin Watson's next little snippet will paint me as suspect number one."

The cat blinked, and then let out a loud meow.

"Well," I sighed, "Josh was right about one thing. It has been an exciting few days in Fox Hollow. Excitement of this nature, though, I could definitely do without."

Purrday jumped off the sofa, stretched out his hind legs, then butted his head against my ankles.

I reached down and stroked his head. I couldn't control what Quentin

Watson might write about me, any more than I could control what those gossip magazines always used to print. Except in those instances, none of that drivel had ever been one hundred percent true.

I had argued with Amelia Witherspoon and accused her of influencing board member votes. I'd intimated to Larry Peabody and Andy McHardy that they might be being blackmailed by her. And I had found her dead body.

Why had Amelia wanted to see me? To clarify details about a certain matter, she'd said. But what matter? Whatever it was, she'd thought I'd known, but I hadn't. I needed to know just what this information was, and what, if any, connection it might have to me.

The question was, how was I going to find that out?

Nine

I changed out of my pantsuit into a sweat suit and decided my time might be well spent making a call list of my aunt's old suppliers. I thumbed through her old-school Rolodex, writing down businesses, names, and any other little notes from Tillie that might be useful. *Takes payment up front, ask about overstock discounts, only ships full cases.* I smiled. I could practically hear her voice. Then I found a card for Scott Aviary, Carl Scott proprietor, that had the note *try to call outside store hours, likes to chat.* Figuring four o'clock on a Sunday was a nice time for a chat, I tapped the number into my cell and then hit Send.

A few seconds later I was connected with Mr. Scott, a pleasant-sounding man with a broad Southern accent. He was thrilled I was taking over Tillie's store, because, as he put it, she was "one fine lady" and "a terrific customer. She paid on time!" I assured him I'd be taking over in every category, and just as soon as things got a bit more settled, I'd set up a meeting to discuss stock. I hung up hoping that meeting would take place sooner than later. I started to thumb through the Rolodex again when I saw my iPhone start to whirl around in a circle on the desk. I hesitated, afraid it might be Quentin Watson again, but it might also be Josh Bloodgood; he'd said he might have more questions. I snatched the phone up and looked at the number.

Lord, it was worse. It was Gary. I sighed. If I didn't answer, he'd only keep calling back. Best to get it over with, else I might find myself taking his call behind bars.

"Hello, Gary."

"Finally!" My ex-costar's usually well-modulated voice held more than a trace of irritation. "Tell me it's not true, and you haven't lost your mind. Tell me this is all just a fit of temporary insanity, and you're coming back here on the next plane."

"Sorry, no can do. I'm a permanent resident of Fox Hollow, Connecticut, now."

"Oh, Good Lord. Max was right. You've lost your mind. Look, if it's top billing on the reboot you want, well then, you've got it, sweet cheeks. Just say the word and Max can get that contract ready by tomorrow. I checked, and there's a ten p.m. flight out of LaGuardia. Is Frog Hollow near LaGuardia?"

"It's Fox Hollow and I have no idea, but it doesn't matter. I'm not coming back to LA. At least not right now."

"No? Then your decision is final? You don't want to do that series on cable?"

"No, Gary, I don't. But you feel free to go for it," I said, trying to put a note of enthusiasm in my voice. "Look on this as a golden opportunity. You can get a hot new starlet as your costar. It'll give the new series a fresh look."

"Yeah, well, seems the producers don't want a fresh look. They want *you*."

"Gee, thanks."

"Aw, Shell, you know what I mean. Look, babe, if you don't return soon, you might as well kiss your acting career goodbye."

"You weren't listening, were you? I meant it when I said I've retired. Look," I said, my tone softening, "you turn on that charm of yours. I'm sure the producers will still want you."

"What if they don't? Would you change your mind then?" When I didn't answer, he added, "Turning this down is so typically selfish of you, Shell. You're only thinking of yourself."

Ah, yes. The guilt trip, and he was so very good at it. But I wasn't exactly in a mood for playing his game right now. "Yes, that's me. Always putting myself first. You would never be guilty of such a thing, right?"

"Is this about what happened at the Emmies? Didn't I already apologize for that?"

I sighed. "No, Gary. It's not about that."

He was silent a few moments and then said, "Is this about Patrick? Because I still talk to him?" Before I could answer he rushed on, "I told you right from the get-go not to get involved with him, but you did anyway. I lent you a shoulder to cry on when it all blew up, and I never said I told you so."

"That's true, you didn't. No, Gary, it's not about Patrick. I'm over him, trust me."

"Maybe you are. I'm not so sure about Patrick."

My breath caught in the back of my throat for a brief moment. "That's his problem," I said firmly.

"Something's going on," he persisted. "I can hear it in your voice, Shell. Talk to me. Maybe I can help."

Not unless you're Perry Mason. "Trust me, Gary, you can't."

His voice took on a wheedling tone. "C'mon, Shell. Didn't we fight crime and trap international spies together for ten years? Of course I can help you, unless you're really involved in international espionage, in which case you should probably call the FBI. You're not, are you?" he asked anxiously.

I pushed the heel of my hand through my hair. "I'm hanging up now. Got things to do."

"Like what? Selling kibble to dogs? Catnip socks to cats? Look, I know a brush-off when I hear one. Well, I guess I'll just have to come out there, find out what's going on for myself."

I knew darn well he wouldn't. Gary just wasn't cut out for small-town life. "Fine. Come on down. You can stay here. I've got plenty of room."

"Say, that's real hospitable of you, Shell. It'll make it easier for me to help, too. I'll see you soon," he said and hung up.

"Sure you will." I tossed the phone back on the couch. Purrday and Kahlua both poked their heads out from under the couch and looked up at me. Kahlua let out a short yowl.

"Men," I said. "Don't worry, he's not really coming. I like Gary, but I know him. He craves excitement, life in the fast lane. He wouldn't be caught dead in Fox Hollow . . ." I stopped and put my fingers to my lips. "Sorry. Poor choice of words."

Both cats gave me a cool look, then Kahlua hopped up on top of the couch and stretched herself full-length. Purrday settled himself at my feet and closed his eye.

The phone rang again, and when I noted the caller's name on the screen, I answered quickly. "Ms. Madison. Hi."

"I just heard," Mazie Madison breathed into the phone. "Amelia's dead, and you found the body? Are you all right?"

"Yes, just a little flummoxed, I guess." I forced out a laugh. "It was my first dead body. My first real one, anyway."

"Good Lord." Mazie sounded as if she were in shock, which she probably was. "What happened? Why were you there?"

"Amelia called me earlier," I said carefully. "She said she had something to discuss with me, that she was certain we could come to an amicable arrangement. I was hoping it was about my proposal."

"I doubt that." Mazie hesitated and then said, "I had a call from

Lawrence Peabody. He said you made some pretty harsh accusations against him, Amelia, and some of the other board members."

Swell. "I just wanted to be sure they were making up their own minds about the collection, not having it done for them."

"Ginnifer called me too. She seemed to think you deserved another chance."

I felt a little bit of relief. "That's good to know."

"Of course, now any decision should wait until we replace Amelia," Mazie went on. "I'll certainly keep you posted."

"I appreciate that."

"Well, I'll leave you to rest now. I can't imagine what it must have been like, finding her body lying there. It must have been horrible."

"It certainly was an experience I wouldn't wish on my worst enemy," I agreed.

I said goodbye and hung up. I sat on the edge of the couch and rested my chin in my hands. Now all I had to hope for was that I'd be available to donate the collection, if the new vote went in my favor. I gave myself a little shake and abruptly stood up, startling both cats.

"Of course I'll be available," I said, stretching both arms wide. "What am I thinking? I'm innocent. I know I didn't kill Amelia."

Oh, yeah, like I would be the first innocent person ever to be convicted of a crime they didn't commit. I plopped back down on the couch and sat, shoulders hunched, my thoughts whirling around in my brain like a tornado.

And then my doorbell rang.

I went into the foyer and peeped out the window. There was no mistaking Rita's flaming hair, or Olivia's dark head. No sooner had I opened the door than I found myself wrapped in an enormous group hug, my face pressed against Rita's generous bosom.

"Oh, my God, Shell, are you all right?" Olivia whispered in my ear. "We just heard."

I managed to raise my head and offer them a lopsided smile. "Wow, gossip sure does travel at the speed of light in Fox Hollow, doesn't it?"

Olivia pooh-poohed that and gave my arm a quick squeeze. Rita released me and held me at arm's length, looking me over like a mama wren might look over a baby bird getting ready to spread its wings for the first time. "I bet you haven't eaten a thing all day. You look terrible."

"Thanks." I swiped at my face with the back of my hand, and then realized she was right. I'd gotten up late, and after Amelia's phone call, food had been the last thing on my mind. As if on cue, my stomach rumbled.

"See," Rita said triumphantly, "I knew it. Ron, get that in here."

I noticed Ron was there too. He'd been standing a little bit away from the other two, on the stairs, and he held a flower-patterned Crock-Pot in his arms. "That's sweet of you, but you didn't have to . . ."

"Oh, you don't know Rita." Ron smiled. "She thinks food is the cure for everything."

"Well, isn't it?" Rita winked at me and stepped inside, dragging me by my wrist. "Ron, put that soup in the kitchen and turn the Crock-Pot on low. It's my own recipe," she said, her eyes soft. "First, though, you've got to tell us what happened."

"Rita," Olivia said in a stern tone. "Maybe Shell doesn't want to talk about it. Or maybe she's under orders not to."

"Nonsense. It's all over town anyway," Rita said.

"Yep," Ron nodded. "In a small town, everyone knows everything, or darn close to it." He gave me a small smile as he turned toward my kitchen. "Not much different from Hollywood, huh?"

I was starting to think Fox Hollow was ten times worse than Hollywood. Rita turned back to me. "I heard you found her in the Sword Room, and she had a saber sticking out of her chest?"

My eyes widened. "Good Lord, no. There was nothing sticking out of her chest, or at least nothing I could see. Her blouse was covered in blood."

"Oh, God." Rita squinched her eyes shut. "Just like on *CSI* or one of those crime shows, right? She was shot?"

"I have no idea. Maybe." Despite the situation, I chuckled. "What, the Fox Hollow gossip mill hasn't pinned down the cause of death?"

"Not yet." Ron grinned back. "Official details haven't been released yet, but speculation's high that since it's Amelia, it must have been gruesome."

"Gruesome enough," I agreed. "I was interviewed by the homicide detective. He said he might have more questions for me."

"Ah." Olivia and Rita exchanged a knowing glance, and then Olivia added, "I see you met Josh."

"Actually, I'd met him yesterday in the park. His dog, or I should say his sister's dog, ran into me."

"Oh, Rocco!" Rita laughed merrily. "He's quite a little prankster, that one. You'd never know he was that affectionate to look at him, would you? With that pit bull face?" She put a finger to her lips. "Olivia, I forget. Is Rocco Sue's dog or Michelle's?"

"Sue's. Michelle lives in a tiny apartment over the Captain's Club. I doubt that landlord of hers would let her have a big dog. She's lucky to have that hamster." Olivia laughed. "She got it at your aunt's store, too."

"Josh has *two* sisters?" I asked. I remembered the bartender at the Captain's Club. "Does one of them work at the Captain's Club?"

Olivia nodded. "Michelle. She's the youngest. She's studying law at the university, and she bartends nights and weekends to put herself through school."

"Sue's the oldest," supplied Rita. "After her divorce, she moved back here. Josh helped her open her store. You might have seen it. Secondhand Sue's?"

Aha. Josh had been standing in its doorway when he'd seen me arguing with Amelia. He must have been returning Rocco. I recalled the anxious look on his face and turned to Olivia. "Josh didn't have any sort of relationship with Amelia Witherspoon, by any chance?"

Olivia's eyes widened. "Relationship?" she asked. "What sort of relationship are you talking about?"

I shifted a bit uncomfortably. "Not what you're thinking," I said. "I thought maybe they might be friends, or, oh, who knows? Distant relatives, perhaps?"

The three of them looked at each other, then at me, and then they all burst out laughing. "What gave you that idea?" Rita finally managed to gasp out.

I lifted my chin. My idea wasn't *that* ridiculous, was it? "Josh was standing in the doorway of the secondhand shop yesterday when I yelled at Amelia that she'd be sorry for not reconsidering my proposal. He had a funny look on his face, like he was upset."

Olivia waved her hand. "He probably was. For a homicide detective, Josh hates arguing and dissention. Besides, it probably got under his skin that another person found a reason to dislike Amelia. Lord knows ninety percent of the town did already."

"He did know her, though. Amelia was a big contributor to the policeman's fund," supplied Rita. "I think she and Josh were on a couple of fundraising committees." She paused and then added, "Along with your aunt."

"Great," I sighed. "He hears us arguing and then hears me scream she'll be sorry, and then I find her dead body. I must look like suspect number one in his eyes right now."

Olivia shook her head. "Not necessarily. There are lots of other people in line ahead of you for that position."

"Yeah?" I leaned forward and rested my chin in my hands. "Make my day. Tell me who?"

"Well, there are those three board members for starters," offered Olivia. "And Mazie Madison's no angel in the hating Amelia sweepstakes, either."

"That's true," Rita agreed. "Mazie got the museum director job via the recommendation of Mayor Hart. The board passed her appointment while Amelia was out of the country on vacation. I don't think Amelia ever forgave any of them for that," chuckled Rita.

"Made her work all the harder to get something on the mayor," observed Olivia. "It's anyone's guess whether she succeeded or not. I know Amelia made a generous contribution to Hart's reelection fund a few years ago. There are times when it seemed as if she had the mayor in her hip pocket, and then others when Hart would just flat-out disagree with her. Funny thing, they always seemed to get along. That relationship's a hard one to pin down."

I was remembering something else, too. "And the other two board members? How did they feel about Amelia?"

"Simone could take her or leave her. Simone is just as, if not more, wealthy than Amelia, so she pretty much marches to her own drum," Rita said.

I racked my brain to come up with the last board member's name. "How about Garrett Knute?"

Ron frowned. "Hard to say. Rita knows him best." He looked at the redhead. "He used to be in business with your husband, right?"

Rita nodded. "They had an accounting firm until Garrett's grandfather passed and left him a bundle of money. He opted out of the partnership and went into business for himself. He opened a specialty dish shop. Did pretty well with it, too, surprisingly." She shook her head. "He always voted the opposite of anything Amelia wanted to do on the museum board. Sometimes I think he did it just to piss her off. There was no love lost between them, that's for sure."

"He was arguing with her yesterday," I said slowly. "I heard them. They were arguing over an envelope. He wanted it, but Amelia stuffed it into her bag. Then he said, 'over my dead body,' and stalked off."

"Oh, that does sound ominous," agreed Rita. "You should tell Josh."

I frowned. "I don't know if I should tattle on Garrett. I'd hate to piss off another board member."

Rita's eyes were wide. "But if he threatened her . . ."

"It wasn't a threat, exactly. He said over *his* dead body."

"But he was pissed at her," persisted Rita. "Maybe he was pissed enough to kill her. You should tell Josh," she repeated.

"Garrett says stuff like that all the time, though," Ron interjected. "You know how he is. He blows up and then, poof! It's over. But I agree, you probably should mention it. If for no other reason, to throw someone else in the suspect pool along with you." At Rita's sharp gasp, he let out a loud guffaw. "You know as well as I do how Josh thinks. Shell's right. I'm sure she is on his short list."

My shoulders slumped even more. "Terrific."

"You know how it is on the crime shows. The most obvious suspect is never the right one," Rita added hastily. "Besides, you know you didn't do it, right?"

"We're supposed to be cheering Shell up, not convincing her that she's going to jail," Olivia said. She turned to me. "Maybe you should start making plans for the store's reopening. It might take your mind off all this."

"I thought about it, but I just can't concentrate on all those details right now. And wouldn't a celebration be in poor taste? I'm afraid Urban Tails's reopening will have to be delayed for a bit."

Rita rose and motioned toward the kitchen. "How about we all have some gumbo now? It should be hot enough."

I shook my head. "I appreciate the gesture, really, but I haven't much of an appetite."

Ron clambered to his feet. "We should let Shell get some rest. She's had a pretty trying day, and it's not even dinnertime."

"Yes," Rita agreed. "Keep the Crock-Pot, dear, you might get hungry later. I can swing by tomorrow or the next day and pick it up."

Olivia squeezed my hand. "You take care, Shell. And call if you need anything."

I breathed a sigh of relief once I'd closed the door behind them. I knew they meant well, but that entire conversation had been tiring and enlightening at the same time. Purrday and Kahlua appeared and both let out loud meows.

"Well, kids, looks as if there are plenty of suspects, but which one had enough of a motive to want to see Amelia dead?"

Purrday cocked his head as if debating that point. Kahlua just opened her mouth in a wide, unlovely cat yawn.

I floated from room to room, unpacking a box here, straightening a few odds and ends there. Eventually I wandered into the kitchen, pulled out a bowl, and sampled some of Rita's gumbo from the Crock-Pot. It was good. Once things settled down, I'd have to ask her for the recipe. I finished the gumbo, put the dish in the sink, and then wandered into my den. I thumbed through my CD collection, found the soundtrack for *Phantom of the Opera*, and popped it in.

The whole time I had the vision of Amelia's dead body, covered in blood, playing through my head.

Purrday had followed me into the den and now he perched atop the desk, his tail grazing the computer keyboard, watching my movements with feline interest.

"Want some treats?" I finally asked him.

He meowed.

"Okay. Just don't tell your sister."

We went back into the kitchen. I retrieved a box of treats from under the sink and shook out a handful, laying them on his place mat. He minced over to them, sniffed, then started to wolf them down. Deciding I needed a pick-me-up as well, I put a fresh pot of coffee on, and as it perked I leaned against the counter, mentally reviewing the day's events.

"I knew I shouldn't have kept that appointment," I muttered. Amelia's words still puzzled me, though. An amicable agreement to what? "I bet the reason behind that meeting is the key to why she was murdered, but how to find that out? And who out of all those people would have the best motive for wanting her dead?"

Purrday finished gobbling his treats and dropped to the floor, resting his head on his paws. His good eye closed and I could hear his even breathing. I sighed. Neither Purrday nor Kahlua had any answers, and I certainly didn't. I went to the sink, washed out the dish, and had just put it back in the cupboard when there was a knock on the back door. I peeped out the window, and my heart did a little flip-flop when I saw who stood on the back stoop. I opened the door and stared into hazel-gold eyes.

"Hello, Ms. McMillan," Josh said. "I hope this isn't an inconvenient time. I just have a few more questions."

Ten

S hades of *Columbo*, I thought. I nodded and moved aside to let Josh in. He stepped over the threshold and stood there awkwardly for a moment. "You seem to have settled in nicely," he said at last. His eyes rested on the Crock-Pot. "I see Rita's been here." At my look, he grinned. "I didn't need to be a detective to figure that out. Rita and her Crock-Pot usually make an appearance for every newcomer in town."

I gestured toward the Crock-Pot. "Would you like some gumbo? Or a cup of coffee?"

"Nothing for me, thanks." He leaned an elbow against my counter, still studying me. "Tillie talked about you quite a bit."

"You knew my aunt, then?"

"Everyone knew Tillie Washburn. She was a large contributor to the policeman's fund, of which I'm a committee member."

I cleared my throat. "I understand Amelia was on that committee, too. You knew her as well."

"Let's just say there are very few people in Fox Hollow who didn't know Amelia." He paused. "I'm curious. Why does a successful actress chuck her career in Hollywood to move to a small town like Fox Hollow?"

I shrugged. "My show was recently canceled. I've been acting most of my life. I decided it was time for a change. I have plans to reopen Urban Tails." *Unless, of course, I'm in jail for a murder.*

He pulled his notebook and a pen out of his pocket, flipped a couple of pages. "You said you'd met the deceased one other time," he asked abruptly, his tone casual.

"You know I did," I replied evenly. "You saw me."

He tapped the end of the pen against his notebook. "I did." He raised his gaze to mine. "You threatened her, if I recall."

I gripped the edge of the counter. "She threatened me first. I was just responding in kind."

"Mind telling me what the argument was about?"

"I attempted to ask her why she'd voted against me, and I didn't agree

77

with her reasoning. I tried to convince her to change her mind, but . . ." I lifted my shoulders in a shrug. "I wasn't successful."

"Apparently." He glanced toward my coffeepot. "I think I will take that coffee, if you don't mind. Black, two sugars."

I motioned for him to take a seat at the table and I pulled two mugs out of the cabinet. I filled them both up with coffee, added half-and-half to one and sugar to the other, and went over to the table. I set his mug down in front of him and eased into the chair opposite, wrapping my hands around my mug. He took a long, slow sip out of his before he set it down and reached for his notebook again.

"I understand you met with the other board members who voted against you yesterday as well."

My, he had been busy! "You must be very good at your job," I said dryly, "to learn so much in such a short space of time."

"It's a small town. People love to talk, and this apparently was a very hot topic yesterday. You got Peabody and McHardy pretty hot under the collar."

I shifted in my chair. "That wasn't my intention. When it seemed Amelia wasn't going to change her mind, I felt I should try and convince one or more of the others to change theirs."

He picked up the mug again, took another sip, set it down. "You told them you intended to file a complaint against them, didn't you?"

"I said I might if they didn't listen to reason. I never actually said I was going to. As it happened, I'd spoken to Ginnifer Rubin and she seemed willing to re-review my request. I was going to hold off on anything until I'd heard from her. I probably should have let her talk to the other two but—" I shrugged. "I've always been a very proactive person."

He scribbled something else on his pad.

I cleared my throat. "I feel I should mention something that I overheard yesterday."

He glanced up. "Go on."

"When I went to confront Amelia across the street from Sweet Perks, she was arguing with another board member, Garrett Knute. Mr. Knute was trying to get an envelope away from her. She shoved it in her tote bag and laughed at him. As I approached I heard him mutter, 'over my dead body.'"

Josh looked expectantly at me as I stopped. "That's it?"

I stared at him. "Yes."

"And you think that's significant?"

"I certainly do. It shows that I wasn't the only person Amelia had an argument with yesterday."

His lips twitched slightly. "Amelia's disagreed vehemently with over half the town on one thing or another. It doesn't necessarily mean that Garrett wanted to kill her over it."

I felt exasperation well up inside me and I bit down on my lower lip, hard. "And just because we disagreed over my aunt's collection doesn't mean I killed her, either. After all, I only just met the woman."

He leaned back in his chair and tented his fingers. I couldn't help noticing how long and slim they were. Perfect piano-player fingers. I wondered how they would feel, twining through my hair, running across my body . . .

"How did Amelia sound when she called you today?"

I shook my head quickly to clear my mind, pursed my lips as I thought. "She sounded smug."

"Smug?"

"Yes. I told you she said she thought we could come to an amicable arrangement. But—" I broke off, frowned.

"What are you thinking?" he prompted.

"I'm thinking that the only thing we could arrive at an amicable arrangement about was displaying the posters. But Amelia denied that was the reason for the meeting. Still, if she had that photograph in her hand . . ." I shrugged. "It doesn't make sense."

"No, it doesn't." Josh flipped a page in his notebook. "What time did you say you arrived at the museum?"

"Eleven ten. I know because I looked at my dashboard clock and then at my watch before going into the museum."

"And Amelia called you at what time?"

"A few minutes past ten. She said she wanted to meet me in an hour, and I looked at my watch when I hung up. It was just ten fifteen, so I assumed I had to be at the museum by eleven fifteen."

"Hm," he said again, and scribbled something else in his notebook. Then he leaned back in the chair. "Per the coroner, the time of death was somewhere between ten forty-five and ten fifty-five." He looked at me and I knew what he was thinking. From my driveway to the museum parking lot was a twenty-minute drive, give or take a few minutes. It would be cutting it close, but it was doable.

"I don't own a gun," I blurted out.

He looked up, startled, and then said, "Good to know."

I tapped at the table with my fingernail. "I want to go on record as voluntarily giving you this information before you ask."

His lips twitched. "Very forthcoming of you; however, a gunshot wound wasn't the cause of death."

"She wasn't shot?" I frowned. "With all that blood, I just assumed . . ."

"The autopsy's not complete, so we can't release details yet, but . . ." He hesitated, then made a slashing motion across his throat. "Two stab wounds. One across the throat, what's often called 'a smile beneath the chin,' and the other in the chest."

"Ooh." I shut my eyes, trying to ward off that vision of Amelia lying there covered in blood. My eyes snapped open as a thought occurred to me. "Well, that should convince you I had nothing to do with it. If I'd killed her, I'd have known she was stabbed and not shot."

His lips twitched slightly. "True. Then again, you are an actress. You could be trying to throw me off the track."

I flushed. "Okay, how about the fact I had no blood on me. If I'd killed her, there would have been some spatter on my clothes and person."

"True, *unless* you wore some sort of plastic covering when you stabbed her and then ditched it before we came."

I leveled a look at him. "Wow, you have an answer for everything, don't you?"

His lips quirked again. "That's why I'm such a good detective. And for the record, I said you *could* have, not that you *did*."

He sat silently for a moment, sipping coffee. Obviously, he'd shared all he was going to. I cleared my throat. "How's Rocco?"

If he was surprised by the change in topic, he gave no outward indication. "He's fine. Hopefully my sister won't require my services for a while. That dog's a handful."

"He belongs to the sister who owns the secondhand shop, right? Not the one who bartends at the Captain's Club?"

He looked momentarily surprised and then let out a soft chuckle. "You're somewhat of a detective yourself, I see. Yes, Rocco is Sue's dog. She got custody of him in the divorce." He gave a rueful grin. "Jason sure knew what he was doing there."

Purrday came out from around a corner, rubbed against Josh's leg, and let out a soft meow. Josh bent over and petted him on the head.

"Hello, fella. Guess you miss Tillie, huh?"

I watched Purrday rub up against Josh. "He seems to know you, and like you, too."

"As I said, your aunt was a regular contributor to the policeman's fund, and she spearheaded a few fundraisers for us, so yeah, I've been here before. Purrday's quite a cat."

"Yes, I'm finding that out."

He glanced up at me. "You plan to keep him, then?"

"So long as he and Kahlua get along. Kahlua's my Siamese. She's been an only cat for two years, but so far so good. Besides, I'm sure my aunt would want me to take care of Purrday."

"Yes, I'm sure she would. And I'm sure your cat will learn to love Purrday. He's the kind of cat that grows on you." He flipped his notebook shut. "That's all the questions I have for now."

I eyed him. "Is this the part where you tell me not to leave town?"

His lips twitched ever so slightly. He wanted to smile, I just knew he did. He pushed his chair back and stood up. "Should I? You're not going anywhere, are you?"

I shook my head. "Nope."

"Then I don't see a problem."

I pressed my palms together. "But I am a suspect?"

"Let's see . . . you argued with the victim in public, you went around threatening to file a formal complaint against her and those other board members, and then you found the body. Let's just call you a person of interest for now."

I let out a silent sigh of relief. "I didn't kill her, Detective."

"Maybe not."

I raised both eyebrows.

"Probably not," he amended. He looked deeply into my eyes. "I still have the sense you're holding something back."

I widened my eyes and returned his gaze. "I've told you all I know."

He gave me a long, searching look, and then turned toward the door.

"Well, hopefully all this will be resolved soon." He reached into his pocket and pulled out a card, which he pressed into my hand. "If you think of anything else, call me. Day or night."

I glanced at the card, then shoved it into the pocket of my hoodie. "I will."

He twisted the doorknob, then paused. "If I have any more questions, I'll follow up with you. In the meantime, my advice to you is be careful. There's a murderer out there. It could be someone hoping that you'll take the fall for what he or she did. If I were you, I'd be doubly cautious dealing with people."

I paled. "What are you saying? That I could be in danger too?"

He quirked a brow at me. "You were pretty public with your dislike of Amelia, and Quentin Watson certainly exploited it. I wouldn't rule anything or anyone out." His hand shot out, briefly grazed my cheek before dropping back to his side. When he was halfway out the door he turned and said, "I'd hate to see anything happen to you. Good night, Shell."

He left, closing the door behind him. I reached up to touch my cheek. It was still warm from his touch. "Good night, Josh," I whispered.

Eleven

A special edition of the *Fox Hollow Gazette* was out Monday morning. I winced as I read the headline: *Foul Play Suspected at Museum. Local Committee Member Murdered.* I took the paper into the kitchen, slapped the teapot on the stove, and read the account, standing up.

> *Fox Hollow—Amelia Witherspoon, local philanthropist and daughter of town scion Winston Witherspoon, was found dead Sunday afternoon at the Fox Hollow Museum, the victim of multiple stab wounds.*
>
> *Resident Homicide Det. Joshua Bloodgood responded to a 911 call made by Fox Hollow's newest resident, Ms. Crishell McMillan, who found the body. No suspects have yet been identified, but Detective Bloodgood is interrogating some "persons of interest" and following several leads.*
>
> *Amelia Witherspoon, who was 87 at the time of her death, is a descendant of one of the original founders of Fox Hollow, Cunningham Witherspoon. Her father, Winston, was a lawyer and then a judge for many years before his passing fifteen years ago.*
>
> *Ms. Witherspoon is survived by a distant cousin, Ms. Aggie Wharton of Kennebunkport, Maine. A memorial service will be held in the town square Monday evening. No funeral arrangements have been finalized.*

I let out a sigh of relief. I'd expected Watson to somehow sensationalize my part in all this, but the article was brief and to the point. I was curious, though, who his source was, who the other "persons of interest" might be, and what leads Josh might be tracking down. I'd spent quite a bit of time looking at his business card the night before. I debated calling him, but I doubted he'd share any information, especially since he'd told me I was one of the persons of interest.

I set the paper down and busied myself making a cup of hopefully soothing English Breakfast tea and putting an English muffin in the toaster. Purrday appeared and lofted onto the counter. He nosed at the paper and flipped it onto the floor, then hopped down and stretched out on top of it, claws curled inward.

"Hey," I admonished the cat. "I wasn't done reading that." I attempted to pull the paper out from under him, but he only rolled over on his side, dug his claws deeper, and blinked his eye at me. I grasped the paper with both hands and gave a hard tug. Purrday rolled off it, shot me an injured look, and stalked over to his food bowl. He glared at the empty bowl and then at me.

"Good Lord, Purrday, what's the problem?" I grumbled. I went to the cupboard and pulled out the kibble. I shook some into his bowl and then Kahlua came running into the kitchen. She stopped, eyed the kibble in my hand, and let out a sharp meow. "Fine," I said. "You too." I poured kibble into her bowl and they both hunkered down, shoulder to shoulder, and dug in. I glared at them, my hands on my hips. "One of these days I'm going to find a cat who'll wait on its owner, not the other way around."

They both stopped eating and swiveled their heads to look at me. I could visualize a bubble over both their heads with the unspoken words *Fat Chance*. I shook my head and bent to gather up the paper Purrday had so unceremoniously knocked down. As I gathered it up my eye fell upon the part Purrday had clawed, the article at the top of the page. I squatted down on the floor in front of the cabinet and began to read, my eyes getting wider with each sentence.

Washburn/Witherspoon Feud Lives On?

> *The years-long feud between the two paragons of our town, Matilda Washburn and Amelia Witherspoon, should have come to an apparent end with the sudden and untimely death of Ms. Witherspoon yesterday, yet this person fears it might not have.*
>
> *Sources tell me that Tillie Washburn's niece, Crishell McMillan, aka Shell Marlowe, was right in the thick of things with Amelia, even to the point of a public argument. A sanction against our own museum board has even been mentioned. Can anyone say sour grapes?*
>
> *Ms. Marlowe, or Ms. McMillan, as she prefers to be*

known now, has not hidden her dissatisfaction at the museum's declining to showcase her aunt's extensive movie poster collection, leaving this writer to wonder just how far she'd take her grudge to exact revenge.

Alas, old feuds do not die, they live on in other guises.

I read the article once, twice, and then a third time before throwing the paper away with a strangled cry. *"Aah,"* I said, so loudly that Purrday put his paws over his ears. "That man is so infuriating. He's practically accusing me of murdering Amelia! I'm going to sue him." I scrambled up from the floor and started looking around for where I'd chucked my cell phone, when it started to ring. I found it behind the cereal box, saw the number, and answered. "Hello," I snapped.

"Uh-oh," Olivia's voice rang out. "Someone's read the morning paper."

"Yes, and I was just about to get my aunt's lawyer on the phone. Quentin Watson is a fungus that's got to be stopped."

"Hold on, Shell. Take a breath. He doesn't actually come out and say you murdered Amelia."

"No, but the intent is there."

"I'm not sure there's all that much you can do. Freedom of the press and all that."

"Are you kidding? This article is libelous!"

"Is it?" Olivia asked in a matter-of-fact tone. "You were right in the thick of things with Amelia, so to speak, and you did threaten Larry and Andy with a sanction. The way he's phrased the article is more along the lines of his opinion than a slur against you. And as we all know, everyone's entitled to their opinion."

Much as I hated to admit it, Olivia was right. "It's just so unfair. It puts me in a very bad light. I'm trying to start a life here. I can't possibly reopen Urban Tails with this hanging over my head. No one will come to the store if they think it's run by a killer."

"Hey, now." Olivia clicked her tongue. "You can't let that creep get the best of you. He wasn't exactly a fan of Amelia's, either. He's just trying to get under your skin because you wouldn't give him an interview. You've got to hold your head up high and act like he's an old coot blowing off steam. Which he is."

I had to laugh. "Yeah, if anyone's holding a grudge, it's him, not me."

"That's right. You be the bigger person, sweetie."

I paused as a sudden thought occurred to me. "Maybe he knows what their feud was all about."

"Possible, but I doubt it. Your aunt always was a very private person, and Amelia was closemouthed as well when it came to your aunt and their disagreement. Quentin Watson probably only knows as much as the rest of us—that something happened a long time ago that made 'em hate the sight of each other."

I sighed. "I guess you're right."

"Of course I am. Are you going to the town memorial for Amelia tonight?"

I blew a stray curl out of my eyes. "You're kidding. Why would I want to attend that?"

"For one thing, to get out and show these people that you don't hold any sort of grudge against the woman. What did we just talk about, being the bigger person? You showing up will take some of the sting out of that little snippet of Watson's, and maybe take him down a peg or two."

As much as I hated to admit it, Olivia was right. "Okay, count me in."

"Great. We'll be by for you at six." She paused. "Wear something simple. And black."

• • •

With an entirely free afternoon, I decided to make some more calls to suppliers. I made great progress, checking off nearly half my list. People said kind things about Tillie and looked forward to receiving my orders in the near future. I found the number for Kathleen Power, the woman who knit items for the store, and she answered on the second ring. I explained who I was and the nature of my call, and she was more than delighted to hear from me. "I was wondering what would happen," she confessed. "I was planning to come down once I saw the store was open with a few samples."

"We could do that now. Say, early next week?" Hey, I'm nothing if not optimistic. I told Kathleen I'd get back to her with a definite date, then shut my cell off and tried to take a nap; however, I wasn't very successful. Every time I closed my eyes, I saw Amelia's body on the museum office floor, her chest covered with blood.

At five o'clock I got up, showered, did my hair and makeup and pulled out a simple pair of black linen slacks, black T-shirt, and a gray and black animal-print jacket. Kahlua and Purrday were both sprawled across my bed, albeit at opposite ends. While Kahlua napped, Purrday watched me dress, and when I'd finished, let out a soft meow of approval, then flopped on his side and a few minutes later started snoring. I left the cats to their snoozing and made my way to the kitchen, where I heated up a bowl of Rita's gumbo and ate it along with some saltine crackers. I sighed. I really had to get to the supermarket, but after recent events, I confess I was afraid to go. I just knew I'd be recognized and whispered about, just as I'd been in the weeks following Patrick's betrayal.

Gosh, this was Hollywood all over again.

Promptly at six o'clock my doorbell rang. Olivia and Rita, both wearing black maxi dresses, stood on my front porch. Rita wore a purple shrug around her shoulders and matching flats; Olivia was bare-armed and had her turquoise sandals on. We engaged in a brief group hug on my stoop before I asked, "Where's Ron? Isn't he going?"

Olivia shrugged. "Amelia wasn't his favorite person, either, but I'm sure he and his wife will be there. Whether they come with or without their dogs remains to be seen."

"Oh, the whole town will show up," Rita said. "Even though most of 'em are glad the old bat is dead, they'll still come with their flowers and candles and what have you. It's a tribute to the hypocrisy of small towns."

For the first time, I noticed that Olivia and Rita each held a small plant in their hands. "Wait just one moment," I said. I hurried back into the house and grabbed a silk peony plant that one of the crew had given me on the last day of shooting *Spy Anyone*. I hurried back onto the porch, pulled the door shut behind me, and held the plant aloft. "Now I'm ready."

We walked the short distance, cutting through the park to get to the other end, near the library and congregational church where the memorial was being held. We passed the spot where, only two days before, I'd seen Amelia arguing with Londra Lewis, and I remembered that I'd forgotten to mention that to Josh. Or maybe I'd wait until I had a chance to talk to Ms. Lewis myself.

We approached the hill overlooking the library. A group of teenaged boys were setting up a makeshift podium where three women and two men stood. Two of the people I recognized. One of the women was Mazie Madison, and the tall man was Lawrence Peabody. I touched Olivia's arm and nodded toward the podium. "Mazie and Larry are here."

Olivia nodded and pointed to three other figures standing off to the right. Even at this distance I recognized Ginnifer's red hair. "All the board members are here. See Andy over there, dabbing at his eyes with his handkerchief."

"Crocodile tears, or real?" I asked.

"A mix of both, maybe. Welcome to small-town America, hon. No matter how much a person might be disliked, it's appropriate to pay one's respects. Unfortunately, it's noticed when you don't." She glanced significantly toward the fringe of the crowd on the opposite end, and I recognized the curly headed figure in his peacoat, leveling his camera at the crowd. "He'd sure have noticed if you didn't show up, and then you'd have made tomorrow's special edition too."

Two more figures made their way onto the podium, a woman and a man. The woman was slight of build and had light hair the same color as Mazie's. Olivia saw me looking and nudged me. "That's Carolyn Hart, our mayor. The other guy is Melvin Feller. He used to work with Rita's husband and Garrett at the accounting firm." She leaned over and whispered in my ear, "He was a member of the Screaming Eagles, One Hundred and First Airborne. I think Garrett thought it lent a bit of prestige to the firm, but they let him go after a few months."

"Really? Why?"

"He's a bit of a gambler, and I think it affected his work. He freelanced for a while after that, and now he only does occasional work." She winked. "He seems to be better at gambling than accounting. No love lost between him and Amelia, either. Mazie nominated him for a spot on the museum board, but Amelia campaigned vigorously against it. That's how Andy McHardy got on."

I peered at the small group, paying particular attention to Melvin Feller. He was a short man, rather squat, with a receding hairline, a large nose and even larger ears. He wore an ill-fitting jacket and slacks. He looked nondescript, like someone you'd pass over in a heartbeat. I wondered how deep his hatred of Amelia had run. Enough to kill, perhaps? Then again, was being passed over for a board chair enough of a motive?

People had been killed for less.

My attention was diverted by the roar of a dark maroon sedan careening up the street. It skidded to a stop, half on the grass, half off. A tall woman with short black hair shot with streaks of purple emerged from the driver's side. She turned her face toward me and I could see that she was quite young, late teens. She had on skintight jeans and an even tighter top, and a pair of leopard heels that had to be at least five inches high. A boy slouched out of the passenger side, hands jammed into his pockets. He didn't walk with the assurance of the girl, but rather more into himself, almost as if he were afraid. His hair was shaggy and a large pair of dark sunglasses covered most of his face, so it was hard to gauge his expression. He wore jeans too, but his were far from tight; rather, they almost looked as if they'd fall off his frame at any given second.

Olivia nudged me. "Who ya lookin' at? Oh, the Hart kids." She waved one hand dismissively. "Those are Carolyn's kids, Selena and Kyle. No doubt they're here to support their mother. It's an election year, after all."

The crowd fell silent as Carolyn Hart approached the podium. I took a moment to study her. She was a nice-looking woman: ash blonde hair cut stylishly short, a trim navy suit and heels, slender build. She tapped the microphone and the crackle blared through the stillness of the evening, silencing the last of the talkers.

"Good evening, everyone." Her voice was crisp, cool, a tone that commanded attention. "Thank you all for coming. Tonight, we are gathered to pay homage to a woman struck down in a horrific way. A friend, a neighbor, a woman with a rich heritage from Fox Hollow. Amelia Witherspoon."

She bowed her head and the crowd did the same. The rest of the little group stood around her as she offered up a nice, tidy little speech. It was a mixture of praise, remembrance, and sorrow, extolling her generosity, her contributions to various charities, and the committees and boards she'd served on. By the time Carolyn was done, she had Amelia sounding almost like Mother Teresa.

I got bored halfway through and let my gaze wander. I started as I spied a familiar face on the fringe of the crowd—Josh. He stood, arms folded across his broad chest, scanning the crowd with his flat cop gaze. Looking for the murderer, no doubt.

A chill shuddered through me, and I gripped my jacket more tightly around me to ward off the evening chill. Sure, it was possible the murderer might be here. Why not? Josh's last words came back to me, full force: *There's a murderer out there. It could be someone hoping that you'll take the fall for what he or she did. If I were you, I'd be doubly cautious dealing with people.*

Olivia nudged me. "What's wrong? You look a little sick."

I shook my head. "No, I'm fine." My gaze traveled up to the podium, skimming over the people clustered there before they settled on Andy McHardy. I recalled his words to Larry Peabody: *We can't go on like this, her expecting us to jump whenever she snaps her fingers.* Had he perhaps decided he'd had enough, and there was only one way to end it? Or what about Londra Lewis? That hadn't been just a small disagreement I'd witnessed in the park. Had it escalated to the point of no return?

Mayor Hart finished her speech and then everyone on the podium joined hands for a moment of silence. And then it was over. I glanced around and saw Quentin Watson, camera in hand, clicking away. He looked up, and our gazes locked. Then he very deliberately snapped my picture.

My chest suddenly felt tight, as if I couldn't breathe. I felt like rushing over and ripping the camera out of his hand, but such a foolhardy action, I knew, would do more harm than good. As the crowd started to disburse, I touched Olivia's arm. "I'm going to go home," I said.

Olivia and Rita both moved toward me. "Do you want us to come with you?" Olivia asked. She inclined her head in Quentin's direction, and I knew she'd noticed him snapping my picture.

I shook my head. "No. I'm okay. I'll talk to you tomorrow."

She pulled me into a quick hug. "Don't do anything stupid."

Even with all that had happened, I was glad to count these women as my new friends. I gave her a weak smile. "I won't."

I moved off to the fringe of the crowd and stood for a moment, taking in great gulps of air. Tomorrow I was making a suspect list, and then . . . well, then I wasn't sure just what I was going to do. But if Josh was right, and someone was setting me up to take the fall for their crime, it was in my best interests to find out who it was as quickly as possible, so I could get on with my life.

I scrubbed at the goose bumps that had popped up on my arms underneath my sheer jacket when the hairs on the back of my neck suddenly started to stand up. I was being watched, I knew it. Slowly, deliberately, I turned my head.

And saw Josh, staring right at me.

I touched my fingers to my forehead in a salute and then deliberately turned away and started for the park. But I could feel his eyes still on me, watching, all the way to my front door.

Twelve

The next morning I awoke to the rumble of a B-52 in my ear courtesy of Purrday, who seemed to have adopted my chest as his new bed. When he saw I was awake, he jumped to the floor, stretched, and started for the door.

"Good idea," I said approvingly. "I slept better than I thought, but I could use a cup of coffee and I bet you're hungry."

"Ma-row," he said.

I pulled on my robe and we went downstairs and into the kitchen, where I opened my refrigerator to two eggs, a half-full carton of milk, and a jar of jelly. My larder was practically bare.

I really had to get to that supermarket.

Purrday leapt onto the counter and watched me, white plume swishing. Kahlua appeared also, coat freshly groomed, and rubbed against my ankles. I opened the cabinet and pointed to the neat rows of cans I'd packed before leaving the store on Saturday. "Don't worry," I told them. "*You two* have plenty of food. It's me who'll starve."

Both cats let out loud meows. I wasn't sure if they were pleased with the fact that they both had plenty of food or that I would be the one doing the starving. I opted for the former.

I set out bowls of tuna and water for them and then sat down at the kitchen table to make a list. A half hour later I jumped into my convertible and pointed it toward town. Instead of the larger A&P, I opted for a grocer I'd seen yesterday called the General Store. As I pulled into the parking lot I realized that this was certainly not like the convenience stores I was used to in LA. This place definitely had more of a homey feel to it. There was a large sign right at the front door, announcing the store's hours. A small stand cluttered with various plants and flowers occupied one end of the porch, and there was a long bench off to one side that looked hand-carved. A small group of teenagers converged by the entrance, snapping their fingers as they bebopped to and fro to whatever tune was coming out of the devices they all had hooked up to their ears. I pushed open the screen door and stepped inside. A bell jingled, signaling my arrival. The inside of the store was busy—not with people, but with things crammed on shelves, peeping out from odd angles everywhere. I could smell the aroma of fresh-perked coffee in the air, mixed with the faint scent of fruit. A gray-haired woman wearing an oversized sweater looked up from behind the counter and beamed at me.

"Welcome to the General Store! Can I help you with something? I'm Agnes, the owner."

I held out my list. "Just about everything, I'm afraid. I just moved to Fox Hollow, and like old Mother Hubbard, my cupboard is bare."

Agnes plucked the list out of my hand and studied it, adjusting her wire-rimmed glasses on her pug nose. "We have meat over there"—she made a motion with her hand—"and Rodney, our butcher, just put out fresh steaks and chicken thighs about an hour ago. The cleaning stuff's down aisle five, and we have a nice selection of fruits and vegetables right by the freezer case." She pointed down the middle aisle. "If you'd like, I can have the stock boy put together a box for you of all this household stuff, while you pick out your meat and veggies."

"Oh, would you?" I cried. "That would be wonderful."

"Sure, no problem." She leaned over the counter and shouted, "Kyle! Come out here. A customer needs some help."

A few minutes later a thin, sullen boy wearing faded jeans and a plaid shirt emerged from the back room. He seemed vaguely familiar, but I couldn't quite place why. He walked up to us, and Agnes handed him the list. "Make this young lady up a box of those sundries. I'll help her with the rest."

He nodded. "Yes, Mrs. Dinwiddie."

He loped off down the middle aisle, my list in one hand, his shoulders hunched, and it suddenly struck me where I'd seen him before. Last night, at the memorial for Amelia. I stared after him wonderingly. "Kyle Hart?" I murmured.

Agnes had started down the side aisle toward the meat case and now she turned and looked at me. "You know Kyle?"

I shook my head. "No. I was at a memorial service last night and he was there with his sister." I glanced quickly down the middle aisle again, but Kyle had disappeared. "I'm a bit surprised to see him here now," I admitted. "Shouldn't he be in school?"

"Probably," she chuckled, "but seeing as he's homeschooled, he can make his own hours."

That surprised me. "He's homeschooled?"

Agnes nodded. "He was in some fancy prep school, and then one day he just showed up here."

"Was there some sort of trouble?"

She shrugged. "Not that anyone knows of. I heard his grades were poor, and his attention span wasn't what it should be. Carolyn thought it'd be better if he had private tutoring, so she pulled him out of school."

"That's a shame," I said, but my thoughts were racing. Was there more to Kyle's being yanked out of school than met the eye, and had Amelia known the reason? Could that have been her bargaining chip with the mayor?

Agnes reached out and patted my arm. "Well, dear. Did you want to see those steaks now?"

"I sure do. And do you sell notebooks here too?"

"Stationery's in aisle three."

• • •

Twenty minutes later I paid for my purchases, which included a vinyl-covered spiral notebook, and Kyle carried the large box out to my car. He deposited it in my backseat, and as he turned away I pressed a five-dollar bill into his hand. He looked at the bill, then at me.

"It's a tip," I said. "Thanks for carrying the box out for me."

"It's my job," he muttered, "but thank you." He shoved the bill into his back pocket and hurried back inside the store. I felt a pang of sympathy for the boy as I watched him. He was a bit sullen, true, but he seemed like a good kid.

I opened my car door and slid behind the wheel. I was anxious now to get home, unpack my purchases, and start writing down a list of suspects and motives in my brand-new notebook. I was just about to turn the key in the ignition when a sleek maroon sedan like the one Mayor Hart's daughter had driven to yesterday's service pulled into the parking lot and slid into a space near the front entrance. It wasn't Selena Hart who exited the car, however.

It was Garrett Knute.

Garrett slammed the car door shut, and as he turned toward the entrance, glanced my way. His gaze fell full upon me, and his expression hardened. He changed direction and walked toward my car with purposeful strides.

"You! You're Crishell McMillan, right?" he shouted as he came abreast of me. "I'm Garrett Knute. We've never met before."

I shook my head. "No, we haven't."

His lips slashed into a thin line, and his eyes were dark with suppressed fury. "Then would you mind telling me why you suggested me as a murder suspect to Detective Bloodgood?"

Of all the things he might have said, that was the last thing I expected to hear. "What? Why? When did this happen?" I stammered.

He leaned back a bit and folded his arms across his chest. "You needn't act so innocent. What were you doing, trying to cast suspicion away from yourself?" He jabbed his finger in the air. "Well, it won't work. There are far better people to cast in a disparaging light than me."

I forced myself to respond in a calm tone. "I'm sure there are. And I wasn't deliberately trying to cast any suspicion on you. I just told the detective what I'd heard."

"He said that you overheard me threaten Amelia."

"That's not exactly true. I told him I saw the two of you arguing over an envelope, and Amelia snatched it away from you and you muttered 'over my dead body.' That's all."

"That's all!" he thundered. "Believe me, young lady, there was nothing sinister about that remark. Haven't you said things like that when you were angry?"

I recalled shouting similar remarks at Patrick more than once, but pushed that out of my mind. And there was no way I was going to clue him in about my own ominous words to Amelia before she died. "I suppose so," I said. "But—"

"No buts," he snapped. "Amelia argued all the time with everybody. She had a lot worse than that said to her, believe me. You could count on one hand the people she *didn't* argue with." He cocked his brow at me. "I didn't kill her," he said flatly.

"I'm sure Detective Bloodgood didn't accuse you."

"He didn't have to. The mere idea he'd even stoop to question me means I'm on that suspect list." He glared at me again. "My only consolation is that you're probably at the top of it. And while we're at it, just where do you come off, threatening to sanction the museum board?"

I lifted my chin. "All I want is to be treated fairly."

He paused and cocked his head to one side. "I can appreciate that," he said slowly. "But there are better ways to achieve that than by threats."

"Look, Mr. Knute. My intention was not to make trouble for you. I mentioned your altercation with Amelia simply in passing, because Detective Bloodgood asked me about my own tiff with her. I certainly didn't intend to point fingers at you."

He stared at me for a second and then said, in a somewhat mollified tone, "Well, I guess I can understand it. Josh can be intimidating at times."

"As for sanctioning the board, I wouldn't have done anything hastily," I continued. "I wanted to find out why those particular four people turned down the display offer." I paused. "Mazie Madison didn't, and neither did Simone Bradbury . . . or you."

Garrett's expression softened, and a bit of the fury went out of his gaze. "Well, I've always felt there's a lot to be said for being one of the crowd. Besides, none of the other museums' displays could hold a candle to your aunt's collection. Unfortunately, not everyone shared my opinion." He paused. "I heard you're going to open up Urban Tails again. That's great news. It's sorely missed by all the pet owners in town, including me."

"You have a pet?"

"A corgi. And he loves that premier brand of dog food your aunt's store carried. The only other spot to get it is the big box store on Highway 12, and that's a pain to get to. Any idea when you'll reopen?"

"As soon as possible."

His eyes held a slight twinkle now. "Translation: just as soon as you're no longer a murder suspect?"

"More of a person of interest. Getting back to our original discussion, I'd heard that Amelia had a certain way with those particular board members," I said carefully. "I just wanted to be certain Amelia wasn't putting undue pressure on them to vote the way she wanted them to. I don't mind losing out on the display opportunity as much as I do the idea I might have been disqualified due to something out of my control."

The puzzled look returned. "What would be out of your control?"

I took a breath. "I've heard Amelia and my aunt, Matilda Washburn, had a long-running feud. I need to be certain that didn't play a part in the turndown."

Garrett Knute reached up a hand to rub absently at the back of his neck.

"First, I hadn't heard about a feud, but it would explain a lot. There was no love lost between those two women, that's for sure."

"I understand it was over a man, but no one seems to know any details other than that."

"Hm," he grunted. "Hard to imagine Amelia getting her knickers in a twist over a man. She always seemed the independent type. As for her exerting influence over the others, I can't speak to that. I can only say that she never tried to sway my opinion, most likely because she realized she couldn't."

I looked him straight in the eye. "Was she attempting to try?"

"What do you mean?"

"The argument you two were having the other day. I caught the tail end of it. You wanted to see the contents of an envelope she had, and she wouldn't let you. Pardon me for asking, but was Amelia holding something over your head?"

His face darkened again. "If you're trying to imply she found out some deep, dark secret about me, think again."

I cocked my brow. "Then why were you so upset?"

He barked out a short laugh. "You think that was upset? That was just a normal argument with Amelia. She did try to get under my skin and succeeded for a bit, but after I cooled down, aw heck, it's all moot now anyway, isn't it?"

"She hadn't dug up something on you, perhaps a secret you didn't want revealed?"

He shifted his weight to his other foot. "Amelia's dug up many secrets on people over the years. She was a nosy old woman. I had no reason to want her dead, but I could think of plenty who did. As a matter of fact, I'll tell you the same thing I told Josh. If I oversaw the investigation, I know exactly who my number-one suspect would be. Melvin Feller!"

And with that, he nodded curtly, turned, and strode into the General Store, leaving me staring after him. After a minute, I climbed back into my car. I started the car and turned it in the direction of Fox Hollow, and I'd gone little more than a mile when it suddenly occurred to me that Garrett Knute had never answered my question.

The envelope he and Amelia had argued over and its contents were still a deep, dark mystery.

Thirteen

I returned home, parked, and started bringing in the groceries. Purrday and Kahlua lofted atop one of the high cabinets to watch me unpack and Purrday let out an approving meow when I held up the large bag of kibble I'd gotten on sale. Once I was finished, I sank down in one of the chairs to catch my breath. The cats jumped down, and Kahlua leapt into my lap while Purrday twined himself around my ankles. I related my encounter with Garrett Knute to them. "He never did say what was in that envelope," I mused. "I wonder what it could be?"

Both cats cocked their heads and meowed softly.

"He seemed awfully anxious to point fingers at this Melvin Feller," I went on. "I think I should find out a bit more about him. What do you think?"

Kahlua burrowed her head into my armpit. Purrday stretched out a forepaw and tapped my knee.

"Glad you both agree." I remembered Olivia saying that Melvin had worked for Garrett and Rita's husband, so I knew exactly what my next move would be. I gently dislodged Kahlua from her post under my arm, pushed back my chair, and reached for my purse.

Time for some coffee at Sweet Perks, and maybe some juicy gossip, too.

• • •

Parking seemed to be at a premium today, but I found a spot across from Urban Tails and slid my convertible into it. The sign, *Reopening Soon*, was still on the door and I noted that something was scrawled in pencil beneath my words. I hurried over for a better look. Someone had printed *Not soon enough* on the sign. I had to agree with their assessment.

Sweet Perks was about a five-minute walk from Urban Tails. This time when I entered, Rita was behind the counter. She looked up and smiled as I approached. "Shell. How nice to see you! What can I get you?"

My stomach rumbled, reminding me that I hadn't had breakfast or lunch. I glanced at the display case and my eye fell on a spinach mushroom quiche. Rita saw me looking at it and grinned wider.

"My niece makes them fresh," she said. "How about a nice piece of quiche and a double mocha latte with skim milk?"

"Sounds perfect." I glanced around, and since there was no one waiting behind me, I asked, "Would you have a minute to talk?"

"Sure. It's time for my break anyway. You go on, get a table and I'll bring your food right over."

I went over and selected a table in the farthest corner of the store. A few minutes later Rita hurried over with a tray on which rested a plate with a generous slice of quiche and two tall mocha lattes. Rita set the plate in front of me and I inhaled the delicate aroma. "It smells delicious," I said.

"That it does. And it tastes even better."

I picked up my fork, broke off a piece, and popped it into my mouth. It was piping hot and delicious, and practically melted in my mouth. "Ooh, you're right," I said. "This is scrumptious." I picked up my latte, took a sip, and let out a contented sigh. "Um. I feel like I've died and gone to heaven." I pushed the coffee cup back. "I decided it was time to stock up, so I did some grocery shopping today at the General Store."

"Oh, don't you just love that place?" Rita gushed. "It's so cozy, not like that A&P. And Agnes makes all those jellies and jams herself."

"Does she? I'll have to buy some next time. I just stuck with the basics this time out." I took another sip of coffee. "I didn't realize Kyle Hart worked there."

"Carolyn's son? Oh, yes." Rita smiled faintly. "His sister works too, at some fancy hair salon over in the next town. I think she wants to become a hairstylist. Or maybe it's a makeup artist, I'm not sure."

I popped another bite of quiche into my mouth, chewed, and then said, "Is Selena homeschooled, like her brother?"

Rita shook her head. "Heck, no. She's a senior at Fox Hollow High. She'll graduate in June. Carolyn wants her to go to college but Selena has other ideas. As for Kyle, he's always been a bit slow. Rumor has it he was flunking out of that fancy school, so Carolyn just yanked him out and hired some fancy private tutors. When he's not studying, he's working at the General Store."

"That doesn't sound like much of a life for a teenaged boy," I said thoughtfully.

Rita laughed. "I can see the wheels turning in that brain of yours, Shell.

You're wondering if there's more to the incident, and if Amelia knew about it."

"Guilty," I confessed. "If Kyle had been doing drugs, let's say, and had been expelled for it, that might be something the mayor would want to keep quiet. And if Amelia found out and was blackmailing her . . ." I let my voice trail off, the implication in the air.

"True, but I doubt either one of those kids would do drugs. Carolyn would kill them if they did. Kyle was just never a very sociable kid, not like his sister. Sorry, Shell, but if you're looking for a deep dark secret there, well, I doubt it."

"Maybe." I scraped up the last bite of quiche. "I ran into Garrett Knute after I finished shopping."

"Yeah? How is he? I haven't seen Garrett in a while. Ever since he and Frank split up the business, he kind of keeps his distance."

"I take it the dissolution of their partnership wasn't amicable, then?"

"Oh, no, it was," Rita hastened to assure me. "Frank was diagnosed with rheumatoid arthritis right around the same time Garrett's uncle died and left him all that money. We sold the business and put our money into Sweet Perks, and we haven't done all that badly."

"Oh, I'm sorry," I said. "Olivia mentioned you took your husband for treatment for his arthritis, but I didn't realize how severe his condition must be. Rheumatoid is one of the more crippling, isn't it?"

"It is," she nodded. "RA is a chronic inflammatory type of arthritis. It is also classified as an autoimmune disease. The joint linings are affected most, but it can also affect organs as well. This new doctor has helped Frank a lot, though. She changed his diet, which seemed to help, and so do the weekly massages." She shook her head. "My husband has a wonderful outlook on life. It's what's seen him through this. If it were me, well, I doubt I could be half as cheerful as he is sometimes." She sighed. "Garrett rarely comes into Sweet Perks, and when he does, it's usually when I'm not around. Sometimes I think he feels a bit guilty over everything that happened, but there's no reason why he should. Frank wouldn't have been able to work much longer anyway." She chuckled. "It's more likely he feels guilty over inheriting all that money. He was struggling, just like us, before his uncle died. Now he lives like a king."

"Well, he wasn't very happy with me today. I saw him arguing with

Amelia over an envelope outside your shop Saturday, and I told Josh."

"Uh-oh." Rita rolled her eyes. "Let me guess. Josh talked to him, and Garrett thought you implicated him to take the heat off you."

"Something like that."

"Sounds like Garrett. He always did like jumping to conclusions." She pursed her lips. "He and Amelia were arguing over an envelope?"

"Yep. He tried to grab it away from her and she stuffed it in the tote she was carrying. I heard him mutter 'over my dead body' before he stalked off."

Rita frowned. "That does sound mysterious. I wonder what was in it."

I shrugged. "Don't know. I tried asking him about it, but he said Amelia had nothing on him, and if anyone should be the number-one suspect in her death, it would be Melvin Feller."

Rita's eyes popped, and then she started to laugh. "Melvin? Why on earth would he say that?"

"I have no idea." I leaned forward. "Olivia said that this Melvin Feller used to work with your husband and Garrett, and that they fired him."

"Well, it was Garrett who fired him," Rita said. "It was a few months before Frank got sick. We'd gone to Aruba on vacation, and when we came back all hell had broken loose. Garrett had fired Mel. He'd gotten too many complaints about him, he said. Two of their biggest clients got contacted by the IRS over mistakes he'd made, and there was some other stuff too, I don't really remember. Frank might. The straw that broke the camel's back was when Garrett decided to check out the college where Mel got his accounting degree; he couldn't find a mention of it anywhere! Told Mel to pack up his stuff and get out. We never saw Mel much after that, but I guess you can't blame the guy, right?"

"Did this Mel Feller have any dealings with Amelia?"

Rita's brow furrowed as she thought. "Amelia used to be one of Frank and Garrett's biggest clients, and your aunt too. Mel never did any of the accounting for either one of them, though. Frank and Garrett always handled the Fox Hollow clients themselves. Amelia and Mel knew each other to say hello to, but that's as far as it went."

"You have no idea why Garrett would think Mel might have something to do with her death?"

She picked a piece of lint off her sweater. "Honestly? He probably just blurted that out. There's no love lost between those two. Mel would probably say Garrett should be the number-one suspect. But if you want, I'll ask Frank about it."

I finished my latte and pushed my chair back. "Would you? I'd appreciate it. And if you think of anything else—"

"Come to think of it." Rita stood up too. "Garrett used to do the museum accounting, exclusively. That's how he got on the board." She reached over and squeezed my hand. "My break's over. Catch you later."

• • •

Back on the street, I started to head toward my car when I happened to glance up and see the Secondhand Sue's sign. Impulsively I crossed the street and walked over to peer into its large bay window. The items displayed weren't vintage antiques, but they were many and varied. Some were vintage kitsch, like a black and blue Batman lunch box, complete with matching thermos. Others looked as if they were waiting to be given a second chance, like the twin lamp set with bases carved out of rose marble, or the bust of Edgar Allan Poe with a raven beside his head. I'd always liked Poe's works and his poem "The Raven" had always been one of my favorites. I could visualize that bust behind the counter at the pet shop—which reminded me, I had to call the parakeet breeder and put off our interview. I pushed open the door, intending to price it, when suddenly a brown and tan blur shot past me. The next instant I was down on the floor, being covered in sloppy doggy kisses.

"Rocco! Down! Where are your manners? Goodness, miss, are you all right?"

Rocco was pulled back and I found myself considering a woman's face that reminded me faintly of Josh. Same jawline, same bump on the nose, same hazel-gold eyes. Only instead of dark hair, hers was a light ash blonde, cut into a stylish pixie crop. She wore an expression of concern on her face as she peered down at me.

Abruptly she pushed the dog into the arms of a young boy who'd come up behind her. "Henry, take him for a walk. He's definitely got too much energy today."

"Wait. I'm fine." I struggled into a sitting position. "Don't blame the dog too much. Rocco and I have met before."

The woman stared at me. "You have?"

I nodded. "Yes. Saturday, in the park. He jumped on me then too. Your brother rescued me."

Her brow furrowed, then cleared, and her thick lips split in a wide smile. "Oh, goodness! You must be Shell Marlowe! Or is it Shell McMillan?"

"McMillan." She helped me stand up, and I brushed at my pants legs. Rocco came up, a bit more subdued now thanks to the leash Henry'd snapped on his collar, and sniffed at my ankles. I grinned wryly. "I guess he remembered me."

"Yes, Bloodgood men seldom forget females they've branded." She extended her hand. "I'm Sue Bloodgood, but I think you already knew that."

"Yes, I heard you own this shop. I think it's fantastic. You have a lot of nice things here."

"Thanks. Second chances are in, you know." She winked. "I hear that's what you're after too, here in Fox Hollow. Or is talk of you reopening Urban Tails only idle gossip?"

"No, it's true. I'd originally planned on next week, but as things stand right now I'm afraid it's been delayed indefinitely."

Sue's tongue clicked against the roof of her mouth. "Oh, you mean what happened to Amelia. Josh said you found the body." She gave a small shudder. "It gives me the creeps just to think about it."

"It wasn't exactly the highlight of my day," I admitted. "Even though Amelia and I didn't exactly start out on the right foot, I would never wish that fate on anyone."

Sue grinned. "Well, for what it's worth, I can't understand why Amelia wouldn't want those posters on display. Why, Tillie even used to bring some of 'em into the pet shop and display them from time to time."

Somehow that didn't surprise me. It sounded like a good idea, and one I'd hopefully be able to continue. "Ones with animals, I'll bet."

"Yep. She had Thin Man posters with that cute little Asta, a *Lassie Come Home* that was real cool, and my favorite, *Turner and Hooch*."

I laughed. "I like that movie too. I like pretty much anything with Tom Hanks. I met him once at an awards show. He's really cool."

"I bet." Sue reached up to scratch behind one ear. "A few weeks before she took ill she had a *Bringing Up Baby* poster in the window. Cary Grant was her favorite, you know."

"I do." I spread my hands. "I still can't believe the museum voted against displaying her collection."

Sue nodded briskly. "Makes you wonder what they were smoking when they held that vote."

"I know. Their decision makes no sense to me. Aunt Tillie's collection would be an asset, not a liability."

"Yeah, well, knowing the board, I'm sure there's more to the story," Sue said. "I for one would love to take a closer look at your aunt's collection." She waved her arm toward the back of her shop. "I carry a few movie things here, but nothing like what's in her—I mean your—shop. Mostly it's Star Wars stuff, aimed at people our age. If you ever want to sell any of her stuff, though, let me know. We could do it on consignment."

"I'll keep that in mind." I craned my neck around. "You have a lot of nice things here," I said. "I think your shop is charming."

"Thanks." She beamed at me. "Your aunt liked it too. She came in here a lot. Even suggested that I should expand my inventory to include more upscale pieces."

"That might not be a bad idea," I said. "Antiquing is very in."

"Oh, I'm not against the idea at all. It's just that first I should scrape up some more capital and get rid of a few leftover bills. Lord only knows when that will be, though. Tillie suggested getting a partner, but so far I haven't run across anyone who'd be interested." Her lips twisted into a rueful smile. "Enough of my problems. See anything you like?"

"Actually, yes. I wanted to price that Edgar Allan Poe bust. I think he and the raven would look great behind the counter in Urban Tails."

"You've got good taste," Sue said appraisingly. "That's made from Sylacauga marble. It's hardy material, but heavy too. You could probably kill somebody with it—oops!" She clapped her hand over her mouth. "Poor choice of words, huh?"

I laughed. "Don't worry, I'm getting used to it."

Sue walked over and glanced at the price tag, then quoted a price so low I was certain she had to be mistaken. "Are you sure? It looks more valuable than that."

"Let's say we're giving you the first-time customer/new resident/Rocco favorite discount," she said. "Plus, these aren't professional pieces. They were made by students at an art school in the city."

I gave the bust another appraising look. "It was made by an art student? You could have fooled me. It's mighty fine work." I pulled my checkbook out of my purse and we walked over to the register for Sue to ring up the sale and fill out a delivery slip.

"If you're not in a hurry, I can get it to you in a few days," she offered. "Should I just bring it over to the store?"

"Hm, better bring it to my house for now. No telling when I'll have my grand reopening. Everything's kind of up in the air."

"Understandable. You don't want any stigma attached to your name when you open for business, right?"

"Exactly."

I leaned my elbow on the counter while she finished writing up the receipt. "So, has your brother mentioned how the case is coming along?"

She frowned. "No, but I for one hope he wraps this up quickly. Josh is usually cool-headed, but this one got him a bit rattled. He worked on a couple of committees for the policeman's fund with Amelia. Believe it or not, he liked her."

"Oh, I believe you. I thought myself he seemed a bit distressed."

"Yeah, well, Amelia might have been public enemy number one to most of the town, but she was always nice to Josh."

Since I honestly couldn't conceive of any woman not being nice to Josh, I had no answer to that. Sue's next words, however, made me stifle a gasp.

"Not like that strumpet of an ex-wife of his. Thank God she left town."

• • •

Driving back toward my house, I reviewed the morning's events, homing in on my adventure in Secondhand Sue's. So, Josh Bloodgood had a strumpet of an ex-wife, eh? I chuckled as I remembered Olivia's words: *Everyone in a small town has a skeleton or two in their closet.* Apparently not even Fox Hollow's homicide detective was immune.

After all, even I had a strumpet of an ex-fiancé, or whatever the male equivalent of *strumpet* was. I could think of several good ones, albeit unrepeatable.

As I rounded the corner and approached my driveway, I let out a gasp of dismay. Parked straight across the entrance was a light blue convertible. I glanced around but saw no sign of the driver. Fantastic. I wondered who I'd make as an enemy now if I called to have that car towed.

I pulled up to the curb and was just about to rummage in my purse for my cell when I heard someone shout from my porch.

"Well, it's about time. Where in heck have you been?"

I froze. I knew that voice, but it couldn't be, could it? Then a familiar dark head came into view, and I saw I wasn't mistaken.

The owner of the convertible was none other than my former costar, Gary Presser.

Fourteen

For a second I just stared, and then I raised my arm, took some skin between my thumb and forefinger, and pinched myself hard.

"Ow!" I cried. Well, that settled that. I wasn't dreaming, or hallucinating. He was really here, along with a large black suitcase propped up against my front door.

Gary tripped down my porch steps and ran over to stand in front of me. "There you are," he said, waggling his finger. "For a second there, I thought that guy at the gas station gave me directions to the wrong house."

I fisted a hand on my hip and shot him a stony stare. "Gary, what are you doing here?"

His lips drooped down almost immediately into a hangdog expression. "Gee, thanks a lot. I fly cross-country and drive all this way and that's the greeting I get? I told you I was coming, remember?" When I didn't answer, he persisted, "I kept asking you what was wrong, and you kept avoiding the issue, so I said I'd come on out and see for myself."

I pushed the heel of my hand through my hair. "You did say that, but I didn't think you really meant it."

His arms enveloped me in a gigantic bear hug. "Oh, come on, Shell. What sort of costar would I be if I deserted you in your time of need?" He pulled back a bit to study me. "This is your time of need, right? I mean, something's up. I could hear it in your voice."

"I'm fine, Gary. You didn't have to uproot your life and come all the way out here to check on me."

He spread his arms wide. "Hey, you decided to uproot your life and change careers. I guess that dark store in town with the reopening sign on it is yours?"

"You guess right. I'd hoped to be getting the store and its stock ready for a grand reopening, but instead . . ."

"Yeah, I know." He reached out and give my hand a squeeze. "That's why you could use my help. After all, right now I've got nothing else to do, other than sign up for unemployment."

The note of disappointment in his tone was unmistakable. "What happened? They didn't go for the reboot?"

"To quote the producers exactly, 'That show just isn't worth spit without Shell Marlowe.' Or similar words to that effect."

I remembered Max's words and a pang of guilt arrowed through me. "That's not true and you know it."

"Yeah, well, it seems they were gearing the show more toward the male audience, and not the action end of it, if you get my meaning."

I wrinkled my nose. "Then I'm glad I turned it down, although I'm sorry it didn't work out for you. You'll get something else, Gary, but only if you go back to LA and start auditioning."

"I'm not so sure." He plopped down on my bottom step and cupped his chin in one hand. "I had a lot of time to think on the plane ride out here. Series TV is getting to be a rat race, and I'm not as young as I used to be. Maybe I should try something different, maybe Broadway, or Off Broadway."

I laughed. "You're considering a play? I thought you always said theater was for people who couldn't make it in Hollywood."

He grinned sheepishly. "I did say that, didn't I? Well, maybe I've had a change of heart. Look, I didn't come all the way out here to talk about me. What's going on with you, Shell?"

I looked down at the ground. "I don't know what you mean."

"Oh, yes, you do." He leaned over so that his nose was only about an inch away from mine. "I could hear it in your voice when we spoke on the phone. You sounded just like you did when Pat left you."

I raised my gaze to his and thrust my jaw out. "I most certainly did not. And I left Patrick, no matter what he told you."

"Whatever." Gary folded his arms over his chest and stood, one foot tapping impatiently on the concrete. "Are you going to tell me what's up with you or not?"

I folded my own arms over my chest. "Not."

"Okay, then, I suppose I'll have to guess." He put a finger to his lips, closed his eyes, and then popped them wide open. "Aha, I have it." He pointed his finger dramatically in the air. "You must be the actress they suspect of murdering the local termagant."

"Wow, is that a fifty-dollar word or what? I'm impressed. And just where did you hear this juicy bit of news?"

He grinned. "It's the main topic of conversation at the gas station out on the highway. It's a veritable hotbed of local gossip." His expression sobered and he reached out and gripped my hand. "Is it true?"

"Is what true? That I murdered the local termagant or that I'm suspected of doing so?"

"Very funny."

He looked so upset that I sighed. "Yes, it's true. That I'm on the suspect list, not that I did the deed—although I had a public argument with the woman the day before her death."

Gary let out a low whistle. "Sounds like you could use a friend." I glanced over at his suitcase, and he added, "If it's inconvenient, I can always find a hotel near here. I'm not leaving, Shell."

My expression softened. "I know you're not, and it's not inconvenient. Come on, grab your suitcase. I'll make you a cup of java and fill you in."

• • •

I showed Gary to one of the guest bedrooms and left him to unpack and freshen up. I went into the kitchen and put on a fresh pot of coffee, then pulled out the wheels of cheddar and Brie I'd purchased at the General Store along with some crackers, arranged them on a tray, and set it on the table. I'd just poured us each a steaming mug when Gary reappeared. His hair was damp from a quick shower, and he'd changed into comfortable sweatpants. He eased himself into one of the chairs and sniffed the air.

"Um, what's that, Kahlua-flavored coffee? You wouldn't happen to have the real thing to add to it, would you? I didn't drink on the plane, and I'm overdue."

Gary had an aversion to air travel, so the mere fact he'd stepped on a plane to come to my aid was quite something, indeed. I opened one of the bottom cabinets and pulled out a bottle of Kahlua. I added a generous amount to both our coffees and then sat down across from him, my hands wrapped around my mug. We sat for a few minutes, sipping in silence, and then Gary set down his mug.

"Care to fill me in on what's going down here now? What was that public argument about that's got you on the suspect list?"

I explained all about the museum board vote and the supposed feud between Amelia and my aunt that I believed to be behind Amelia's crusade. I also recounted my meetings with the other three board members and Garrett Knute. Gary listened intently, and when I'd finished, ran his finger around the rim of his cup.

"Sounds to me like you might have painted a target on yourself," he said grimly.

I bit down on my lower lip. "Funny. Josh hinted at pretty much the same thing."

Gary's eyes widened a bit. "Josh?"

Heat seared my cheeks and I ducked my head. "Detective Bloodgood. He's investigating the murder."

"I see. And are you often on a first-name basis with detectives investigating you for murder?"

"We'd met briefly before all this mess. His sister's dog ran into me in the park. I had no idea he was a detective."

"Of course not." He let out a low chuckle. "And what does this Detective Bloodgood look like? I'm betting he's not paunchy with gray hair, like most of the detectives on TV."

I narrowed my eyes. "No, he's not."

"So?" Gary persisted as I remained silent. "Is he as good-looking as me?"

I made a face at him. "No one's as good-looking as you, Gary, except maybe Hugh Jackman. I've already had to assure some of the local women that marvelous head of hair is all yours."

He reached up to give his hair a swift pat and laughed. "Nice try at a diversion, but I'm still interested in a description of your Detective Bloodgood."

"He's not my Detective Bloodgood," I protested. "Besides, I have a new man in my life."

Gary almost dropped his mug. "You do?"

"Absolutely. I was worried he and Kahlua might not get along, but they seem to have effected a truce."

Gary's brows drew together. "Kahlua? Your cat? Why wouldn't he get along with your cat? Is he allergic?"

"No, far from it."

I lapsed into silence, and Gary's frown deepened. "So, details, Shell. What does this fellow look like?"

I put my finger to my lips. "He's very hairy," I said at last.

110

Gary gave me a puzzled stare. "He's hairy? You hate facial hair . . . or was that just so I'd shave the beard I grew for season six?"

"You look better clean-shaven anyway. I did you and all your female fans a favor." I inclined my head toward the doorway. "Here he is now. Come here, Purrday, and say hello to Gary. He's going to be staying with us a while."

Purrday glided into the kitchen and hopped up on the vacant chair next to Gary. He cocked his head to one side and blinked at him. "Merow."

Gary stared at Purrday and then burst into laughter. "Oho, another cat, eh?"

"He belonged to Aunt Tillie. I couldn't turn him away."

Gary bounced both eyebrows at me. "Just be careful this doesn't start a trend, Shell. I'd hate to see you become the neighborhood crazy cat lady." He reached out his hand. Purrday sniffed at the tips of his fingers, then his pink tongue darted out and gave them a quick lick. "Friendly fellow. Lots friendlier than Kahlua. She usually hisses at me."

"She doesn't like your cologne. You've got Purrday's stamp of approval, at least."

Gary selected a piece of cheddar and started to put it on a cracker when the cheese slid from his fingers and landed—*plop!*—on the floor. Purrday eyed the cheese, then cocked his head at Gary.

"Okay if I let him have it? It fell on the floor."

"Go ahead, but you'd better practice your *whoops, I knocked it on the floor* routine. For such a good actor, that was beneath you."

Gary's eyes widened. "Shell! I'm shocked! You think I did that on purpose?"

I laughed right at him. "I know you did. You would never drop a piece of anything edible on the floor."

He raised both hands. "Okay, I'm guilty. But Purrday appreciates it, don't you, boy?"

Purrday didn't answer. He'd already snatched the bit of cheddar in his paws and was nibbling happily at it.

Gary turned back to me. "Well, now that I've met the main man in your life, let's get back to number two. Your detective."

"Let's not and say we did." I rose and walked over to the cabinet and pulled out the bottle of Kahlua. "Refill?"

He held out his mug. "Sure. And don't bother with the coffee this time."

Once I'd refilled both mugs with Kahlua we adjourned to the parlor, leaving Purrday happily noshing on his cheese. Feline Kahlua was stretched out across the top of the love seat. She lifted her head, took one look at Gary, let out a loud hiss, and promptly vanished up the stairs.

"Great to see you again too," Gary called after her retreating form. He looked over his shoulder at me. "Some things never change." He plopped down on the brocaded sofa and I sat on the love seat across from him. "Let's think of this logically," he said. "You said most of the people in Fox Hollow hated this woman, Amelia?"

"So I've heard."

"Okay." He leaned back against the sofa cushions, his eyes slitted in thought. "First things first. Who might have hated her enough to do her in?"

"Well, there are the aforementioned board members: Larry Peabody, Andy McHardy, and Ginnifer Rubin. And Garrett Knute is hiding something as well. I heard him say 'over my dead body.' And Amelia was determined he shouldn't get his hands on that envelope."

"Hm." Gary laced his hands behind his neck. "That definitely piques my interest. Anyone else?"

"I saw Amelia arguing with a woman in the park. Olivia thinks it might have been Londra Lewis, who works at the museum as the administrator. Amelia disliked her because of her loyalty to the museum director, Mazie Madison." I tapped the edge of my mug. "Olivia said that Mazie was no angel when it came to Amelia either. Then there's the mayor."

"Oho, the mayor, eh?" Gary bounced his eyebrows. "You just can't trust those public officials."

"It might be nothing, but Amelia might have something on one or both of the mayor's kids, I'm not sure. And Garrett Knute mentioned this guy, Melvin Feller, but so far I haven't been able to make a concrete connection between him and Amelia. And Garrett said half the town hated the woman, so who knows who else might have a motive." I paused. "Then there's the editor of the town paper, Quentin Watson. He's a smarmy little weasel who's already printed two less-than-flattering snippets about me in his paper because I wouldn't give him an interview. Lord knows what *his* relationship with Amelia was."

"Well, there doesn't appear to be a dearth of suspects," Gary said wryly.

"And the reason you're at the top is . . . ?"

"I'm not even sure I'm at the top. Josh—I mean, Detective Bloodgood—told me I was a person of interest, primarily because I argued with the deceased in public."

Gary gave a short laugh. "Well, person of interest is better than suspect, if you ask me. Now, what we have to do is systematically go through all of those people and determine which of them had the best motive for wanting Amelia dead."

"No doubt J—the detective is doing that already."

Gary shrugged. "Maybe. Or maybe not. In any case, our considering it can't hurt, right? I mean, after all, the sooner this gets cleared up, the sooner you can open up your little store."

Purrday ambled into the parlor just then, batting the button between his paws. I reached down to retrieve it.

"It looks like one of Aunt Matilda's buttons. Where he got it from is a mystery."

"It probably just fell off something. You know cats. They can be real scavengers. Remember when Kahlua had a stash of all your rhinestone pins?"

I started to reply when the doorbell rang. I excused myself and went to answer it, and my eyes widened in surprise when I saw Josh on my front stoop. His lips were slashed into a straight line, and he had his cop face on.

"Mind if I come in?" he asked. "Something's turned up, and I need to speak to you about it."

I pushed the door wide and motioned for him to enter. As he stepped into the foyer, Gary emerged from the parlor. The two men started then stood and stared at each other.

I cleared my throat. "Detective Josh Bloodgood, may I introduce my former costar—"

Josh waved his hand. "I know who he is." He turned back to Gary. "Gary Presser, right? Or should I say Douglas Doolittle?"

Gary beamed and held out his hand. "Ah, you've watched our show?"

"When my schedule permitted."

Josh took Gary's hand and Gary pumped it up and down. "Always happy to meet a fan. I take it you're Josh the detective?"

"That would be me." He released Gary's hand and shoved his deep into the pockets of the light khaki jacket he wore. "It might be best," he said, with a meaningful look at me, "if we discussed my news in private."

"Not necessary," Gary said breezily. He stepped right up to me and slipped one arm around my shoulders in a protective gesture. "I came out here to Fox Hollow to help Shell, so . . ." He paused and looked expectantly at me.

I sighed and turned to Josh. "Anything you have to say you can say in front of Gary. It won't go any further."

Josh frowned. "Okay, then," he said at last. He reached into the inside pocket of his jacket and pulled out a small plastic bag, in which rested a slip of paper. "My men did a thorough sweep of the murder scene, and we found this under the desk near the body."

He held the baggie out to me. I took it. Inside was a note printed in block letters:

I'VE DISCOVERED YOUR LITTLE SECRET. UNLESS YOU WANT ME
TO EXPOSE YOU, I SUGGEST WE TALK.

S

I read the note twice and then looked at Josh, puzzled. "I'm sorry. I don't get it."

His gaze bored into mine. "Did you write that?"

I took a couple of deep breaths before I answered. "Absolutely not. For one thing, I don't print that neatly, and I've never seen this before in my life."

He turned the bag over in his hand. "Then you weren't planning to expose Amelia? The purpose of that meeting wasn't blackmail?"

I stared at him, shocked, and drew myself up to my full height. "Definitely not," I snapped. "I've never blackmailed anyone in my life. Besides, I don't know anything I could have blackmailed her with."

"That's true," Gary interjected. "Shell is one of the most honest people I know."

I gestured toward the note. "Evidently someone wanted you to think otherwise."

Josh scratched absently at his jaw. "We dusted it for prints, and the only ones we found were Amelia's. Obviously, whoever wrote it must have worn gloves."

"What in the world could I have been going to expose about her?" I asked. "I didn't know the woman."

"Well, you were going around asking people if they were being blackmailed by her," Josh answered. "And you accused Garrett Knute of having a secret."

"That's true, but they're legitimate concerns," I declared.

"Well, it seems pretty obvious to me," said Gary. Josh and I both turned toward him.

"What does?" asked Josh.

Gary spread his hands. "This murder was no accident. Someone planned it out carefully, and decided to use Shell as a scapegoat. Think about it. The photograph Shell gave her was clutched in her cold, dead hand, plus this note, conveniently signed by S?" He jabbed his finger at Josh's face. "And your job, my friend, is to find out who would do such a thing."

"I agree," Josh said grimly. He turned to me. "For what it's worth, Shell, I don't think you killed Amelia. But it sure does look as if someone wants us to think you did."

I shuddered. The thought that someone might deliberately have set me up as a murderer was not an appealing one. "If I could take back speaking to those people, I would, in a heartbeat. But I can't. What happens now?"

"What happens is you keep your mouth shut and keep a low profile while I work on finding out just who did kill Amelia," Josh said softly. He looked as if he wanted to say more, but instead just nodded curtly to both Gary and me and then turned and exited out my front door.

I set my lips. Now I was more determined than ever to do some digging on my own. Someone had used me to get Amelia alone at the museum and kill her. Someone had planned it with malice aforethought, and I was betting it was someone I'd met, someone I'd spoken with.

I wouldn't feel safe until I found out who.

Fifteen

"Oh, this is so exciting. I feel like I'm a character on one of your *Spy Anyone* episodes!"

After Josh had left I called Olivia and asked her to bring Rita and Ron over to my house pronto for a powwow on how to proceed with our "investigation." They were all thrilled and a bit speechless, too, when they found Gary there. Olivia in particular. She spent most of our little meeting staring at Gary's fabulous thick head of hair.

"This isn't television," Gary said in a stern tone, although the half smile he shot Olivia was, I was sure, intended to take the sting out of his words. "This is reality, and one of these people is trying to frame Shell for a crime she didn't commit. We have to help Detective Bloodgood by narrowing the suspect pool."

I'd abandoned my notebook idea and instead dragged the whiteboard out from the den and set it up in the parlor. Gary had drawn boxes with each suspect's name in one of them, and arrows pointing to the center box, which read *Victim: Amelia Witherspoon*. Under each suspect's name he'd printed a possible motive. Now he stood in front of it, pointing to each box with the tip of a ruler, like someone teaching Criminology 101.

"Let's look at each one logically," he said and pointed to the first box. "Lawrence Peabody. He consistently voted with Amelia on museum matters. Did Amelia have something on him to buy his loyalty? Ditto his friend, Andy McHardy." Gary tapped the second box. "Shell heard him saying it couldn't go on. What, exactly? Why did these two constantly side with Amelia?"

I stepped up to tap at the third box. "Ginnifer Rubin seemed very nervous when I confronted her. She said she'd talk to Amelia, but I could just feel the fear emanating from her. It was quite a different feeling than the one I got from Garrett Knute." I pointed at the fourth box. "Even though he acted as if Amelia had no hold on him, that argument I witnessed over the envelope suggests otherwise."

Ron squinted at the board, then pointed. "You've got Quentin Watson on there?"

"Why not?" Olivia leaned back and tucked her knees under her. "He's a despicable character who delights in dishing out dirt on people. Who knows, maybe he had something on Amelia. We know he dislikes Shell. Maybe he wrote that note to deliberately incriminate her."

"Right. Then there are others with murkier motives." Gary pointed to the boxes on the bottom. "Londra Lewis. Shell saw her arguing with Amelia in the park. We've yet to determine over what or just how deep that hatred runs. And over here, we've got the three long shots: Mazie Madison, Mayor Hart, and Melvin Feller."

Rita wiggled her fingers. "I know why Mazie and the mayor are on the board, but Feller? I double-checked with Frank like you asked me to, Shell, and he couldn't recall Melvin ever even meeting Amelia."

"He's on there because Garrett Knute told me that Melvin would be his choice of a number-one suspect. Of course, he could have said that to throw me off the track."

Rita shook her head. "I know he can flare up and all, but I just can't see him killing anyone. Garrett probably just said that 'cause he doesn't like Mel."

Gary tapped his forefinger against the board. "Until Shell's name is completely cleared, no one's name goes off this board. One of these people killed Amelia and is trying to frame Shell."

Ron stretched his arms wide and laced his fingers behind his head. "Don't see what Mazie's doing on there."

Olivia nodded. "True. She disliked Amelia, but murder? She's such a little mouse."

"And why is Mayor Hart on there?" Ron pointed to the box. "She and Amelia weren't buddy-buddy, but I doubt she hated her enough to kill her."

"I'm not sure if Amelia had something on her children or not," I said. "If she did, and threatened to expose it, that would be a powerful motive for murder."

"Exactly," Gary said. "The next step is spelling out everyone's motives, try and see who had the best reasons for wanting Amelia dead." He paused and tapped against the mayor's box for emphasis. "And *no one's* name goes off."

"Well," Ron said and rose. "As it happens, the mayor has a floral arrangement delivered to her office every Tuesday. I'll just make the delivery in person and see what I can find out. I'll take an extra spray of roses for her admin. Janie loves to talk, once you get her going."

"Excellent," Gary said. He looked pointedly at Olivia and Rita. "Anyone else?"

"Garrett usually goes to the diner for lunch. It's right near Sweet Perks," Rita offered. "I'll try to grill him, see if I can find out why he mentioned Mel Feller as a suspect. He may not talk to me, though."

I gave her an encouraging smile. "It's worth a shot, and I appreciate that you're willing to try."

"Ginnifer Rubin does a Zumba class this afternoon at my studio," Olivia piped up. "Maybe I can get her talking about Larry and Andy. It's a sure bet neither one of them will open up to anyone." Olivia turned to Gary and gave him the benefit of her full-wattage smile. "Perhaps you'd like to tag along? She was a big *Spy Anyone* fan, I know. Your presence might make her feel more at ease."

"Fine." He patted his stomach. "Maybe I could use some Zumba myself. Unemployment sure makes a fellow overeat." He glanced at me. "What about you, Shell?"

"It just so happens I got a text from Mazie earlier. She'd like me to drop by the museum today, so it will be the perfect opportunity to feel out her and Londra Lewis."

Gary rubbed his hands together. "It sounds as if we have a plan!"

Olivia chuckled. "And like the best laid ones, let's hope ours don't go astray."

• • •

When I pulled into the parking lot of the museum shortly after one o'clock, I must admit I had a brief attack of the willies. I made sure to park in a completely different spot than the one I'd parked in on Sunday, although I did notice as I got out of my car that Amelia's black Caddy was still in the same spot. The sight of it gave me a chill as I walked up the short flight of steps to the front entrance and pushed open the door.

After I paused to admire the lovely oil paintings hanging in the foyer, I walked down the short hall into a bigger room from which corridors branched out in all directions, and gilt-edged signs pointed the way to different attractions: The Saber Room, The Egyptian Room, Fox Hollow Heritage Room. A woman wearing a blue blazer and thick glasses sat behind a massive desk square in the center. I walked up and introduced myself and said I had an appointment with Mazie Madison.

"Oh, yes." Her fingers flew over the keyboard, and she squinted at her monitor. "Crishell McMillan, right? Just take that corridor all the way down to the back"—she pointed at the center aisle—"and her office is on your right-hand side."

I followed her directions and moved down the corridor, walking swiftly past the closed door marked *Library*—although just seeing the closed door conjured up too many memories for my taste. I found the door marked *Office* without any problem. I pushed open the door and walked into a large, brightly lit room. A woman with dark brown hair was seated behind a cherrywood desk. She looked up as I approached, and I recognized her instantly as the woman I'd seen arguing with Amelia in the park on Saturday. My eyes automatically strayed to the marble nameplate on the desk: Londra Lewis.

For her part, Ms. Lewis gave me a wide smile. "Ms. McMillan? Nice to meet you." She held out her hand, and I shook it. Her grip, for a petite woman, was surprisingly strong. "Ms. Madison will be with you in just a moment." She gestured toward one of the chairs. "Would you like some coffee?"

I shook my head. "No, thanks." She shrugged and turned back to her computer. A few minutes later the connecting door opened and Mazie Madison stood framed in the doorway. She motioned to me, and I got up and followed her into a much larger office that held an oaken desk, matching bookcase, and file cabinet. The Queen Anne chair in front of the desk was upholstered in a light pink brocade. She waved me toward the chair and settled herself behind her desk. She pulled a fat file in front of her and folded her hands on top of it.

"First off, I want to say again how very sorry I am that you were the one to find Amelia," she said. "That must have been a terrible shock for you." Mazie adjusted her readers on her nose and leaned forward. "I can't imagine how upset you must have been."

"It's an experience I wouldn't care to repeat," I said. I crossed my legs and leaned forward a bit. "Seeing her car here gave me a bit of a start, I must say."

Mazie peered over the tops of her readers and frowned. "Her car? Amelia didn't own a car. She didn't drive."

Now it was my turn to frown. "That black Caddy that's parked out back isn't hers? I thought . . ."

"Oh, dear, no." Mazie laughed lightly. "That Caddy is Londra's. She only lives around the block, and so parks her car there most of the time. Some weeks she rarely even moves it."

Londra lived that close? The thought flashed through my mind that the assistant probably had a key, too. It certainly wouldn't have taken much for her to come here, kill Amelia, and beat it before I arrived. I cleared my throat again. "Well, at the time I thought it was Amelia's, so I went to the side entrance because she'd said she'd leave the door opened, but it was locked. I ended up going in the service entrance. I walked down the corridor and finally saw a light coming out of the library. I saw her the minute I walked in. Once I got over my initial shock, I called 911."

"Well." Mazie picked up the folder and tapped it against her blotter. "It's a misfortune, to be certain. Amelia could be tough to deal with, but she had good ideas. She will be missed. At any rate, I'm hopeful her replacement will be appointed before the week's end." She leaned across the desk and said, "Anyway, the reason I wanted to meet with you is to tell you that I've polled the other members, and it appears the motion to display your aunt's posters will pass this time." She paused dramatically. "Ginnifer Rubin has changed her vote. She was on the fence anyway, and only voted with Amelia because she was afraid to cross her."

I smiled. I'd had a feeling Ginnifer had been won over by my plea. "What about the other two?"

Mazie raised an eyebrow. "Larry and Andy? I'm afraid they're sticking with their original vote." She hesitated and then added, "They are apparently not too fond of you."

I grimaced. "I know. It's my own fault. I'm afraid I got a bit pushy with them."

Mazie made a clicking sound with her tongue. "It's understandable. I want you to know that I'm going to do everything I can to ensure that things go smoothly."

She rose, an indication the brief interview was over. I hesitated, wanting to broach the subject of her relationship with Amelia but not quite sure how to do it. She noticed my hesitation and smiled at me. "You look as if you want to ask me something else, Crishell. What is it?"

I decided that perhaps a straightforward approach might be best. "How did you get along with Amelia?" I asked her.

For a second she looked startled. Then she smiled again. "As well as could be expected. We weren't friends, but we weren't enemies, either. I think deep down we probably respected each other. Why do you ask?"

I shrugged. "No reason. From what I've heard, Amelia seemed to know most everyone's secrets in this town."

Mazie laughed. "She did, didn't she? Fortunately I had no secrets for her to hold over my head." She sat back down and opened her file folder. "If you'll excuse me, I have some matters I must attend to right away."

I took the dismissal with good grace and walked back into the main office. Londra was at the file cabinet. She pulled a fat folder from it, but as she turned, her sleeve caught on the edge of the drawer. The file fell to the floor, scattering papers across the carpet.

"Damn," she muttered and then, realizing I was standing nearby, choked out a soft, "Sorry."

"No need," I assured her. "I say lots worse, especially when someone cuts me off driving."

I bent down to help her gather up the scattered papers. I noted that most of them were bills and memos, all signed by Mazie Madison. I also noticed that after some of the signatures there was a miniscule checkmark, positioned so it looked like part of the M in Madison. Londra saw me looking and smiled.

"It's my code," she said, taking the papers I'd gathered up.

"Your code?"

She nodded. "Yes. Mazie's so busy that most times I sign the memos and correspondence. Occasionally, even a check."

"You can imitate her signature that well?" I knew such a thing wasn't unheard of. I'd heard my mother complain many times that her admin could sign her name better than she could.

"Oh, yes. Mazie's often joked she has to hide her personal checkbook from me." She lifted her chin. "That's why I add that little checkmark. It's hard to spot unless you know to look for it, but it's how I can tell what ones I've signed." She shoved all the papers back in the folder and tucked it under her arm. "I guess things are looking up for you, Ms. McMillan, what with your aunt's posters being a shoo-in now." She paused and then added in a low tone, "Amelia Witherspoon was a terrible person."

I decided what the heck and leaned closer. "I noticed you arguing with her in the park on Saturday. You certainly seemed upset."

A look came into her eyes. Fear? But it was gone in an instant. "I happened to run into her and I made the mistake of voicing my opinion. I told her that I didn't think the vote against you was fair."

"You did? Well, thank you." I paused and then added, "I understand that you wanted a docent position here."

Her laugh was bitter. "I tried several times, and each time Amelia had a better candidate. She was just pissed because I would take Mazie's side instead of hers. Amelia hated it when she couldn't bend people to her way." She picked up a pen and shoved it into a pencil cup, then raised her gaze to meet mine. Her eyes were as hard as stones.

"I'll tell you the same thing I told Detective Bloodgood when he asked. At the time of Amelia's death, I was home, making breakfast. I'm afraid the only person who saw me was Happy, my parakeet. I have no alibi. I didn't kill her, but I can't say I wasn't tempted at times. I'm not sorry she's dead, not one whit. It couldn't have happened to a better person."

• • •

I returned home to find Gary and Olivia sitting in my parlor, having a drink. I flopped down on the edge of the love seat and looked at them. "You two are back early. How did your investigation go?"

"Everything depends how you look at it," said Olivia. "Ginnifer never showed up for class."

"No, but I got a good workout." Gary patted his stomach. "And we had an interesting afternoon, anyway."

"Oh? How so?"

"When we were leaving the studio, I suggested going out the back way and cutting across over to the bike run in the park," said Olivia. "Guess who was there! Your pal Quentin Watson."

"Ugh," I said. "What did he want?"

"Oh, he didn't see us," Olivia said with a smile.

"No," cut in Gary. "We walked around behind him. He was so intent on his phone conversation he never noticed us. But we sure paused when we heard him say the word *dagger*."

I sat up straighter in my seat. "Dagger?"

They both nodded and then Olivia said, "He was talking to someone on the phone about, quote unquote, the dagger that killed Amelia. He was describing it to someone. I heard something about it being serrated with a double edge."

"Really?" My brow wrinkled as I thought. "I don't recall seeing anything anywhere about the murder weapon itself. Every account I read just said she'd been stabbed multiple times."

Olivia's lips curved in a triumphant grin. "Exactly."

"So, the question is, how did this guy know that?" Gary waved his finger in the air dramatically. "I can think of one way: if he were the one who used it to kill Amelia."

Sixteen

As appealing as the thought of Quentin being Amelia's killer was, I hesitated. "We still don't know if he had a motive," I said. "As for knowing about the knife, that man's like a bloodhound, or a stalker. For all we know he could have a mole in the police station."

Olivia snapped her fingers. "I know how I can find out. Gladys Ficke takes my evening modern jazz class. She works the reception desk at the *Gazette*. Quentin always has her running his errands. She hates him, and she'll be more than happy to share any gossip she can."

"Okay," I said. "That sounds like a plan."

Gary looked at me. "You didn't tell us how you made out down at the museum."

I related my interview with Mazie and Londra Lewis's parting comment to me. When I finished, Gary let out a low whistle. "Sounds as if this Lewis woman certainly had an axe to grind. Plus, she has no alibi for the time of death."

"True, but I can't see it. Londra's pretty petite, and shorter than Amelia," Olivia hastened to point out. "I can't really see her attacking Amelia and slashing her throat from ear to ear, like Josh described."

"Oh, I don't know. I looked that 'smile' wound up on the internet," said Gary. "You would bend the head forward and cut deep all the way across from ear to ear. If she attacked her from behind, she'd have the element of surprise. Strength would have nothing to do with it."

"Yuck." Olivia suppressed a shudder. "It's amazing what one can find on the internet."

I pursed my lips. "I'm not entirely sure I buy her explanation of the argument I witnessed between her and Amelia in the park. It certainly seemed like more than just a mere difference of opinion."

"Probably not, but with Amelia dead and no other witnesses, there's no way you'll be able to find out for sure," said Olivia. "Not that Amelia would have told you anything anyway." She rose and stretched. "I guess I should be getting back to the studio. I'll let you know if I find out anything from Gladys."

Once she'd gone I looked at Gary. "What's next?"

He rubbed his stomach. "I don't know about you, but detective work gives me a ravenous appetite. Plus, I skipped lunch."

My stomach chose that moment to growl, reminding me I'd only had a piece of quiche. "Well, I bought some nice steaks and chicken breasts at the General Store," I offered. "I could whip us up a nice steak salad, or a chicken Caesar."

Gary made a face. "No, thanks. I've sampled your cooking, remember?"

I swatted at his arm. "That dinner party was two years ago. I've vastly improved since then."

"What, so now you don't burn the steaks? You just overcook them so they taste like shoe leather?"

I wrinkled my nose at him. "Very funny."

He rose and grabbed my hand, pulling me up alongside him. "Come on. The least I can do is treat you to dinner, since you're giving me free room and board. What's a good restaurant around here?"

Free room and board. Heck, I'd forgotten about that. With my luck, Gary might never leave. I put that depressing thought from my mind and said, "Good question. Since I've only lived here a week, I haven't had much opportunity to find out."

"Tsk tsk. You certainly have changed in a short space of time. The Shell Marlowe I knew would have all the local restaurants on speed dial by now."

I laughed at him. "True. But Crishell McMillan is much more discerning."

He pulled out his iPad. "No matter. I'll just look some up."

"There is an upscale pub in town. The Captain's Club. That's where I had my unfortunate encounter with Peabody and McHardy, as a matter of fact. And met Quentin Watson for the first time." I paused and then added in an offhand tone, "The bar looked really nice. One of Josh—Detective Bloodgood's sisters bartends there."

Gary wasn't buying my casual act. He bounced an eyebrow at me and crowed, "Oho, so that's the big attraction there, is it? You figure the good detective might stop by for a drink and to see his sister?"

"No, that's not what I was thinking," I protested. "You asked about a nice place to eat. That seemed like a nice place."

"Uh-huh."

I widened my eyes as much as I could without looking like the victim of a serial killer. "What, you don't believe me?"

"I believe you'd like to see the good detective again, and not when he's questioning you about the case. You do know you could pick up the phone and call him, right?"

"I could," I said, "but I really shouldn't. After all, I am technically a person of interest in a murder case he's investigating. I don't want to put him in an awkward position."

"But it's okay to accidentally run into him, right?" He glanced at his iPad. "Well, maybe some other time. I've found a better place for us to try."

He passed me his iPad. I looked at the screen and burst out laughing. "The Hairy Lemon? Really?"

"It's in a town called Appleton, about twenty minutes from here." He fiddled some more with the screen. "It says they serve the best Reuben in the county. And look, they've got your favorite, shepherd's pie." As I hesitated, he gave me the eye. "I doubt we'll hear from Rita and Ron today, and we can stop by Olivia's studio on the way back, see what she found out."

"How can I refuse shepherd's pie," I said. I threw up my hands. "Okay. You win. Let's go check out the Hairy Lemon. Maybe a change of scenery is what we need to get our detecting juices flowing."

• • •

I changed into beige linen slacks and a sleeveless back-button tangerine-colored top, and Gary put on dark green dress slacks and a matching open-collared polo shirt. Purrday and Kahlua were squatted shoulder to shoulder at the bottom of the staircase, and meowed loudly to remind me they hadn't been fed since this morning. I was happy to see they appeared to be getting along, although I was a bit resentful of their ganging up on me. Purrday's loud yowl of approval when I filled his bowl to the rim definitely rivaled Kahlua's.

"That should hold the two of you. Oh, and don't wait up," I told them. "After dinner we're going to stop by Olivia's dance studio. Maybe Quentin Watson will turn out to be a viable suspect after all."

"Merow," said Purrday. Kahlua was too busy gobbling down food to respond. I noticed the button lying not far from Purrday's dish. There appeared to be a fresh toothmark in the wood.

"I'm not even going to bother taking it away from you this time, but I've got to get you some new toys," I said, giving his head a pat. "I wonder what else you might have hidden somewhere around here."

Gary stood behind me, arms crossed over his chest. He shook his head. "Do you really think they understand you?"

I straightened up and turned. "As crazy as it sounds, yes."

Gary rolled his eyes. "When either one of them answers you, let me know. I'll get you all on late night and we'll make a fortune. Oh, wait." He threw his hands up. "I forgot. You've retired from show business. Guess it'll just be me and the cats."

I stuck my tongue out at him. "Very funny."

We piled into Gary's convertible and less than twenty minutes later found ourselves in the Hairy Lemon's overflowing parking lot. "Must be a great place," he said, pocketing the keys. "You can always tell how good a restaurant is by how full their parking lot is. Or how many cop cars are here."

I glanced around at the sea of cars. There were two cop cars parked near the back entrance. "Then this place must be five stars at least."

The building looked like a traditional British pub. It was made of polished stone, a British flag and an American one waving above its mahogany doors. Gary held the door for me and made a low bow. We walked into a large room that was wide open, with tables scattered all around. The bar was a shining block of mahogany wood, accentuated by droplights and a long mirror. Padded stools in gold and purple flanked it. The lighting was dim, but cozy. On a small stage near the back, a band was in the process of warming up. A blackboard to the left of the bar listed a large variety of specials. We hadn't been standing there for more than two minutes when a young girl with long black hair, wearing a bright red maxi dress that matched her lip gloss, sidled up to us, menus tucked under her arm. "Welcome to the Hairy Lemon." She gave us both an appraising glance. "First time?"

Gary gave her his triple-wattage full-grille smile. "Yep."

"Excellent. You'll enjoy it, I'm sure. Will you be having dinner?"

"Oh, absolutely." He leaned forward and closed one eye in a wink. "We're dying to try your shepherd's pie and the Reuben. Best in the county, right?"

She smiled, showing off teeth I was certain had been professionally whitened. "Absolutely. Would you like a table for two? Or would you like to have a drink at the bar first?"

My gaze flicked to the bar, and I started as my eye fell upon a man seated on a stool directly off to the left. I knew that prominent nose, and those ears, even though a cell phone seemed glued to one of them.

It was Melvin Feller.

"We're pretty hungry, so I think a tab would be best." He flinched as I grabbed his hand and squeezed it hard. I inclined my head toward the bar and widened my eyes. Gary turned back to the hostess and smiled. "Maybe we will start off at the bar."

She moved aside and I pushed forward, homing in on the two empty stools three seats down from where Melvin sat. I hopped up onto a stool and Gary slid onto the one next to me. The bartender, a young man with close-cropped blonde hair and a tiny mustache, turned to us with a smile. "Good evening, and welcome to the Hairy Lemon. What are you two drinking tonight?"

"A good question." Gary made a low bow to me. "Ladies first."

There was a small book shoved off to one end, the words *Drink Menu* engraved in embossed gold on its cover. I snatched it up and thumbed through it. "Oh, my," I said. "There's a drink called the Hairy Lemon?"

The bartender laughed. "Sure is. Fresh lemon and blueberries, seltzer, vodka, and ice. Want to try one?"

I set the book back. "Sure. Why not?"

"Frozen or straight up?"

I cocked my head to one side. "Frozen."

He glanced at Gary. "And you, sir?"

"I'm not that adventurous," Gary said. "I'll just have vodka and tonic with a twist."

"Coming right up."

Once he'd moved away Gary leaned into me. "Okay, Shell, give. Why were you so anxious to sit at the bar? I thought you were hungry."

"I am, but"—I raised my hand and made a pointing motion—"don't look now, but Melvin Feller is three seats over." As Gary turned casually in that direction I added, "He certainly seems engrossed in his phone conversation. I sure would like to know who's on the other end."

The bartender returned and set our drinks in front of us. I had to admit, the Hairy Lemon certainly looked cool and refreshing. I picked it up, took a sip, and set it back down. "Whew. That's strong."

"Too much?" The bartender reached for the glass. "Sorry, I can tone it down a bit if you want. The owner doesn't like us to skimp on the liquor."

I pushed the glass toward him. "That's odd. Usually they want the drinks watered down. Makes for more of a profit."

"True. Not this owner, though. He thinks full-bodied drinks make for happy customers, and happy customers keep coming back."

I glanced around the crowded area. "He might have something there, at that."

The bartender picked up the glass and turned to add a bit more seltzer.

Gary took a sip of his vodka and tonic and made a wry face. "A little on the strong side, but I can handle it. Although it'd be a lot easier if I had a Reuben in front of me," he grumbled.

"Just one drink, and then we can get a table." I nibbled at my lower lip. "I'd love to know what he's talking about. Judging from his facial expression, it seems intense."

Mel's brows were drawn together, and his lips were pressed together as he listened to whoever was on the other end. His short, stubby fingers fiddled with the handle of the frosty beer mug in front of him. He seemed engrossed.

Gary glanced down at the other end of the bar. "Say, there's a bowl of pretzels down there. You want some pretzels?"

I frowned. "Not really."

Gary slid off the stool and surreptitiously closed one eye in a wink. "Sure you do." Before I could utter a word of protest, he'd ambled off. I watched as he pushed himself in between Mel and another man and reached for the small bowl of pretzels on the edge of the bar. He pulled it quickly toward him, just as Mel started to set down his mug. Bowl collided with mug and both tipped over, spilling pretzels across the bar and onto the floor, and frosty ale right onto Melvin Feller's lap.

Mel jumped back, dropping his phone. Gary swooped down and caught it before it could hit the floor. The bartender came over with two towels. He handed one to Mel and started wiping up the spilled beer with the other. Gary leaned over and pressed the phone back into Mel's hand, whispered something to him. The older man waved him off, slid the phone into his pocket, then whipped out his wallet and slammed a bill on the bar. He said something to Gary and then pulled on his jacket and weaved his way toward the exit. Gary watched him for a few minutes before he made his way back to me.

I eyed him as he slid back onto the stool. "That was no accident," I said.

Gary's eyes widened. "Shell! Are you saying I bumped into the guy on purpose? What sort of person do you think I am?"

"A klutzy one," I responded, and Gary's lips quirked slightly. I fisted my hand and put it on my hip. "So? Just what did that accomplish, besides getting beer splattered on your shirt?"

He chuckled. "Well, for one thing, I heard a bit of his conversation. He was explaining to whoever was on the other end the difference between a straight-edge and a serrated-edge knife."

My eyes popped. "Oh my God! Are you sure?"

Gary tapped at his ear. "Mine might not be big, but they are in very good working order. I know what I heard. Perhaps your friend Knute's assessment of him as suspect number one isn't so far off the mark after all." He whipped out his iPad. "My memory's in excellent working order as well. I paid attention to the phone number on the screen when I rescued his phone. All we have to do is a reverse lookup, and we'll know who he was talking to."

I gave my former costar an appraising look. "Gary, I never realized how sneaky you were before!"

He shot me a boyish grin. "Stick with me, kid." He pulled up the reverse lookup site and tapped the number in. A few minutes later he handed me the iPad. "We're in luck. It's not unlisted."

I glanced at the name on the screen and stifled a gasp. The person Mel Feller had been talking to was Londra Lewis.

Seventeen

"That's amazing," I said, passing the iPad back to Gary. "Why on earth would he be talking to her about those types of knives?"

"Never mind that," Gary said, slipping his iPad back into his pocket. "Why would he be talking about knives period?" He paused, frowned, pulled the iPad back out and started tapping at the screen.

Curious, I leaned closer. "What are you looking up now?"

"Tuareg knife. I heard him say that just before I spilled the drink on him." Gary's fingers flew across the tiny pad.

"It's a short dagger kept in a sheath, usually attached to the forearm." As Gary shot me a look I added, "I remember going to a shop with Aunt Tillie, and there was a huge collection of various knives on display."

He passed me the iPad. On the screen was a photograph of a nasty-looking dagger with a crooked serrated blade. I glanced at it and a shudder ran through me.

"That's it, all right." I nodded. "Look at that blade. Could you imagine being stabbed with that?" I tapped the iPad against my chin. "Makes you wonder, though. Since when is he an expert on this type of dagger? And why would Londra Lewis ask him about it?"

"True. He has no connection to the museum, right?"

"He worked for Garrett Knute and Rita's husband when they had the accounting firm, and the museum was one of their clients, but Rita said Garrett did their accounting exclusively."

"Still, he would have known the people who worked there, right?"

"I'm not sure of the timeline of Mazie coming on board, but he probably would have known Londra." I stifled a gasp. "Could they have planned to murder Amelia together?"

"Whoa, let's not jump to conclusions," Gary said. My cell rang just then, and I fished it out of my bag. It was a text from Olivia: *Got some info from Gladys! When can we meet?*

I glanced up at Gary, who was peering over my shoulder. He sighed. "I know that look. Text her we'll be there in twenty." He patted his stomach. "That Reuben's gonna have to wait."

131

• • •

The Niven School of Dance was located on the second floor of a low-slung stone building, not far from the park. The bottom floor was a large crafts store that displayed local artists' work. The second floor was divided into three units: the dance studio, another that served as a pottery class, and one used for yoga and meditation. We pushed through the door marked *Niven School of Dance* and found ourselves in a large, mirrored room. Olivia was leaning against the ballet barre that stretched against one wall, doing some exercises. She stopped when she caught sight of us in the mirror and hurried over. "Wow, you got here pretty fast," she exclaimed.

"We're anxious to hear your info," Gary said. He gave his stomach a significant pat. "So much so we skipped dinner."

"You didn't have to do that," Olivia protested. "It would have kept."

Gary rolled his eyes. "Now you tell us."

I gave him a quick poke in the ribs and turned to Olivia. "Pay him no mind. He gets cranky when his stomach isn't full."

Olivia laughed. "Don't all men? But to tell the truth, I haven't eaten myself yet. I could go for one of the Captain's Club's buffalo chicken salads. They make one that's to die for."

"Yeah?" Gary appeared interested. "How are their Reubens?"

"Good, but not as good as the Hairy Lemon's."

He shot me a look. "That's what I was afraid of."

Olivia looked decidedly puzzled so I said quickly, "We were just at the Hairy Lemon, as a matter of fact. We were going to have dinner but we got a bit sidetracked."

"Shell saw one of her suspects at the bar, so that ended our dinner plans," Gary supplied. "The guy named Melvin Feller."

Olivia's eyes widened. "Mel was at the Hairy Lemon? Really?"

"Really," I answered. "And you'll never guess what Gary heard him talking about!" Without waiting for her to answer, I pushed my lips close to Olivia's ear. "Knives!"

To my surprise, Olivia started to laugh. "Wow, that seems to be a hot topic of conversation around Fox Hollow. Wait until I tell you what Gladys heard. She said—"

"Ladies, ladies," Gary interrupted us. "Maybe we could do this over a nice Reuben sandwich, or whatever your food of choice is at this Captain's Club?" He turned to me and wagged his finger under my nose. "Just so we're straight, young lady, we are eating first, and *not* sitting at the bar. No matter whose sister is bartending or who else might be there."

Olivia grinned and I felt my cheeks grow warm. I floundered for a witty remark, but a stifled "Ha ha" was all I could manage.

Olivia walked over to a small table and snatched up a jacket and tote bag. She shrugged her arms into the jacket, then fished in the tote and pulled out her iPhone. "I'll text Rita and Ron. Maybe they can join us, and we can all exchange notes."

"Great idea," I said, avoiding Gary's gaze. "Who knows, maybe we'll find the answer to who killed Amelia tonight."

Gary rolled his eyes. "Only in the movies," he muttered.

• • •

Rita was waiting for us in the foyer of the Captain's Club. "Ron will be along shortly," she assured us. "Marva's got a class at the adult school tonight, so he has to walk the dogs."

Mollie, the hostess, was the same girl who'd been there on my one and only other visit to the restaurant. Tonight, she had on a brown maxi dress with a matching crochet shrug, and she'd teamed it with a chunky turquoise necklace and bracelet. Her lips glistened with a mocha-colored gloss, and they parted in a wide smile as we approached her podium and her eyes rested on Gary. "Welcome to the Captain's Club. Table for four?"

"Five, actually. We're expecting another gentleman shortly," Olivia said.

"Hm." She frowned at the sheet on the lectern in front of her, then glanced up and craned her neck at the wide dining area. "All the larger tables are filled right now, but one should open up shortly. Would you like to have a drink at the bar while you wait?"

I glanced quickly over at the bar. I didn't see Josh, but I recognized Michelle behind the wide counter. She was serving a good-looking guy in a sweatshirt a beer, laughing at something he said.

"Can't get away from bars tonight, can we?" grumbled Gary in my ear.

I noticed a group of stools at the far end of the bar and motioned toward them. "The bar will be fine," I said.

Gary reached into his pocket and I saw him press a bill into Mollie's hand. "Be sure and call us the minute you get a table," I heard him say right before his stomach let out a loud rumble.

"Well, that was embarrassing," he growled, when we were all settled on stools. Rita positioned herself so that she had a good view of the front entrance, to signal Ron when he arrived.

"Oh, that girl was so taken by your charm she didn't even notice," I said with a brisk wave of my hand. "It wouldn't surprise me if she actually rushes someone along with their food just so we can sit down."

Gary chuckled and plucked the drink menu up. Michelle came toward us with a smile. "Good evening. What can I get y'all?"

Gary flipped the menu back on the counter and trained a dazzling smile on Michelle. "Vodka with a twist." He cut me a side glance. "Since I only had a couple of sips from my other one tonight."

"White wine spritzer for me," Olivia sang out.

Rita nodded. "Make that two."

Michelle looked at me. "And for you?"

I really wanted another Hairy Lemon—the little I'd had had been very tasty—but since that wasn't an option at this bar I decided to just go with the flow. "I'll have a spritzer too." I leaned forward and said in a low tone, "Do you know if your brother's on duty tonight?"

Michelle's smooth brow furrowed a bit. "Josh? I believe so. Why?"

I leaned back on the stool. "No particular reason. If you should hear from him, could you ask him to please call Shell McMillan?"

Michelle's eyes widened a bit. "You're Shell? The girl from the park?" She let out a low chuckle. "I heard you had a run-in with Rocco."

I laughed. "Sure did. He's a sweet dog, though."

"Yep, he's just a big sloppy bundle of doggy love. Most people get frightened by the pit bull face but you'll never find a gentler animal." She cocked her head to one side. "Sue mentioned you visited her shop."

"I did. It's very quaint. She has some nice things in there."

"Yeah, she does. Sue said you're going to reopen Urban Tails." Without waiting for an answer she went on, "I know a lot of folks can't wait. Your aunt gave lots of them personal service with their pets' needs. They miss that. Sue too. Tillie always kept a stash of Rocco's favorite liver and bacon treats on hand."

"I'm hopeful to continue the tradition. Eventually. And I'll make it a point to order those treats for Rocco."

"I'm sure he'll be glad about that. Sue too." Michelle's eyes twinkled. "She also said you bought that bust of Poe for the store. She's been trying to unload that for, like, forever."

"I'm surprised no one else snatched it up. It's a beautiful piece of sculpture. She said she got it from an art school?"

"Yeah, cool, right? There were three of 'em, in that set, if I'm not mistaken. Shakespeare and someone else, Lincoln maybe? They sold like that." She snapped her fingers in the air.

"It's exceptional workmanship."

"Sure, is, except for—oh, sorry." Michelle frowned as two older gentlemen signaled to her from the opposite end of the bar. "Two of my regulars. I'll take care of them and then be right back with your drinks."

Gary eyed me as Michelle moved off. "Getting in good with the siblings, eh?" he said.

I cut him an eye roll and turned to Olivia and Rita. "Shall we start comparing notes?"

Olivia nodded. "Might as well. Who wants to go first?"

I raised my hand. "I will," I said. I filled them in on my earlier meeting with Mazie and Londra, and then our encounter with Melvin Feller. When I'd finished, Rita let out a low whistle.

"Wow, that is something. I didn't realize they'd even found the murder weapon yet."

"They haven't," Olivia cut in. She gave a brief recounting of what she and Gary had overheard Quentin Watson say. "I talked to Gladys Ficke. They have *not* found the murder weapon yet, but from the shape of the wounds, they've narrowed down the type of blade they think might have been used. And top of this list is—"

"A Tuareg knife," I finished. "Did she mention how her boss acquired that information?"

"She came up with a big fat zero on that," sighed Olivia. "No one quite knows where Quentin gets his info from, but he's something like ninety-nine percent accurate."

"He's got to have bugs planted all over town," Rita agreed. "Either that or the guy's psychic."

I shot her a wry grin. "Psycho sounds more accurate, actually. And how did you make out, Rita?"

"Well, Garrett seemed very surprised to see me, and even more so when I sat down at his table and started chatting." She laughed. "We really haven't spoken all that much since he and Frank dissolved the business, so I just used that as an excuse and segued into Amelia's murder. He wasn't all that broken up about it."

Olivia let out a snort. "Did you think he would be?"

"Heck, no. I tried to get the conversation around to Mel Feller. That took some doing. Finally, I said that I'd seen Mel at the service for Amelia, and I was a bit surprised, since they hadn't known each other." She paused. "He just stared me right in the eyes and said, 'Oh, yeah? Shows how much you know, Rita.' So then I said, 'Well, it's not like he ever did any accounting for her,' and he said that Mel had, one time when he and Frank were both out, but he put an end to it fast—all he needed was Amelia complaining! Then I mentioned the museum board fiasco and he just snorted and says, 'You don't think that she'd ever let him on the board? Not after—' And then the waitress came over and asked if we wanted anything else, and he looked at his watch and said he had to get going. Picked up the check and left."

"Oh, too bad," I cried. "So now we know Mel *did* do some accounting for Amelia. I wonder if that was for her personally, or for the museum?"

Rita shook her head. "He didn't say. I can ask Frank, though."

"I'm more interested in his last comment," cut in Olivia. "It sounds as if there might have been more to his being rejected from the museum board than just his reputation for gambling."

"Hey, did I miss anything?"

We all turned as Ron joined our group. We'd been so engrossed in swapping stories that we hadn't seen him come in. He slid onto the empty stool next to Olivia. "Sounds like you're talking about Feller."

"Yep. Garrett intimated to Rita there might be more to that museum board story than meets the eye."

"Well, sure there was," Ron said. "You mean you two never heard the rumors?"

Everyone leaned toward Ron. "What rumors?" demanded Olivia. "About Mel and Amelia?"

"No. Mel and Londra."

I had to grab Olivia's arm to keep her from falling out of her chair. "You're kidding. When did those start?"

He waved his hand carelessly. "Oh, awhile back. There was talk of Mel being involved with someone at the museum, and folks spotted him and Londra meeting in out-of-the-way places. No way would Amelia condone something like that, particularly with Londra being in Mazie's pocket. She figured that Mazie could get to Mel through Londra and there would go her advantage, so—she made damn sure Andy McHardy got in."

Gary leaned forward. "Do we know why she was so anxious to get McHardy in?"

Ron stretched his long legs out underneath the bar. "Well, Andy's father had a gardening business and he was pretty sweet on Amelia. I think he even dated her for a while after his wife passed. I guess Amelia always considered Andy family, and I imagine he felt the same way."

"Ah, so loyalty was behind it." Gary shook his head. "I think that might eliminate him, then, although one never knows for sure."

"Oh, I doubt Andy did it," agreed Olivia. "He got disgusted with her high-handed manner, but deep down he actually cared about her. And Simone didn't give her much thought one way or the other."

"We still need more clarification from Garrett, and we need to find out what she had on Larry," I said.

"Larry's another odd one to figure out," Ron said. "As far as I know, he never had any dealings with Amelia save for after he got on the board. Why he always votes for her is a real mystery."

"Which we should solve, if we expect to find out who did kill Amelia," I said. I glanced at Ron. "How did you make out with the mayor?"

He chuckled. "I managed to engage one of the admins in a brief conversation when I dropped off the arrangement. She said that Selena's a handful, but basically a good kid. Now Kyle is another story. Supposedly his mom pulled him out of that fancy school because he has a learning disability. She felt he'd be better off with tutors."

I wrinkled my nose. "Supposedly? The admin thought there might be another reason?"

"She wasn't sure, and she didn't want to talk out of turn. She did say Kyle got in with a rather fast crowd when he first went to the school, though."

"Hm." I pondered this. "Fast teen crowds sometimes mean drugs. If that were the reason, and the mayor was trying to keep it quiet and Amelia found out, she might have been using that as a bargaining chip."

Gary nodded. "Mother cubs kill to protect their young, and if Amelia threatened young Kyle . . ."

Michelle reappeared, cutting off the rest of Gary's thoughts. "Mollie said your table will be ready in a minute, so I'll have your drinks sent over there. I hope that's all right."

"That's fine," Gary said with a smile. "Thanks." To me he muttered, "I sure could use a drink, how about you?"

"I could use a whole truckful."

Ron put his order in for a Michelob just as Mollie swung by to tell us our table was ready. As I slid off my stool, the front door opened and Josh walked in, super yummy in a dark blue blazer, dress shirt, and blue and gray striped tie. Our eyes met, and he inclined his head perceptibly. I nodded and, as the others moved into the dining area, I hung back. Josh walked over to the end of the bar where I stood and ruffled his hair with one hand.

"You wanted to talk to me?"

"Yes, but how did you—" I stopped speaking and turned my head toward the bar. Michelle grinned, reached into her pocket and held up her iPhone. "Your sister texted you."

"Yep. So?" He leaned against the edge of the bar and crossed his arms over his broad chest. "What's up?"

I hesitated, then decided to plunge right in. "You haven't uncovered the murder weapon yet, right?"

He nodded, his eyes never leaving my face. "Right."

"But you've made a determination on what type of knife was used, right?"

Josh's brows drew together and he pursed his lips. His whole demeanor was wary, as if he were trying to decide how much or how little information to impart. Finally, he said, "That Tuareg knife blade most closely resembles the marks found on Amelia's neck. We're trying to track down who might have gotten their hands on one, so we've been canvassing dealers and specialty shops. Why did you ask? Have you heard something?"

I quickly filled him in about Quentin Watson, Mel Feller, and the knives, and pulled out my iPhone to call up the image of the Tuareg knife. He listened impassively, and when I finished cleared his throat.

"It doesn't surprise me that Quentin found out. That guy is relentless when he's after a story." He hesitated, then added, "A Tuareg knife was supposed to be included in a shipment of rare knives the museum received a few weeks ago. I stopped by the museum late yesterday afternoon and asked Mazie Madison about it. She said that when she examined the shipment, there were three knives missing. She advised the store but hasn't heard back yet." He paused. "Mazie's door was open, and there were people in the outer office. Anyone might have heard and tipped off Quentin. As for Melvin, well . . . Londra was sitting at her desk, and I know for a fact her hearing is exceptional. She probably told him. They're rumored to be rather close."

His hand shot out suddenly, and his long fingers wrapped around mine. "You and your friends shouldn't be getting so involved in all this. You're not trained investigators."

I liked the feel of his fingers wrapped around mine, so for a minute I couldn't think of a thing to say. Then I blurted out, "Some people, though, think I did it. How else am I going to clear my name and reopen Urban Tails unless I investigate?"

His gaze softened a bit as it swept over me. "Not all people think that," he said quietly. "Believe me when I say I want this solved just as much as, if not more than, you do."

It was on the tip of my tongue to ask just why he wanted the case solved, but before I could utter a word he added, "I've told you before, I'd hate to see anything happen to you." Abruptly he pulled his gaze from me to study the toe of his shoe. "Rocco's quite fond of you. That dog needs all the friends he can get."

"Just Rocco, huh?" I blurted it out before I realized I'd spoken my thoughts out loud. I clapped a hand across my mouth. Josh's lips twitched and he started to say something.

Just exactly what, I was destined never to know, because Gary chose that moment to yell over from the dining area.

"Shell? Are you coming or what?"

Josh patted my arm. "Thanks for the information. You go on with your friends, now, and remember my advice."

"Oh, I'll remember it," I said. Josh gave me a tight smile and then went over and sat at the far end of the bar. I watched him ease his lanky frame onto a stool. After a few moments, Michelle walked over to him. She leaned forward and whispered something to him. He threw back his head and laughed.

Well, at least someone could make him smile. Until this cloud was lifted from over my head, it was a sure bet he'd never laugh like that at anything I said.

If I ever wanted to get anywhere with Josh Bloodgood—and, I admitted to myself, I did—I had to get rid of the "person of interest" label damn fast.

"Oh, I'll remember your advice, all right," I muttered as I headed for the table where the others sat. "But that doesn't mean I have to follow it."

Eighteen

Purrday woke me before my alarm went off the next morning. I opened my eyes to find his flat white face next to mine as he gently swatted at an errant curl with one paw.

I let out a gigantic yawn. Not to be outdone, Purrday opened his mouth in one as well. I got a whiff of cat breath and it made me sit up straight in the bed. Purrday rolled off my chest and lay on his side on the comforter, looking as annoyed as a cat can look.

"Yowzah," I said to him. "We've got to get you some breath mints, or else cut back on the tuna."

"Ye-*owl*!" The elegant white plume flicked back and forth, double time. His majesty was *not* pleased with that remark.

I chuckled, stretched, and leaned back against the pillows. My thoughts wandered back to last night. We'd certainly learned a lot, but there were still a ton of unanswered questions. Thinking of unanswered questions made me think of Josh, and his parting warning. Beside me on the bed, Purrday made a sound in the back of his throat that sounded a bit like a disgruntled *humpf*.

"Yes, it certainly was nice of Josh to be concerned about my safety," I told the cat as I absently scratched him behind one ear. "But if he thinks a little danger is going to stop me, well, he doesn't know me. After all, on *Spy Anyone* I took down international bad guys every week. One knife-wielding murderer isn't going to discourage me from finding out the truth of who killed Amelia."

I paused in my scratching ablutions as Kahlua hopped up on the bed. She gave Purrday a wary look but didn't raise her paw. Purrday, for his part, apparently knew who the boss was. He shot me a sidelong glance and then hopped off the bed, allowing Kahlua to take his place. I scratched the Siamese under her chin and received a contented rumble in return. Purrday, resigned to not getting any more scratching for a while, lofted up onto the highboy and started grooming his tail.

"There's some connection between Mel Feller and Londra Lewis other than knives, but just what that is remains to be seen," I mused. "And just what is their fascination with them, anyway? The mayor's son might be involved with drugs, which would give her a motive. Garrett Knute seems darn suspicious to me too. He never answered me when I asked him about the contents of that envelope he and Amelia argued over."

Kahlua let out a sharp meow. Purrday blinked his good eye.

"So far, I believe I can eliminate Simone Bradbury and Andy McHardy," I went on. "Simone doesn't seem to figure into any of this. She has no motive, and Andy doesn't either, unless you count getting disgusted doing Amelia's bidding." I pushed the heel of my hand through my tousled curls. "Larry, though, is still on my list. He's hiding something, I just know it. Mazie Madison? I'm not certain, but I'd tend to eliminate her. She and Amelia didn't agree on museum business, but there's nothing to indicate she had any sort of reason to want her dead, other than it would be an annoyance out of the way."

Kahlua wriggled free of my grasp, stretched, and settled next to my hip.

I stretched my own arms wide and laced my hands behind my neck. "It was nice of Josh to be concerned," I continued. "There were definite sparks between us that day in the park, but all that dissipated the minute I found that body, and Josh found that note." I let out a long sigh. "There's no concrete evidence to prove I killed her, but there's none to prove I didn't, either. If there's ever to be any hope for me to reopen Aunt Tillie's shop, let alone have a normal relationship with Josh, I've got to clear my name. Right?"

Both cats sat up straight. "Er-owl," they chorused.

"I knew you'd agree." I threw back the covers, swung my feet over the side of the bed, and slid them into my well-worn scuffs. I reached for my robe and motioned to both cats. "Let's get some breakfast, what do you think about that?"

They both took off, a white blur and a coffee-colored one, through the door. I shook my head. Food. It'll do it every time.

• • •

The aroma of fresh coffee assailed my nostrils before I was halfway down the stairs, and it got stronger as I entered the kitchen. Gary stood in front of the stove, cracking eggs into a pan. He looked up, smiled, and motioned toward the old Corningware percolator on the stove.

"Keurigs are great, but nothing beats a fresh-perked pot of java, am I right?"

I stifled a yawn. "You sure are. Aunt Tillie felt the same way about fresh-perked too."

"See, great minds think alike." He waved the spatula in the air. "And it's nice to see you up and about, sleepyhead. If you hadn't rolled out of bed by the time I finished, I was going to bring you breakfast in bed."

I went to the stove, grabbed a mug, and filled it with coffee. I added a little cream and sugar and took a large gulp. "Delicious," I said, sinking onto one of the stools beside the counter. "To what do I owe this special service?"

He grinned. "I was hungry, and it seemed the least I could do." He gestured toward the pan. "Scrambled okay? I used some of that cheddar in the fridge, and diced up a red pepper."

"Ooh, an omelet. I haven't had one of those since I breakfasted in the commissary at the studio." I licked my lips. "Jose's were darn good."

"Yeah? Well, if you liked his, you'll *love* mine!"

While Gary puttered at the stove I got up, pulled a loaf of rye bread out of the breadbox, and put two slices in the toaster. "Did you sleep all right?" I asked.

"Like a rock, when I finally drifted off. My mind was pretty busy, counting suspects," he said and chuckled.

Kahlua was busy gobbling down food. Purrday, however, lay on his side, batting his paw against the edge of the place mat that held his food and water bowls. Gary had pushed the mat a bit farther back so that it was almost flush with the wall, and Purrday didn't seem to like that too much. He dug his claws into the mat's edge and gave a sharp tug. His water bowl jerked, spilling water all over the tiled floor.

"Purrday. Bad cat!" I admonished him.

"Guess he didn't like that I moved his mat," Gary observed. "I just wanted to get it out of the way."

"Purrday does have very definite ideas about things," I admitted, eyeing the cat, who didn't look upset in the least at the mess he'd made. He wedged himself in between the mat and the wall and lay down, then stretched his paws out to the wall and started digging his claws into its base. "Goodness, Purrday, what on earth are you doing! You are a bad cat this morning."

Gary leaned over and squinted. "Say, it looks like a portion of the wall is raised there."

I frowned. "Where?"

Gary pointed. "See that little separation? It almost looks as if there's a cavity behind it." Gary knelt and gently gave Purrday a little shove. The cat's head jerked back and he opened his mouth and bared his fangs, emitting a loud hiss.

"Purrday!" I cried. "Don't be rude to our guest, even if it is Gary."

Gary shot me a look over his shoulder. "Thanks a lot." He squinted again at the wall over Purrday's head. "There is a separation there," he said and chuckled. "Well, well. No wonder the little fellow got upset. I bet we've found his stash."

"His stash?" I couldn't help it, I giggled. "What, you think Purrday made off with Aunt Tillie's jewels?"

"I don't know. Is any of her jewelry missing?"

"Aunt Tillie never wore jewelry," I shot back, rolling my eyes. "And the little she owned is all costume. His stash, as you put it, is probably more buttons."

Purrday had apparently tired of us making disparaging remarks about his hiding place. He rose and with a brisk shake of his plume-like tail, strode to the opposite end of the kitchen and sat, tail wrapped around his forepaws. He blinked his good eye twice, almost as if daring us to take further action. Purrday's movement, however, was all the consent Gary needed. He stretched out full length on the floor and started to pry at the opening with his nails.

"Man, this is wedged in tight," he grumbled. He glanced at Purrday over his shoulder. "That cat must be supercat to even move this thing."

I gave him a little push. "Let me try."

I knelt beside Gary but it was soon evident the opening wasn't getting any wider.

Gary got up and walked over to Purrday and looked down at him, his hands on his hips. "His paws are pretty big," he said. "I can't see how he ever got 'em in that tiny opening to hide anything."

"Well, then, maybe it's not his hiding place after all. Maybe the wall just has a crack."

"Aw-arr," cried Purrday. He got up, crossed over to the wall, raised his paw, and it landed—*thunk!*—square in the middle. With that, the section of wall gave a loud creak and groaned inward, revealing a dark cavity.

Gary and I both stared, our jaws open. "Well, I'll be," I muttered finally. "It is a hiding place, but it's got to be manmade. He just happened to find it. I'll bet it was Aunt Matilda's. She always used to talk about hidey-holes."

"Great." Gary gestured toward the stove. "The omelet's getting cold. Want to eat first?"

I made a face at him. "Are you kidding?"

He laughed. "Me neither. I can whip up another one later." He knelt on the floor and peered into the hole. "Jeepers, it's dark in there." He stuck his hand tentatively inside, kept going until half his arm was swallowed up in the wall. "This runs pretty deep. Got a flashlight?"

I found one in the drawer and handed it to him. He flicked it on, shone it inside. "I see a few buttons—a little ball—oh, and a catnip mouse. Maybe this is Purrday's hiding place after all."

Maybe, but I didn't think so. "Keep looking," I encouraged him. "You said it ran deep."

He shot me a dirty look and then thrust his arm inside all the way up to his elbow. "Noth—Wait! There is something all the way in the back." He wiggled the light around. "Looks like a box."

"A box!" I leaned forward excitedly and tried to peer over his shoulder. "Can you grab it?"

"I think I can get both hands in there if you hold the flashlight."

He passed it to me. It took a few minutes, because I kept jiggling the light around and he had to stop every few seconds to chastise me, but eventually Gary pulled out a long, rusty metal box. He also pulled out Purrday's toys. Purrday walked over, picked the catnip mouse up between his teeth, and went over to lay in front of the refrigerator, happily chewing away on his toy. Gary set the box on the counter and we examined it. It wasn't very deep, but it was long. Actually, it looked like the type of container you find inside bank safe-deposit boxes. There was no lock on the box, just a little lever that you flipped up. Gary looked at me questioningly.

"Want me to end the suspense?" he asked.

I hesitated, then shook my head. "I'll do it." I held my breath, then flipped the lid back.

Inside lay two books. The top one was leather-covered, with faded gold embossing on the cover. I picked it up and turned it over in my hand. The embossing was faded, but I could still make out the title: *My Diary*.

"Oh, goodness." Suddenly I felt guilty, as if I'd invaded my aunt's privacy. "This—this has got to be Aunt Matilda's diary."

Gary let out a low whistle. "The old girl kept a diary? Wow."

He reached for it, but I held it back. "I'm not sure we should look at it."

He stared at me. "You're kidding, right? There might be something important in there."

I raised one eyebrow. "Like what? A combination to a secret vault loaded with diamonds?"

"Hey, you never know. It was important enough for her to hide it in a place no one would have ever found, if it hadn't been for Purrday, here." Gary gestured with his jaw toward the cat, who was now lying on his back, his hind legs in the air, his forepaws wrapped firmly around the catnip mouse. His tongue lolled out of one side of his mouth, and I swear I saw a bit of drool spill out onto the tiled floor.

"Yes, Purrday, you were very helpful," I said dryly. "Thank goodness you led us to the secret panel *before* you got high on catnip." I tapped my forefinger against the gold embossing. *Should I or shouldn't I?*

"Did you ever think that maybe you were meant to find that?" Gary said suddenly. "That Purrday was sent by your aunt to lead you to it?"

I stared at him, open-mouthed. "That's a line from our next-to-last show," I said, pointing an accusing finger at him. "When I found the sacred medallion among Captain Ruddy's things. That's what you said to Destiny, only you substituted Purrday for Lola and my aunt for Ruddy."

He shot me a sheepish grin. "Yeah, okay. But you have to admit, it's sort of the same situation."

Abruptly I thrust the book into his hands. "Okay, then. You look at it. It won't seem as much of an invasion of her privacy if you read it."

"Okay, fine."

Gary pulled out a chair and settled himself at the table. I busied myself at the sink, throwing the congealed and cold eggs out and washing out the bowls, because it was a sure bet Gary wasn't going to continue with his chef duties anytime soon.

After a few minutes he said, "This goes back years. Your aunt made her first entry when she was seventeen."

I chuckled. "Aunt Matilda always did come late to the party. Most girls start diaries when they're in fourth grade."

He cast me a quick glance over his shoulder. "Is that when you started yours?"

"No, fifth—" I stopped, realizing how easily I'd stepped into that trap and stuck my tongue out at him.

He continued flipping pages. "Not a lot of excitement in your aunt's life. It's mostly church stuff, and socials, and, oh, wow! She planned a church event when she was twenty-one. Guess event planning runs in your family's bloodline, Shell." He flipped a few more pages, and then let out a whistle. "Here's an interesting entry." He glanced up to meet my gaze. "Her first mention of a man."

Curious, I moved closer. "Who?"

"Doesn't say, just gives an initial. 'Today *R* and I went to the movies. He wanted to see an action picture but finally agreed to the romantic comedy I suggested. Later on, we went for a soda at Parker's.'" He flipped a few more pages and read a few more passages out loud, all of which hinted at a burgeoning romance between my aunt and this mysterious *R*. Gary let out a cry: "Here's something interesting. Come look at this."

I didn't need any further urging. I went and peered over his shoulder and read:

> Today I thought *R* might ask me to marry him. Instead I find out he's been two-timing me with Amelia. That witch pretended to be my friend, and all the while had her sights set on my boyfriend. I don't see how I can ever forgive either of them.

"Oh my God," I cried. "This must be the reason for the feud! Mother said it was over a man. Amelia stole Aunt Matilda's boyfriend away from her." Suddenly I started to laugh.

Gary looked at me. "What's so funny?"

"Sorry. I was just thinking about the last time I saw Amelia. She certainly didn't appear to be the man-stealing type."

"Maybe she just didn't age well," said Gary. He flipped another page and a faded photograph slid out and onto the floor. He snatched it up quickly and we looked at it. From the style of dress, I figured it must have been taken in the early fifties. My aunt would have been in her twenties then. The photo depicted two women, dressed stylishly, their hair worn in long bobs. Standing between them was a tall man with a high forehead, wide eyes, and a killer smile. I frowned as I looked at the photo. Something about the man struck me as familiar, but I couldn't think why.

Gary flipped the photo over. "*Me, Amelia, and R before the church social, September 9, 1951,*" he read. "Which one's your aunt, I wonder?"

"I think the one on the left. She looks like other photos I've seen of Aunt Tillie when she was young." I stared at the other woman. "Amelia wasn't half bad herself." I tapped at the photo. "Wish I knew more about this *R* guy, though."

"Well, let's see what this other book has to offer."

Gary set the diary aside and pulled the other volume from the box. He looked at the cover. "*Fox Hollow High, Class of 1947.* This must be your aunt's high school yearbook. Man, she kept it all these years?" He shook his head. "I couldn't even tell you where my high school diploma is."

I gave him an impish grin. "Are you sure you've got one?" As he sputtered, I reached for the book. "It does seem odd, though, that she'd lock her diary and this book away in such a—a unique hiding place."

"She obviously didn't want to part with it, but the memories it brought up were too painful."

I nodded. "Maybe." I set the book down on the table and started thumbing through the pages. It was typical high school stuff. Lots of candid photos, sports, different clubs. I looked carefully through the various photos but didn't see any of those three in any of them.

Gary noticed my disappointed look and patted my shoulder. "Maybe they weren't very active in clubs," he said. "But for sure you'll find them in the class photos; unless, of course, they were absent the day they were taken."

"Thanks for the encouragement." I found the section on class photos and went immediately to the Ws. Matilda Washburn's and Amelia Witherspoon's photographs weren't far apart from each other and I had to admit, they were both very pretty. Gary was right—Amelia hadn't aged well. No doubt her disposition could account for some of that.

"Since we only know the boy's first initial, *R*, we'll have to look through these photos," I said and sighed. "And there were almost a thousand kids in this class."

Gary flipped a few pages. "Say, maybe not. Look at this photo. He looks like the guy."

I looked, and indeed the figure Gary pointed to was the same man in the photograph with my aunt and Amelia. I sucked in a breath. The man's most prominent feature wasn't discernible in the faded photograph, but there was no missing it in the formal portrait.

Big bug eyes. Like a frog's.

I looked at the name below the photo.

Robert Lawrence Peabody.

Well! That explained a lot!

Nineteen

I made a few quick calls and learned that Lawrence Peabody, aka *Robert Lawrence Peabody*, breakfasted this time nearly every day at Minnie's House of Pancakes, out on Route 81. Gary needed no further urging, since our breakfast plans had long since been abandoned. After we both showered and changed, we set out in Gary's convertible to not only get breakfast but hopefully some answers as well.

We had no trouble finding Minnie's. The building was made of gray stone with a huge stack of pancakes perched on the roof right next to an enormous sign. The parking lot was jammed with cars, and we had to drive around for about fifteen minutes before Gary spied an SUV pulling out of a space at the farthest end of the lot. The entrance was obscured by a sea of people; I finally asked a tall man wearing Bermuda shorts holding a small baby in his arms, and he told us that we had to give our names at the register inside, which meant that we had to push through a veritable wall of people.

"This place either serves food on a par with Wolfgang Puck or no one wants to cook their own breakfast anymore," grumbled Gary. "And this is a weekday."

"It's what the natives would call a tourist hotspot."

Gary cut me an eye roll and then sighed as he looked at the sea of people clustered around the building's railing. "You might as well wait here. No sense both of us getting crushed."

"Okay," I said. "While you're at it, see if you can spot our guy anywhere. Maybe he's at the counter?"

Gary's eyes narrowed. "Even if he's not there, we're having breakfast," he growled, and then turned on his heel and started to elbow his way into the restaurant.

I walked over to the edge of the railing surrounding the building and leaned against it, letting my gaze rove over the crowd. After a few minutes, I saw the front door open and a group of people exit—a young couple with a toddler, an elderly man and woman holding hands, a group of chattering girls who looked to be not more than seventeen, and at the very end of the conga line, Larry Peabody himself.

"Mr. Peabody," I cried out. He paused and looked around, apparently trying to figure out who'd called his name. "Mr. Peabody," I called again and this time I waved.

Larry's head swiveled in my direction and his gaze locked with mine. His lips twisted into a sneer, and then he deliberately turned on his heel and pushed past a young couple to walk briskly down the steps and into the parking lot. I glanced toward the doorway. Through the plate glass I could see there was a line at the register, and Gary was nowhere in sight. After only a moment's hesitation, I hurried down the steps too. I paused for a moment to get my bearings and looked around. I saw Larry heading toward the far end of the lot, not far from where Gary had parked. I quickened my stride, but the old guy walked darn fast. I was halfway across the lot when I saw him get into a dark maroon sedan about three spaces away from Gary's convertible. Geez, did everyone in this town own dark maroon sedans? I broke into a run and reached him just as he backed out of the space.

"Mr. Peabody," I yelled. "Please wait. I need to speak to you."

He lowered his window and leaned out, his face as dark as a thundercloud. "I don't believe we have anything to say to each other, Ms. McMillan."

I positioned myself directly in front of his car. "Oh, I think we do."

"Get away," he growled. "I've no qualms about running you over."

"I wish you wouldn't do that, before I have a chance to ask you about your relationship with my aunt, and Amelia."

His frown deepened. "Relationship? What relationship?"

I glanced around the parking lot. "I'd prefer to have this conversation in private."

"Really?" He sneered. "I'd prefer not to have it at all. Now, *move!*"

"You led my aunt to believe you wanted to marry her, but you were dating Amelia," I burst out. "Just how serious was that relationship, Mr. Peabody? And how long did it go on? Until Amelia's death?"

His eyes narrowed, but his face paled a bit. He waved one hand in an imperious manner. "What sort of nonsense are you babbling?" he said, but his tone lacked conviction.

I moved from the front of the car over to the driver's window and leaned inside. "I found my aunt's diary," I said. "I think it's time you and I had a little talk."

For a few moments Larry didn't say one word, he just sat staring straight ahead through the windshield. The knuckles of his hands were white from gripping the steering wheel, and I could see a muscle working in his jaw. "Diary, huh?" he said at last. He turned his head slightly and glared at me. "My house, two p.m. Be on time." Then he shifted the car into gear and took off, tires squealing.

I stood for a moment, watching the sedan as it sped out of the parking lot and took the corner sharply, then I started back to the restaurant. Gary was leaning against the railing, twirling a small plastic box in his hands. He cut me an anxious look as I approached. "Let me guess," he said. He motioned with his chin toward the exit. "That was Peabody."

"Yep. He was all set to ignore me until I mentioned my aunt's diary. He told me to be at his house at two o'clock."

One of Gary's eyebrows winged skyward. "And that's a good thing, right?"

I set my jaw. "One way or another, yes."

"Good." He jumped as the pager lit up in his hand, and then eyed me. "We're still having breakfast, right?"

My own stomach growled. "Sure, we might as well."

"Good. I hate interviewing suspects on an empty stomach."

• • •

Robert Lawrence Peabody's house was located on a side street near the edge of town, a narrow two-story structure. Gary parked his convertible in front and we walked up the short walkway onto the latticed porch and rang the bell. It echoed eerily through the house. We waited a few minutes and Gary was just about to ring again when the door jerked open and Larry stood there.

"Right on time, I see," he said. He moved aside to let us enter. "Come in."

We stepped inside the dimly lighted foyer and Larry ushered us into a large sitting room that had a long sofa, a love seat, and a La-Z-Boy recliner grouped around a low-slung coffee table. A massive flat-screen TV took up almost one entire wall, and the other had what appeared to be a working fireplace. The older man settled himself into the recliner and motioned us to take seats. We settled onto the love seat, and then I reached into my tote bag, withdrew my aunt's diary, and laid it on the coffee table.

Larry stared at it for a few minutes without saying anything. Then he said, very softly, "That was your aunt's?"

I nodded. "Yes."

"You found it in her house?"

"Not exactly." Gary stretched his long legs out underneath the coffee table. "Purrday found it."

"Huh?" Larry looked puzzled. "Percy, you said?"

"*Purrday*," I corrected. "My aunt's cat."

"Oh?" The angry expression melted away, and he barked out a short laugh. "That figures, that Tillie would have a cat as smart as she was." He leaned back and steepled his fingers underneath his chin. "What do you want to know?"

I scooted to the edge of the love seat. "You were the reason for the feud between Amelia and my aunt," I said.

He considered this a moment. "I guess I was." He blew out a long breath. "I never meant for any of that to happen."

"Why don't you tell me just what did happen? From reading some of my aunt's entries, it appears she was madly in love with you—she expected you to ask her to marry you."

"Did she? Sometimes I wish I had." He stared off into space for several minutes before he spoke again. "Your aunt was a real beauty back in the day. You look quite a bit like her, Ms. McMillan. Anyway, we dated all through junior and senior year in high school. We were quite the item."

"I gathered. How did Amelia figure into this?"

"Matilda and Amelia became friends in high school; they belonged to the Business Club, and they had a lot of the same interests." He pulled at the lobe of one ear. "Amelia wasn't too good at making friends, so she spent a lot of time with Tillie. Once we started dating, Tillie didn't have as much time for Amelia. I knew it irked her, but—" He spread his hands. "What could I do?"

"The notation in my aunt's diary said that she thought you were going to ask her to marry you. It was dated a few years after your high school graduation."

"Tillie and Amelia both went to business school, and I went on to college," Larry said. "NYU is only an hour away by train, and the business school they went to was located two towns over, so we still kept on seeing each other. During my senior year at college I was planning to ask Tillie to marry me—I even went to look at diamonds one weekend. While I was shopping around, I ran into Amelia."

My eyebrows rose and I gave Gary a sidelong look. He looked surprised as well.

"You just ran into her?" I asked. "That seems sort of odd."

"Looking back on all that now, I can see that it was, but then, when I was twenty-one and foolish . . . Anyway, I spent the day with Amelia. When she wanted to be, she could be damn charming. I found I enjoyed her company, so much so that I asked her out."

"I assume you abandoned your plans for an engagement ring for my aunt?"

"I put it on hold," he confessed. "Anyway, Tillie was busy with her new job—she worked a lot of weekends. So when I was home and she was busy, I-I started seeing Amelia. Before I knew it, I was head over heels for her. She kept pressing me to let Tillie down gently, and to announce *our* engagement, but I guess deep down there was a part of me that still wasn't quite sure what I wanted. I kept putting it off, and she kept getting annoyed with me."

"I see," I said tightly. "How did my aunt find out you were dating Amelia? From the notation, it didn't seem as if you told her."

"I didn't. Amelia invited me to her house one evening, and one thing led to another. We ended up, oh, heck, I'm sure I don't have to draw you a picture," he said roughly, pulling his hand through his hair. "What I didn't know was that Amelia had invited Tillie over for a sleepover when Tillie got off work. She phoned her late that afternoon and said she had an errand to run for her mother, but she'd leave the back door open and Tillie should just come on up to the bedroom and make herself at home."

"Oh my God." I put my hand to my mouth as I realized just what Amelia had done. "She caught the two of you in a compromising position."

"To say the least. She told me she wanted nothing more to do with me, and then she blasted Amelia and told her that she was no friend of hers. Amelia tried to tell her that it wasn't anyone's fault, things just worked out that way, but . . . Tillie wasn't having any of it. She never spoke to either of us again, not unless she had to."

I shot the man a disgusted look. "I can't say I blame her," I said.

"Of course, later I realized Amelia had set the whole thing up, and I dumped her," he went on. "I finished college and moved away, out to Arizona, where I met my wife. Ona is a wonderful woman. She changed my life in every way." He gestured toward some framed photographs on the fireplace mantel. "We have two wonderful children, and three grandchildren. We're happy. There's no way I could ever endanger that."

"Endanger that?" Gary frowned. "What do you mean?"

Larry looked at both of us. "What do I mean? I mean blackmail. Pure and simple."

I gasped. "Amelia blackmailed you? Over what? Surely not what happened with my aunt?"

He shook his head. "No, not that. That was old news, over a long time ago. When my father took ill, I had to come back East to take over the family business. In the beginning, I would just fly in for the weekends. The kids were still living at home, and there was a lot to be done, packing up our house in Tempe to move back here. Ona was great. She took care of all those details so I could concentrate on what needed to be done here. Well, one weekend, who should come knocking at my door but Amelia. She'd heard I was in town and wanted to offer her sympathies about my father. I figured she was sincere, so I accepted her apologies and her offer to help." He let out a long breath. "You have to remember, I was under a lot of stress and wasn't thinking clearly. One thing led to another and before I knew it . . ."

"Oh God," I burst out. "You didn't! You slept with Amelia *again*!"

He had the grace to flush. "I'm not proud of what I did, and Amelia swore no one would ever know the truth." He rubbed at his chin. "Fast-forward to a few years ago, when my wife underwent a brief illness. It was around the same time I got on the museum board. Mazie had been appointed director, and Amelia was fit to be tied because it had been done in her absence. Anyway, a post opened and Mazie nominated Melvin Feller. Amelia came to me and asked me to side with her voting against him. She said that he wasn't the type of person she wanted on the board." Larry shook his head. "She always talked about that board like it was her personal property. Anyway, I told her that I didn't see anything wrong with him and I'd vote the way I damn well wanted to. That's when she showed me the photos, and the video that she'd taken when we were making love."

Gary and I both let out a gasp. "She filmed it?" Gary cried.

Larry nodded. "Oh, Amelia was a clever one. She had a camera set up in her bedroom, can you believe that? I didn't even know you could *buy* a home video recorder back then. She told me that unless I voted with her, and continued to give her my support, she'd tell my wife about our brief liaison." His gaze met mine, and I'd never seen a man look so miserable. "I couldn't let that happen," he whispered. "Ona's heart is weak. Something like that, well, it could kill her." He curled his fingers into a fist and banged it against the side of the recliner. "Don't you see! I had no choice! I *had* to go along with whatever she wanted, damn her."

I bit down hard on my lower lip. While I simply couldn't condone this man's behavior, I could see how tortured he was, and how much he did love his wife.

I also saw that Amelia's blackmail gave him a perfect motive for murder.

Gary leaned forward and said, "I'm sorry, sir, I realize how upsetting all this is, and how much courage it took for you to tell us the entire story, but I have to ask: where were you between eleven fifteen and eleven forty-five last Sunday morning?"

Larry stared at us, and then broke into a laugh. "Of course, you have to ask. I've got the perfect motive for murder, right? Well, Josh Bloodgood already asked me, and I'll tell you just what I told him.

"Between eleven fifteen and eleven forty-five every Sunday I am at church with my wife, our daughter, her husband, and her two children. We go to the eleven o'clock service every Sunday and it doesn't get out until five minutes to twelve—even later if Father Randall gets wordy. Last Sunday I was there until five minutes past twelve. My wife wanted to talk to Father Randall about his sermon. I've plenty of witnesses who will swear I was in plain sight at that time. I couldn't have killed Amelia, although don't get me wrong. I wanted to kill her, many times. She always said that if anything ever happened to her, those photos would be made public. I must tell you, when I heard she was dead I was on pins and needles but, apparently, her threat was an empty one. Had I known that sooner, things might have gone a lot differently for a lot of people." He pointed his finger at me. "I'd have voted to display your aunt's posters. I know how proud she was of that collection, and it's one of the more extensive ones around." He spread his hands. "Things just didn't work out that way."

"What about Andy or Ginnifer?"

He passed a hand across his eyes. "Hard to tell with those two. Amelia had something on them, too. I couldn't tell you what, just like I couldn't tell you if their voting against you was their own opinion or Amelia's. But it doesn't matter. Neither of them could have killed her."

"Why do you say that?"

"Because," he chuckled, "we all go to the same church, and they happened to be at the eleven o'clock service that day as well. I saw them when they arrived around a quarter to eleven, and they were sitting together two aisles in front of my family. Neither of them moved a muscle."

I sighed. Just like that, three of my suspects were eliminated. I wasn't sure whether that made me happy or sad, or just plain determined to ferret out the real killer from the ones who remained.

Twenty

"Okay, three down. How many more to go?"

Gary took his eyes off the road and his hand off the wheel long enough to give me a wink and my arm a quick squeeze. For my part, I'd been relatively silent ever since we'd left Larry's house. Now I shifted slightly in my seat to look at him.

"You know, I was kind of hoping it was him," I said. "There's just something about that man that irritates me."

"No doubt you sense he's a kindred spirit to Patrick," Gary said.

"If you mean they both suffer from overactive libido, then absolutely."

Gary chuckled. "Pat never was very good at resisting temptation, and Peabody seems cut from the same cloth. Your aunt was probably all the better off for not marrying him. He obviously didn't love her."

"True," I agreed. "She and Uncle Bertrand were much better suited to each other. Now there was a real love story. Uncle Bertrand was her boss for years, did you know that? They ran the gamut from boss to subordinate to friends to lovers. They had one of the best marriages I've ever seen, unlike my own parents'."

"But they're happy now, right?"

"I suppose so." I drooped forward, chin in hand. "Dad and Darlene certainly seem to be happy, anyway. Mother is, well, Mother. I doubt she'll ever change."

"People rarely do," Gary remarked. "Now, getting back to our original subject. Who's left in our suspect pool?"

"Not enough," I said grimly. "I would really like to have another chat with Garrett Knute. He never answered me on the contents of that mysterious envelope."

"He might feel it's none of your business."

"To quote Inspector Godfrey from our show: 'Murder makes everything my business.' Particularly when I'm still in that suspect pool."

"I'd still like to know how your friend Quentin Watson found out about the murder weapon."

"Probable murder weapon," I amended. "They haven't found it yet."

"Hm. That could mean the murderer took it with him or her. Indicating to me this was definitely something premeditated and not a crime of passion."

"Yeah." I slumped down farther in my seat. "Premeditated with me as the intended scapegoat. You know, it really galls me that someone would go to such lengths to frame someone they hardly know."

"They probably thought it would be easier than framing someone they did know," Gary said and laughed. "Ships that pass in the night and all that."

"I suppose I have no one to blame but myself," I said. "Arguing with her on the sidewalk in the middle of town was a poor decision. But Quentin Watson didn't help things with his little article about me in the paper."

"It's more likely whoever murdered Amelia witnessed your tiffs with her and with Peabody and McHardy, instead of learning about it in the next day's paper," said Gary.

"The way gossip flies around this town, that could be anyone."

He clucked his tongue. "You should have stayed in LA, Shell. At least there the gossip's out front, not behind your back."

"Yeah, usually on the front page of some supermarket rag." I slumped back against the leather headrest. "You know, I was really looking forward to leading a quieter life, and then this had to happen."

He reached across again and lightly brushed my fingers with his. "If that's what you really want, Shell, then you shall have it. We'll get your name cleared and find the murderer, or my name isn't Gary Presser."

"It's not." I slid him a glance. "Correct me if I'm wrong, but per your official studio biography, you changed it from Philip Tewksbury, didn't you?"

His grin was enigmatic. "A mere technicality."

• • •

I was still full from our hearty breakfast of a double stack of pancakes, sausage, and bacon, but Gary of the bottomless pit stomach wanted a snack, so we pulled up in front of Sweet Perks. Rita's niece was behind the register and she gave us a wave as we walked in. I assumed it was aimed more at Gary than me. I saw Olivia sitting at a table near the window and made a beeline right for her while Gary went to put in our orders: a skim mocha latte for me, God knew what for him.

"Hey, Shell," Olivia said as I approached. She frowned as she studied my face. "You look a bit upset. Anything wrong?"

"Nothing much, except the suspect pool is getting smaller. Soon I may be the only one left in it."

"Uh-oh." Olivia pushed her cup to the side and propped her chin in her hands. "Tell Auntie Olivia all about it."

I recounted the day's adventures, starting with Purrday's find and ending with Larry's alibi for Amelia's time of death. I ended it with, "So now it appears he, Ginnifer, and Andy all have alibis."

"Well, we never really figured on Ginnifer and Andy anyway, right? It's just Larry's alibi that's frosting your cookies." Olivia waved her hand. "That type never murders. If he were the kind to do violence, he would have offed Amelia long ago, photos or no photos."

Gary appeared, balancing a tray on which rested three coffee cups and a plate containing a very appetizing muffin. He set my latte in front of me and passed one across to Olivia. "I'm sure you're ready for a refill." He smiled. "Rita told me what you were drinking."

Olivia took the cup and smiled. "Bless her heart, and yours too."

I sniffed the air and eyed the muffin. "That smells great. What is it?" I asked, reaching for it.

He swatted my hand away. "Oh, no. It's an apple crumb muffin. Go get your own." He picked it up and deliberately took a huge bite. I stuck my tongue out at him.

"Children, children, calm down. So, what's our next step?" Olivia asked. "Who do we investigate now?"

"I would love to know what's in that envelope that Garrett Knute and Amelia had the shouting match over," I said. "But I have no idea how I'm going to get that information. Garrett just ignored me when I asked about it."

"Whdugeweassatsn," Gary mumbled around his mouthful of muffin.

I gave Olivia an eye roll and turned to him. "Chew, swallow, and then repeat that."

He did and then said, "Why don't you ask Watson? He seems to have his finger on the pulse of everything that goes down in this town."

"Haven't you been paying attention? Quentin Watson does not like me. He wouldn't give me the time of day."

"No, Quentin Watson merely got back at you the only way he knew how because you didn't jump to give him an interview. That's happened to you before, Shell."

"That's true," I said slowly. "Remember Emily Burgess from the *LA Examiner*?" I chuckled. "She printed that story about me and Nathan Fillion having a torrid affair, and I'd never even met the guy."

"Exactly. And how did you handle that situation?"

"Well, first Max talked me out of suing them." I laughed. "And then I called her and said that I was sorry, I had a busy schedule, but I'd love to get together with her. And she printed one of the best articles that's ever been written about me." I looked at Gary. "So, what. You think I should wave the white flag at Quentin?"

"Can't hurt. After all, look what happened with Emily." He popped the last of the muffin into his mouth.

"Emily was reasonable, at least. Quentin is a sleaze."

Gary grinned at Olivia. "It's a prerequisite in Hollywood. Every actor refers to every reporter as a sleaze. It's in our contracts." He turned back to me. "Give the guy an interview, get on his good side, and maybe you can catch him off guard and find out where he got his info on the murder weapon."

"It's a nice plan," I admitted. "I can think of one downside to it, though."

"What's that?"

"If he turns out to be Amelia's murderer, I might find out about that murder weapon firsthand."

"I wouldn't want you to have a go at him alone," Gary said.

"What did you have in mind? A double interview? You and me?"

"I was thinking more along the lines of you wearing a wire."

I goggled at him. "A wire? Now who's watching too many detective shows?"

"Hey, it would work. We'll have a code word, and if things start getting too sticky, you say it and I'll get there with the police faster than you can say *Gary Presser's a star*."

I looked at Olivia. She shrugged. I looked back at Gary.

"Say I agree to this cockamamie plan, just where are you going to get a wire?"

He grinned mysteriously. "Leave that detail to me. You just arrange a time and place with the sleaze."

I chewed my lip, thinking, and then whipped out my cell phone. "Why do I think I'm gonna be sorry for this?" I punched in a number, then wiggled my fingers at Gary. "You'd better know what you're doing—hello, Mr. Watson? This is Shell McMillan. Shell Marlowe. If you're still willing, I'd love to give you that interview you wanted."

Twenty-one

I arranged an interview with Quentin Watson at noon the next day at the Captain's Club. True to his word, Thursday morning Gary had a wire all rigged up—inside a Victoria's Secret push-up bra.

"Do I want to even know how you accomplished this?" I asked, staring at the apparatus dubiously.

Gary chuckled. "Probably not."

I held the bra up, turned it over in my hand. "This had better work."

"It's been tested. Trust me," he said with a maddening grin and then took off before I could quiz him any further.

Olivia came by and helped me get ready. I chose a flowing black tunic with a split neckline over a pair of deep coral crop pants. I did full makeup: foundation, blush, eyeliner, shadow, mascara, the works—something I hadn't done since I left Hollywood. Olivia helped me style my hair into a low chignon at the nape of my neck. Gary greeted me with a wolf whistle when I finally walked down the stairs.

"I know, I know." He grinned as I cut him a look. "It would mean so much more if it were another male making eyes at you. Like, say, Detective Bloodgood, perhaps?"

I stuck my tongue out at him and self-consciously patted my bust, where the wire reposed. "You're positive this will work?"

"I'll go into the kitchen, and you and Olivia say something. You can talk about how fabulous I am." He gave us a broad wink and vanished.

I looked at Olivia. "Gary is fabulous," I said. "A fabulous pain in the butt."

Olivia started to giggle. "With an even more fabulous head of hair."

"And a fabulous giant-sized ego."

Gary emerged from the kitchen, a frown on his face. "Enough about my butt and my ego." He smiled, though, when he looked at Olivia. "You, however, can talk about my hair, and anything else you want, anytime."

"Great, you can hear the conversation," I cut in, as the two of them started to make goo-goo eyes at each other. Olivia was more age-appropriate than some of Gary's past girlfriends, but that didn't mean I wanted to watch them flirt.

"Yes, I can not only hear you, I'm taping you." He pressed a button on the tiny device he held, and Olivia's voice came over, clear as crystal: *"With an even more fabulous head of hair."*

"Okay," I said. "So, what's my code word for if I get in trouble, or Quentin decides to pull a knife on me?"

"I doubt he'll be pulling a knife on you in the middle of the day at a public place."

"No, but he can pull one out under the table and tell me to walk outside. Now, what's the code word?"

"Oh, I don't know. It should be something fairly easy to use in a sentence." He tapped his chin with his forefinger. "You seem to like the word *fabulous.*"

"Fine," I grumbled, as I snatched up my light jacket. *"Fabulous* it is. Let's get this party started."

•   •   •

Sure enough, Quentin Watson was waiting at a table near the kitchen door when I arrived. Another girl, a lanky blonde with legs that seemed to go on forever, was the hostess this afternoon, and she showed me to the table with a quizzical look that said more plainly than words, *Why are you wasting your time with him?*

I slid into the seat opposite Quentin and flashed him my megawatt television star smile. "Thank you so much for agreeing to meet with me, Mr. Watson," I cooed. "I just feel as if we got off on the wrong foot."

Quentin studied me, his beady eyes taking in every detail of my outfit, lingering perhaps a moment too long on my more than generous expanded bustline. "Don't mention it, my dear. I am always more than willing to give people a second chance."

I had to bite down hard on my lower lip to stop the nasty retort that wanted oh so badly to come out. I set my purse down and leaned across the table, cupping my chin with one hand, and batted my eyelashes (lengthened within an inch of their life with my Mally mascara) at him. "Where would you like to begin?"

The waitress appeared at that moment. Quentin glanced up at her and then turned to me with a smile. "I think I'll begin with a Manhattan, very dry. Ms. Marlowe?"

Straight Scotch would have been good, but I needed all my wits about me. I gulped and smiled. "White wine spritzer, please."

Quentin tapped at the menu. "We'll need a few minutes before we order," he said. The waitress nodded and withdrew to the bar area. I gave a quick glance over in that direction. There was a girl tending bar, but she had bright red hair. Not Josh's sister. Damn.

Quentin was wearing his customary peacoat. Now he unbuttoned it so that I could see a brown V-necked sweater underneath. He reached inside the pocket of the coat and whipped out a thick notebook and pen. He flipped through the notebook until he found a blank page and then looked expectantly at me, his pen poised.

"So," he said. "What's a nice actress like you doing in a town like Fox Hollow?"

I smiled, letting my fingers toy with the stem of my water glass. "Looking for a fresh start," I said. "It's as simple as that."

He looked up from his scribbling and frowned. "Not that simple, surely. My readers would get bored." He leaned over and said in a stage whisper, "C'mon, throw me a juicy bone. Any truth to the rumor that you moved cross-country to avoid Patrick Hanratty?"

I mentally counted to ten, swallowed, and pasted that plastic smile across my face again. "There's always a grain of truth in rumors," I said sweetly.

"Hm. More than a grain in this one, I think. Didn't you find him in bed with one of the stagehands on the eve of announcing a definite date of marriage?"

I could feel my jaw clenching and unclenching of its own volition. "Yes."

"And you never suspected this guy had a roving eye? There had been rumors of him involved with other women before."

"Yes, but that was before we became a couple." I coughed lightly. "I made the mistake of falling into a very common trap. I assumed that because our love was so strong, he'd be different with me. But people basically don't change."

"That's very true."

I took a deep breath and fixed my best moonstruck gaze on him. "Haven't you found that to be true in your experience? I've heard that you've interviewed half the people in this town at one point or another. I'll bet there's plenty you could say about each one of them."

He set down his pen and looked at me. "I can't deny that. I'm quite tenacious when it comes to digging up facts."

Or making them up, I thought. "Take someone like, oh, I don't know—Garrett Knute, for instance. You've interviewed him, right? He seems like a very private person. How'd you get him to open up to you?"

"Garrett is indeed a private person. I interviewed him once for an article about an exhibit the museum was putting on display."

"Really? I would have thought you'd have interviewed Mazie Madison for something like that."

"Mazie is somewhat of a scatterbrain when it comes to interviews. She manages to conveniently forget details. I personally think she prefers to avoid the spotlight. Fortunately, her admin has no such qualms."

"You mean Londra Lewis?"

"Yes. Londra has no problem speaking her mind on many matters. As a matter of fact, I've quoted her on several occasions—some of which she's not even aware of." He leaned back, a pleased expression on his face.

The waitress returned with our drinks. I took a long sip of my spritzer; Quentin knocked back half his Manhattan and raised his glass to the waitress. "I'll have another," he said. "Make it a bit drier, please." He raised a questioning eyebrow in my direction and I shook my head, pointing to my nearly full glass.

"I'm fine, thanks," I said. The waitress withdrew again and Quentin brandished his pen.

"So, it's my understanding that you plan to pick up the pieces of Urban Tails?"

"Yes. As you probably know, my aunt left her house and her business to me, and I think continuing the business she so lovingly built up is the best way for me to honor her memory. My aunt was a big animal lover, and she was also a very big collector of movie memorabilia. Her poster collection is legendary. She has many signed by famous stars."

Quentin shot me a knowing look and cleared his throat. "Isn't it true Mazie Madison recently told you that the museum will take you up on your offer to display your aunt's Cary Grant posters after all?"

"She did mention something, but I don't believe it's public knowledge yet. I'm assuming your source on that is Ms. Lewis?"

He waggled his finger. "Now, now, Ms. Marlowe, or I guess I should call you Ms. McMillan? A good reporter never reveals his source."

"Of course." I did some more eyelash batting. "And please call me Shell."

"Very well. Shell. How's that murder investigation coming along? Are you still at the top of the suspect list?"

Now I almost did lunge across the table at him. "I'm sorry, where did you hear that? If anything, I'm a person of interest, nothing more."

"Yeah? Well, you did find the body, and you did have a vicious argument with the deceased the day before."

I gave my head a toss. "I'm not the only one who did," I said. "Garrett Knute and Amelia had a pretty big blowup right on this very street the day before her death."

He waved that away. "That's nothing. Knute's always blowing off steam at one person or another. He's harmless."

"You might not say that if you'd witnessed the same argument I did," I declared. "They were arguing pretty vehemently over the contents of an envelope Amelia had in her possession."

Quentin chuckled. "Amelia always did know how to push Knute's buttons," he said.

I cocked a brow at him. "Then you don't think obtaining the contents of that envelope would be a strong motive for murder?"

"Of course, it would depend on what the contents were, but I doubt it was anything to kill over. Knute was one of the few people on that board who spoke his own mind and didn't accede to Amelia's wishes. I can only recall one time he did side with her, and that was when Mazie Madison recommended Melvin Feller for a seat on the board."

Now I was getting somewhere. I leaned forward. "Really? I'd heard that this Feller used to work for Knute. Apparently there was some trouble?"

"Trouble? You might call it that, I guess." Quentin let out a snort. "Feller worked for Knute and Frank Sakowski's accounting firm for a time, and they got more complaints about his work than Carter had liver pills. Sakowski felt sorry for the guy, so they kept him on until one day when Frank and Rita were away and some questionable accounting of Feller's came to light. Knute had no choice but to fire him after that."

"Questionable accounting?"

"I've never been able to get out of Knute exactly who was involved, but it was the proverbial straw that broke the camel's back. Feller never seemed to mind being out of work, though. From what I understand, he was injured in the Screaming Eagles, so he gets a good pension; plus, he apparently does pretty well at the blackjack table." He coughed lightly. "Enough about town gossip. It's you my readers are interested in. Do you intend to stay here permanently, or will you be making your way back to Hollywood the minute you get tapped for another series?"

I waved my hand. "I'm totally committed to making a life and a new career for myself here in Fox Hollow. It seems to be a very well run little town. I imagine the mayor has a lot to do with that?"

"Carolyn's a good mayor, despite what some people think," Quentin said. "I myself give her my full support. She's always been very outspoken on her views about freedom of the press, which makes my job a lot easier."

I leaned forward and said in a confidential tone, "I understand she had some trouble recently with her kids?"

His head jerked up, and for a minute he reminded me of a bloodhound sniffing a scent. "Her kids? Really? I can't think what that might be. Her daughter's doing very well in school. Top of her class." He let out a deep chuckle. "She wants to be a hairdresser, though, and it's a sore point with Carolyn. She was rather hoping to have a lawyer in the family, and Selena's her only hope."

I saw my chance and took it. "Why? Is it because Kyle has a learning disability?"

Was I imagining it, or was that a look of unease on the reporter's face? "Right," he said quickly.

I pounced on his discomfiture like Purrday on his catnip mouse. "Except that's not true, is it? Kyle doesn't have a learning disability. He got involved with drugs, didn't he?"

He hesitated, then threw down his pen and crossed his arms over his chest. "Fine. I'll tell you, but you can never repeat it. If you do, I'll deny it, as will Carolyn. Six months ago, Kyle was caught smoking and attempting to sell marijuana on the grounds of that fancy schmancy school she'd enrolled him in. Long story short, another kid, the son of one of her competitors, framed him."

Wow! "Did Amelia know about this?" I asked.

"Who do you think helped hush it up? Amelia went to Detective Bloodgood and had the kid cleared of all charges."

I stared at him. "She did?"

He nodded. "Amelia and the mayor might not always see eye to eye, but Amelia did like her kids, Kyle especially. He used to run errands for her sometimes. And, of course, Mayor Hart requested my cooperation in keeping this indiscretion quiet, because Kyle was a bit unhinged by the whole episode. She pulled him out of school and got him private tutors, and Amelia helped him get that job at the General Store. He's really come a long way." He eyed me. "I trust you will be discreet with this information? There are whispers, of course, but no concrete evidence."

"Of course," I murmured. Well, there went any chance of Carolyn Hart having a motive for wanting Amelia dead. No wonder she'd sounded so effusive with her praise of the woman at the memorial.

Quentin cast me a shrewd look. "And make sure your friends keep it quiet, too."

I started. "My friends?"

"Yes, that costar of yours, and Olivia Niven, and God knows who else." He inclined his jaw toward my chest. "What's your watchword?"

My hand flew automatically to my breast. "Pardon?"

"Your watchword. Oh, please, Shell, what sort of a newsman do you take me for? We've had extra ears listening ever since we sat down. That's a wire you're wearing, right?"

"I—what—how on earth did you know?"

He grinned, showing off his uneven yellowed teeth. "You don't get to my position without having learned a few tricks. You were so reluctant to give me an interview, and then suddenly you call me up, all smiles, and want to meet. It's only logical that I assume you've got an ulterior motive in mind, and it's not the pleasure of my company." He leaned so far over the table his nose was almost level with mine. "You wanted to pump me for information about some of the people you believe are suspects in Amelia's murder." He leaned back, a self-satisfied smirk on his face. "Did you get everything you needed?"

I slashed my lips into a thin line. "Not quite."

"Then let me help you out." Before I knew what was happening, his hand shot out, dipped down the front of my tunic, and a second later he held the wire aloft. "My, my," he said. "This is a nice one. Expensive too. Wherever did you get it?"

I clutched at the front of my blouse. "Why, of all the nerve . . . how dare you . . . fabulous! Simply fabulous, fabulous!" I burst out.

Quentin looked as if he were having trouble trying to stifle a laugh. "Yeah, yeah. Don't worry, I wasn't trying to cop a free feel. I just don't want any other ears listening in on what I'm about to tell you, because I'll deny it to the hilt. And I guess I'd better hurry up. *Fabulous* was your watchword, right?" He leaned over and said in a stage whisper, "If I were you, I'd check out that Feller-Lewis connection very thoroughly. Not many people know this, but one of Feller's hobbies, in addition to gambling, is his extensive knowledge of antique knives. And he's shared that information on more than one occasion with someone else who also has an interest in antique cutlery."

"Londra Lewis?"

He let out a laugh that sounded more like a cackle. "Oh, come now, Shell. What fun would it be if I did all the work for you? I've given you a nice lead. What you do with it is entirely up to you." He gestured with his hand. "Oh, and you and your friends feel free to have lunch on me. Just tell the waitress to put it on my tab."

"Wait." I grabbed at his arm as he started to push past me. "Do *you* know who killed Amelia?"

His grin was laconic. "If I did, it would be front-page news by now, sweetums. I'm counting on you to get me the scoop on that one. Believe me, it's been tough being the only Sherlock Holmes around this burg. I'm happy to have someone else to share the honors with."

He glanced significantly toward the entrance just as Gary and Olivia burst through the door. He raised two fingers to his forehead in a salute. "And here, if I'm not mistaken, is your cavalry. I'd best leave. We wouldn't want to cause another scene, would we?

"Have a nice day . . . Shell. And don't bother to let me know how you fare questioning Feller." He closed one eye in an exaggerated wink. "As I'm sure you've already guessed, I'll find it out on my own."

Twenty-two

"Quentin Watson sprang for lunch! Will wonders never cease?"

Olivia took a last bite of her hot turkey sandwich and popped a French fry into her mouth. When she and Gary had rushed into the Captain's Club, they immediately made a beeline for Watson's retreating form. I had to jump up and literally pull them back and over to the table, where I quickly explained what had happened. Needless to say, my friends didn't waste any time once they learned a free lunch was in the offing. Gary immediately signaled the waitress and ordered a Michelob and a Reuben, while Olivia and I both opted for the hot turkey sandwich with fries and Cokes. Since all our stomachs started to growl at the same time, we decided to halt further discussion on the case until we had all been well fed.

I polished off the last of my turkey and pushed my plate off to the side. "I know, right. He actually seemed to be a bit human, there, at the end." I picked up my Coke and took a long sip. "I still think he knows a lot more than he lets on, though."

"Oh, absolutely," Gary said, his mouth full of Reuben. He took a quick sip of his beer before he spoke again. "I still can't believe he knew you were wearing a wire!"

"Oh, yeah," I said, my cheeks coloring as I remembered him leaning over and ripping it out of my blouse. "Hence my use of the word *fabulous*." I eyed him. "BTW, you need to work on your power walk. If he had been the murderer, I could have been dead by the time you two got here."

"Hey, we were across the street in the car, and then we had to put quarters in the meter," Gary grumbled. "Anyway, what are you complaining about? It all worked out, didn't it?"

"Maybe." I twirled another fry in the turkey gravy and popped it in my mouth. "That was quite a revelation, about Melvin Feller and his antique knives. I imagine the other person with an interest in antique cutlery would probably be Londra Lewis."

"Makes sense, in light of the rumors about their relationship," Olivia said and nodded. "Do you think he and Londra could have planned it together?"

"If they did, it was probably Londra's idea," I said. "She certainly looked angry enough at Amelia the day I saw them in the park."

"Yeah, I've never heard about Mel being involved in any way with Amelia," Olivia had to agree. "If he had a hand in this, he did it for Londra."

"He did it for luuurve," I said, rolling my eyes and making sloppy kissy sounds. "He's her willing patsy."

"A shame how love makes people do all sorts of foolish things they wouldn't do if their brains were functioning properly," cut in Gary. "Like murder."

Olivia burst out laughing. "Wow, how romantic! Gary, have you ever been seriously involved with anyone?"

He grinned from ear to ear. "Many times. However, not to the extent where I did anything for love, as that Meat Loaf song goes."

I picked up my water glass and looked at him over the rim. "I have two words for you. Andrea Spicer."

He flinched and took the last bite of his Reuben. "Ouch," was all he said.

Olivia looked from me to Gary and back to me again. "Who's Andrea Spicer?"

"No one important," Gary said hastily.

"Oh, I wouldn't say that," I declared. I turned to Olivia with a twinkle in my eye. "She was someone Gary met in one of those online chat rooms."

Olivia flopped back in her chair and stole a glance at Gary. "You went on one of those? For heaven's sake, why?"

"It was a dare," he mumbled.

"Yep, Max dared him at a party and he did. He kept up a correspondence with Andrea for what was it, Gary? Two months, three?"

He took a long swig of beer. "Four."

As both Olivia's brows rose I went on, "Anyway, they got quite friendly, and they made arrangements to meet. Of course, he had to drag me with him, and it's a good thing I went. I don't know what he would have done if I hadn't been there."

"Well, for goodness sakes, what was wrong with her?" Olivia burst out as I stopped speaking. Gary, for his part, looked about ready to slide under the table and never come out.

"Well, for starters, she had trouble dragging around her oxygen tank," I said.

Olivia's jaw dropped. "Oxygen tank?"

"She was a bit older than she'd led me to believe," Gary mumbled.

I laughed. "Yeah, like forty-five years older. Except for the tank, though, Andrea was in pretty good shape for an eighty-year-old."

Olivia clapped a hand across her mouth. "Oh my God."

"In my defense, her profile photo must have been taken when she was around twenty-five," Gary said. "And her emails sounded very young. I still think she had a ghostwriter."

Olivia stared at him and then burst into a fit of the giggles. After a minute, I joined her.

"Fine," Gary said, his brows drawn together like a thundercloud. "Waste time making fun of me."

"We're not," I finally gasped. "But you'd gotten really attached to Andrea, right? So, when you say you've never had a love experience . . ."

"Fine," he snapped, "I stand corrected. You know, if you want to throw around stupid things people in love do, I can think of a few you've done."

That sobered me right up.

"Okay, kids," Olivia cut in. "As fascinating as all this is, we're getting away from the original topic, which is Amelia's murder. What's our next move?"

"I agree it wouldn't hurt to question Mel Feller," I said. "But I still can't shake the feeling that Garrett Knute is involved to some degree. You didn't see his face that day, but I did. He was *really* angry. Despite his assurances to me that there was nothing of interest in that envelope, I can't help but feel otherwise."

"But was it enough to warrant killing Amelia over? That is the question," Gary said.

"Maybe, maybe not. At the very least, I'd like to see if I can get him to tell me why he thinks Mel should be suspect number one—besides the obvious reason, that he fired him for incompetence. I just feel in my gut"—I tapped at my stomach—"that there's more to it."

"Okay, so which one first? Garrett or Melvin," asked Olivia.

Before I could answer, my cell phone vibrated. I fished it out of my pocket and saw the number for Secondhand Sue's on the screen. "Hello, Shell McMillan."

"Hey, Shell, it's Sue Bloodgood. I've run into a bit of a scheduling problem. Would it be all right if I had your Poe bust delivered this afternoon instead of tomorrow?"

"Sure." I glanced at my watch. "What time?"

"Is it okay if they make you their last delivery? Around five thirty?"

"That'll work out good, thanks." I hung up and relayed her message to the others. "That gives us a good four hours."

"We should be able to question both of 'em in that amount of time," Gary said. "Or my name isn't Gary Presser."

I rolled my eyes. "Let's not start *that* again."

• • •

A few minutes later we pulled up in front of Melvin Feller's house, a small bungalow that looked in need of some major upkeep. The yard was scrubby and not well kept, and I wrinkled my nose at the faint smell of dog urine. A large tree stretched out across the weedy lawn and lifted feeble limbs to hover over the house. We walked up the dirty drive and onto the rickety front porch, where a trace of cigarette smoke lingered. I made a face as Gary rang the bell. We stood for a few moments, waiting. When nothing happened, Gary pressed the buzzer again. We could hear the chimes echo eerily through the house.

He glanced at us over his shoulder. "Seems like no one's home."

We turned and started down the steps. Out of the corner of my eye I saw a woman walking toward us across the lawn of the next house. "Say," she shouted. "You looking for Melvin?"

I paused to study the woman. She was heavyset, with brassy blonde hair, squinty little eyes, and a bulbous nose. I put her age at late fifties early sixties, maybe a bit older. She wore a loose-fitting housedress and bright pink flip-flops, displaying unpolished toes. "Yes. He's not home?"

"It's Thursday," she said, and then placed her hands on her ample hips and cocked her head at us as if that explained everything. We all must have looked totally blank, because she shook her head. "Thursday's the day the Boar Lodge has their trip to the Indian Casino. They never get back till late. The last trip, he got back around midnight." She chuckled. "Freddie Manson drives the van, and the return depends on how he's doing at blackjack."

"Oh," I said, trying to conceal my disappointment. "Thanks."

"I'm his neighbor, Mrs. Miller. If you want, I can leave him a note and tell him to call you," she offered.

"That would be great," I said. I opened my tote and fished out a piece of paper and a pen. I scribbled down my number and handed it to the woman. "The top one's my cell, the bottom my home."

Mrs. Miller squinted at the card. "Shell McMillan?" She peered at me over the rim of her glasses. "You look familiar. Have we met before?"

"I don't think so. I only moved here a week ago. My aunt passed away and I plan on taking over her business."

"Your aunt?"

"Matilda Washburn."

Mrs. Miller's eyes lit up. "Oh, yeah, Urban Tails. I love that store. My little Pookie-Poo especially loves the liver treats Tillie used to order special for him. Pookie is my poodle," she added. She squinted her eyes at me again. "You remind me of someone," she said. Her head swiveled and she turned her hawklike gaze on Gary. She pointed a stubby finger at him. "You too. I'm sure I've seen the two of you somewhere before."

Gary shrugged. "Sorry, not me. I only got here from LA a few days ago myself."

"LA, huh?" She scratched at her head. "It'll come to me." She started to shove my slip of paper into the pocket of her jacket, stopped as she pulled out another piece of paper. "Oy, I almost forgot. His friend was here earlier. She musta forgot today's his casino day too."

"His friend?"

"Yeah. Nice lady. Why she hangs around him, I'll never know." Mrs. Miller's tone clearly said what she thought about Mel. "I think she picks his brain, what there is of it, that is, on certain things." She shook her head. "That man's head is full of the most useless facts, unless you want to be a contestant on *Jeopardy!*"

Gary, Olivia and I exchanged a look. "You must mean Londra Lewis," said Olivia.

The woman shrugged. "Dunno her name," she said.

"Short, a bit on the plump side, dark hair and glasses," I offered.

"Hell, no. This one's got light-colored hair, and she's middle-aged, in her fifties, maybe? Always drives up in a maroon car." Mrs. Miller shoved the paper and my card back into her pocket, then paused as the sound of a dog barking reached our ears. "Oops, I gotta go. Pookie wants his lunch."

She shuffled off, and Gary touched my arm. "Feller apparently has a way with the ladies."

Olivia wrinkled her nose. "Yeah, makes you wonder what they see in him."

"Especially that lady," I said. "She just described Mayor Hart down to a T. Classy, light hair, maroon sedan."

"Mayor Hart and Mel?" Olivia's laugh tittered out. "It *must* be some other woman. What would she want with him?"

"I have no idea, but I wouldn't be surprised, seeing some of the turns this mystery has taken." I made a checkmark in the air. "One more thing to quiz him about."

"At this rate, we're going to need a scorecard," Gary said.

Olivia glanced at her watch. "Well, I hate to cut this short, but I have a dance class in less than an hour."

"We might as well head back," I said. "I can do some straightening up before Edgar Allan arrives."

"Edgar Allan? Oh, the bust." Gary pulled his keys out of his pocket. "No problem. While you're cleaning, maybe I'll do a little internet surfing. I want to check out some knives of my own and see if I can get a handle on specialty shops in this area that might carry them."

"Good idea." I chuckled. "You know, you have a bit of a flair for this sort of work."

"I ought to. I devoured the entire Hardy Boys series when I was a kid." He waggled one eyebrow at me. "You're not too bad either, Nancy Drew."

"Yeah, except Nancy always solved her cases. This one's a long way off."

We dropped Olivia off and as Gary turned past the park, I suddenly spied a familiar figure ambling down the trail in the park.

"Wait, let me out," I cried.

"What? I thought you wanted to clean?"

I pointed. "That's Garrett Knute. I want to try again, see if maybe I can get why that envelope was so important out of him."

"You are like a dog with a bone. Or in your case, a cat with a mouse." He craned his neck around. "Well, it's a busy day in downtown Fox Hollow today. Not a parking space in sight."

"You don't have to come with me," I said. "You can go back to the house and start your research. It's only a ten-minute walk back if I cut through the park." I fished the house keys out of my purse and dropped them in the cup holder. "I won't be long."

His arm shot out. "Wait, I'm not sure I like the idea of you going after him alone. I should come with you. What if he's the murderer?"

I glanced around. There was a small group of girls clustered around a nearby knoll, a young mother over by the bench with a toddler, and two older gentlemen taking an afternoon stroll down the trail. I pointed. "We're in plain sight in the park, and there are lots of people around. I doubt he'll pull his knife on me here."

He gave me a funny look and then said in a low tone, "Be careful, Shell. I'd never forgive myself if anything happened to you." His lips twisted into a lopsided grin. "I've kind of gotten accustomed to your face, you know, after ten years of working together. Not to mention your lousy one-liners."

"Yeah, yeah. Wish me luck."

"Luck." He hesitated, and I was sure he wanted to add *you'll need it*, but he didn't.

I hopped out of the car and set off at a brisk pace through the park in the direction I'd seen Garrett heading. For a minute I feared I'd lost him and then I spied him sitting on a bench not far from the spot where I'd seen Londra and Amelia arguing. I quickened my steps and soon came abreast of him. He glanced up, did a double take, and then frowned.

"Ms. McMillan. You certainly are persistent."

"Good afternoon, Mr. Knute. Mind if I join you?"

He indicated the seat next to him. "You will anyway."

I seated myself and then said casually, "I was just wondering if you wouldn't mind clearing up a few things for me."

He didn't even look over at me. "What things?"

"You mentioned the last time we met that if you were overseeing the investigation into Amelia's death, you'd look at Mel Feller. I was wondering why."

His head jerked up, swiveled in my direction. "Why? Because Feller is an untrustworthy son-of-a-you-know-what, that's why."

"What leads you to make that statement? Does it have something to do with the museum's bookkeeping?" At his surprised look, I added, "I asked

Rita Sakowski to check with her husband. Frank remembered that Mel did do the museum books briefly, but you took the task away from him, and fired him shortly thereafter."

Garrett nodded. "That's true." He gave a quick glance around and then, apparently satisfied no one else was within hearing distance, said, "I never mentioned anything. I didn't want people knowing what a fool I was, to trust Mel with that account. Frank was away, and I had an opportunity. I trusted Mel with the books, then I found out while we were gone he'd siphoned some of the museum money to cover a large gambling debt he'd racked up. I was furious. I tried to cover it up as best I could. I gave him another chance, but when I did an audit, I found he'd moved money out again. I had no choice. I had to let him go." He took a breath. "I replaced the money out of my own pocket. It was my responsibility."

"You kept it quiet all this time to save face."

"I tried." He sighed. "But she found out."

"You mean Amelia?"

He nodded. "She slammed me with it a few months ago, when she wanted to have Dr. Klein, a noted archaeologist, give a talk at the museum. She needed another vote. Said she knew I'd replaced the money so she couldn't bring criminal charges, but she could tell people I was incompetent. Oh, she looked so smug."

"Is that what was in the envelope? Evidence that you'd fixed the books?"

"So she said. She threatened to tell the other board members, said they might even vote to kick me out. I told her over my dead body. Oh, I was so mad that day."

"Mad enough to kill her?" I asked softly.

He pinned me with his gaze. "Sorry to disappoint you, young lady. But at the time Amelia was murdered, I was in the back room at the Captain's Club with some of the Lodge guys, playing chess. I've got at least eight witnesses who'll swear I got there at nine thirty and didn't leave until well after twelve. I've told Josh too." He leaned down, brushing a piece of lint from his slacks. "Maybe you and the detective should talk to each other. It'd save you a lot of trouble."

I rose. "Maybe so, but I doubt he'd appreciate my help. Thanks, Mr. Knute."

I turned and walked back down the trail. Another dead end, and another suspect eliminated. I bit my lip in frustration. The pool was getting smaller by the second. I certainly hoped I'd fare better talking to Mel Feller, because as it stood right now, he was my only viable lead.

Twenty-three

I was halfway home when I got a text from Kathleen Power. She was in the area, could she stop by the store with some samples? I texted back, *Sure. Meet me at Urban Tails in fifteen minutes.* Might as well get something constructive done.

Kathleen was an attractive woman in her early fifties. She was an accountant, and she did all the kitty and doggie clothing in her spare time. She commented briefly on *Spy Anyone's* cancellation, saying that although she'd never watched the show, she'd certainly heard about it enough from Tillie. I appreciated her honesty and the fact she didn't try to suck up just to get a consignment deal. Actually, she didn't have to. The booties and capes she showed me were adorable, and I was already seeing in my mind's eye how I'd display them. I told Kathleen I'd definitely be getting back to her with firm details, and we both left the store happy campers.

Purrday was lounging by the front door when I arrived home. He wound his fat furry body around my ankles, then held up one front paw and blinked his blue eye.

"My day was just great," I said. "Not only do I keep losing suspects, I keep running into dead ends. Not exactly the kind of detective work that will clear my name, now, is it?"

Purrday put his paw on my knee. "Ow-owrr," he warbled.

"Why is clearing my name so important, you ask? Well, for one thing, I doubt people will want to buy pet supplies from a person who's a murder suspect."

Purrday cocked his head. "Ow-orr?"

"Okay, okay. The main reason for me is so that Josh won't look at me with that little bit of doubt in his eyes. I-I kind of like him, ya know. I mean really like him."

The corners of Purrday's lips tipped up, and he leaned in to my hand. I gave him a quick scratch behind his ear. "On the plus side, I met with Kathleen Power. She makes the most adorable dog and cat clothes. I can't wait to feature them in the store. Maybe you could even model one of the outfits?"

Purrday looked at me, then turned his back.

"Or not," I said. "Anyway, I know I can always count on you to sympathize. Not like the other men in my life."

Purrday turned around and butted his head against my knee in reply.

I got up and wandered into the den, Purrday at my heels, where I found Gary hunkered over my laptop, his fingers flying over the keyboard. Kahlua was perched on the edge of the desk, watching him. I flopped into the chair beside the desk; Gary was so intent on what he had up on the screen that it was a few minutes before he even acknowledged my presence, which he did with a quick glance and a muttered, "Huh."

"Wow, what a greeting!" I scooted forward in the chair and placed my hands on the desk. Kahlua sauntered over, butted her head against my hand. "I can only imagine it's because you've found something really, really interesting."

"You could say that," he murmured. He tapped at the keyboard again, then reached for a pad and pen next to the monitor and started to scribble something down.

I waited a few more minutes, and when I got no other response, hitched my chair closer. "Care to share?"

He stretched his arms wide, then laced his fingers behind his neck. "I found a few specialty shops in New York City that carry antique knives, but none of 'em had a Tuareg. One guy, though, recommended this store in New Hampshire. He said the owner goes on trips three times a year to find all sorts of odd knives, and if he didn't have one, he'd know for sure where you could get one. I called, but I got an answering machine. I left a message."

"That sounds promising. Maybe we'll get lucky."

"Maybe we will." He gestured toward the pad. "I've got a couple more leads to track down and then we can think about dinner."

I rose, hands on hips. "Do you ever think of anything except your stomach?"

He bounced both eyebrows. "Sure, but you told me those topics are off-limits."

I made a face at him and returned to the parlor. I'd just started to sort through the day's mail—advertisements, circulars, more advertisements—when the doorbell rang. I opened the front door and found a tall guy wearing jeans with holes in the knees and a well-worn sweatshirt standing there, holding a clipboard. "Shell McMillan? We've got a delivery for you from Secondhand Sue's?"

"Oh, right, thanks." I took the proffered clipboard and signed my name by the X. The delivery guy took the clipboard, initialed the bottom, and then ripped off the pink copy and handed it to me. He hurried down the stairs to the large truck parked in my driveway, and a few minutes later he returned, a large box clasped in his arms.

"Where do you want it?" he asked.

I frowned. Since I'd planned on eventually bringing the bust to the pet shop, I hadn't really thought about where to put it in the interim. I motioned to a small space by the staircase. "This'll do for now."

He set the box down, then pulled a jackknife out of his pocket and slit open the lid. Out came the bubble wrap and Styrofoam, and a few minutes later Edgar Allan and his pal the Raven were sitting comfortably on my floor. I closed my eyes, visualizing where in the store I wanted to put it, and suddenly my eyes flew wide open.

"Drat," I said. "Now that I think about it, this bust is too big to fit behind the counter space." I tapped at my chin with my nail. "I could set him up off to the side, by that display of cat wands, but I'll need a really nice table to put him on."

"Sue has a tall, thin table with a marble top. That might still be there. Want me to have her hold it for you?" the deliveryman asked.

"That would be great," I said. "Please tell her I'll try to get down there tomorrow or the next day to look at it."

He left and I stood for a minute, admiring the bust. It really was a terrific piece of workmanship, and it deserved to be displayed to advantage, not hidden behind a counter. Purrday ambled out of wherever it is cats amble from, walked over to the bust, put his nose next to Edgar's, and sniffed.

"Like him, Purrday? That's Edgar Allan Poe. He wrote a famous story called 'The Black Cat.' They made it into a horror movie with Boris Karloff. As a matter of fact, I do believe the original lobby card is part of Aunt Tillie's collection."

Purrday swiveled his head around to look at me, then returned to his sniffing. He circled the bust once, twice, three times, and then flopped on his side next to it and lay, his paw grazing Edgar's chin.

Gary emerged from the den, followed by Kahlua. He saw Purrday and the bust and grinned. "Looks like your cat has adopted Edgar."

I chuckled. "What can I say? He knows quality, right, Purrday?"

The cat lumbered to his feet and started circling the bust again. He stopped when he got to the back and put his paw up, tapped twice at Edgar's neck.

"Purrday," I said sharply, "stop that."

The cat looked at me, tapped the neck of the bust again, then stretched out beside it and glared at me with his good eye. Kahlua stared at Purrday, then turned and made a beeline for the living room, apparently distancing herself from her new brother's strange behavior. Or else she just wanted first dibs on the back of the couch. It was hard to tell.

I shook my head. "Why on earth is he tapping it?"

Gary shrugged. "Who knows why cats do anything? Maybe he's trying to decide if Edgar is edible or not."

"You'd better not scratch Edgar, Purrday. He's going to be the official greeter at Urban Tails. If we ever open, that is." I turned to Gary and gestured toward the papers in his hand. "Did that store call you back?"

He shook his head. "Not yet. I tried a few more, but none of them carried a Tuareg knife." He rolled the papers up and tapped them against his palm. "Looks like a dead end, at least for now."

I let out a giant sigh. "We seem to be hitting a lot of those."

"Yep. You know what they say, when you keep hitting your head against a brick wall . . ."

I eyed him. "What's that?"

He grinned. "You eat a good dinner and suddenly the world seems brighter, everything gets put in perspective." He unrolled the papers and passed the top one to me. "There's an excellent Japanese restaurant two towns over, and a Thai one on the highway that got good reviews. What's your pleasure?"

"*That* was your research? Local restaurants?" I shook my fist playfully at him. "I suppose we could have an early dinner," I said. "Maybe even swing by Melvin Feller's house again on the way back."

Gary's grin morphed into a frown. "I thought his neighbor said he wouldn't be back until midnight."

"No, she said *last time* they got home at midnight because the van driver got lucky. So maybe this time Lady Luck will smile on us, and the driver will have a bad day at the blackjack table. It's worth a shot, right?"

"Would it do me any good to argue?"

"No," I said. "And while we're at it, maybe we should pay a call on Londra Lewis too. I think we might get more out of her, especially if you turn on your charm." I laid my hand on his arm and battled my eyelashes double time.

"Okay, okay," he grumbled. "Fine, we'll pay both of 'em a visit. Right now, we've got a decision to make. Japanese or Thai? Oh, and there's a good Chinese restaurant right in Fox Hollow, too. This food critic online gave it four stars."

"Fine. Let's try that. I could go for some shrimp with lobster sauce and a nice egg drop soup." I grabbed my purse and added, "You do realize that eventually we're going to run out of restaurants, and I *am* going to cook dinner for us, right?"

"I do," he said. "I'm just trying to delay the pain. Hey, like you said, the Big Apple is only an hour away." He smacked his lips loudly. "Hundreds of good restaurants there."

I shook my head. "Always thinking of your stomach, Presser?" My phone pinged and I glanced at it. It was a text from, of all people, Londra Lewis.

Can you stop by museum early tomorrow and see me? Must talk to u in private.

I showed the text to Gary. "Well, well. I wonder what she wants to tell you?"

"I don't know," I said as I slid the phone into my pocket. "But maybe we're gonna catch a break."

• • •

The Red Dragon turned out to be a small, quaint building located down the street from the library. The outside was done in red and gold, and the red and gold sign above the door featured a red fire-breathing dragon. The foyer had glass cases on either side, displaying statues and paintings of dragons in various stages: breathing fire, attacking a helmeted soldier wielding a sword, two dragons kissing (I kid you not). The interior of the restaurant was dark, as were most Chinese restaurants, and there was a smattering of tables with wooden chairs with red and gold seat cushions and red tablecloths with gold trim around the edges in the center of the dining area, and some red upholstered booths along one side. We asked for a table and the pretty Chinese hostess in a tight-fitting sheath (red and gold, what else?) seated us at one near the large picture window, then placed red velvet menu books in front of us before she smilingly withdrew.

A Chinese boy who looked to be a teenager in a white coat appeared almost instantly, filling our water glasses and placing a huge bowl of noodles and dipping sauce in front of us. The waitress, also attired in a tight-fitting sheath, appeared a few minutes later. We ordered—shrimp with lobster sauce for me, four seasons for Gary—and I'd just finished pouring us each a cup of tea when Gary's cell rang.

He pulled it out of his pocket, glanced at the number, frowned, and answered it. "Gary Presser. Oh, yes. Thank you for calling back." He listened for a few moments and then he said in an excited tone, "Are you sure? Can you fax me the copy of the bill of lading?" He fumbled in his pocket, pulled out a pen, and thrust it at me. He tapped at his napkin and mouthed, "Fax number." I took the pen and wrote it down on the napkin. He repeated it to the person on the other end of the phone and said, "Thanks so much. I'll be in touch." He disconnected and looked at me. "We just may have gotten a break," he said, leaning back with a smug expression on his face.

"What kind of break?" I asked, my curiosity piqued. "Who was that on the phone?"

"That was one of the leads I was following. It's the specialty shop out in Wyoming the Fox Hollow Museum bought a collection of rare knives for display from. Remember, Mazie Madison said the Tuareg knife was missing from the shipment?"

I nodded. "She said that knife and two others."

"That was the store manager. He said that he's positive *all* the knives were accounted for when the shipment left the store. He can't find any record of the museum claiming items were missing—but he had a temp doing office work that week and a lot of his records have been misplaced. He said he had a request for confirmation from Bloodgood, too. He's looking for the paperwork, and as soon as he gets it he'll fax us both a copy."

"Very interesting," I agreed. "But assuming he's correct, why would Mazie lie about receiving the knife in the shipment?"

"I can give you three guesses," Gary said dryly. "And the first two don't count. She wanted to use that knife to ice Amelia."

I frowned. "It doesn't make any sense, though. Mazie, a killer? She really has no motive that I'm aware of."

Gary inclined his head toward the doorway. "We could ask her."

I followed his gaze and saw Mazie herself standing at the take-out counter at the front of the restaurant. Never one to waste an opportunity, I scraped my chair back and hurried over to her.

Mazie glanced up as I approached. "Ms. McMillan. How nice to see you."

"Hi, Ms. Madison. I was wondering if I could have a word with you."

"Certainly." She glanced over my shoulder at Gary, who'd come up behind me. "You're Gary Presser, right? I heard you'd come to town too. Fox Hollow is certainly overrun with celebrities these days."

"Gary is helping me investigate Amelia's death," I said.

Mazie looked surprised. "You're a detective now?" she asked Gary.

He chuckled. "Strictly amateur. I'm trying to keep Shell out of prison, you know, just in case a new TV series opens up and I can talk her into coming back to the West Coast with me."

I gave his arm a hard squeeze and then turned to Mazie. "You told Detective Bloodgood that a Tuareg knife was supposed to be in a shipment you recently acquired for the museum."

She nodded. "Yes. That and two other knives were missing when it was unpacked. I was pretty upset, as we'd prepaid for the items."

"I checked with that shop," Gary said. "The manager said he packed the items himself, and the shipment was complete." He paused. "He said he has no record of you sending in a complaint."

"Then he's mistaken," she snapped.

"He sounded pretty positive."

Mazie nibbled at her lower lip. She looked very uncomfortable. Finally, she said, "All right. I don't advertise this fact, but Londra is the one who unpacks the shipments. She said the shipment was complete, and I trusted her. She had to leave early that day, though, so I did the unpacking and I noticed the three items missing. That's when I sent the corrected invoice and request for refund. I've been meaning to speak to her about it, but what with all that's being going on . . ." She spread her hands helplessly. "I guess I forgot. Truly, it didn't seem that big of a deal. We deal with that store all the time."

"Are you saying Londra lied about the items in the shipment?" Gary asked.

"I'm not saying anything. It could have been an honest mistake."

"Or she could have removed the items herself," I said thoughtfully. "But why would she do that?" I gave Mazie a sharp glance. "To show them to someone, perhaps? Maybe she thought she could put them back before they were noticed?"

Mazie shifted her weight uncomfortably from one foot to the other. "I'm not saying she did or didn't. Londra has always been a very loyal employee."

Gary and I looked at each other, and I could tell the same thought was running through our minds. If Londra had taken the knives, perhaps that was what she and Amelia had argued over that day in the park. Amelia might have threatened to prosecute Londra for theft, and Londra might have taken matters into her own hands. After all, by her own admission she didn't have an alibi for Amelia's time of death.

"Londra sent me a text earlier. She wants to talk to me tomorrow," I said. "I can ask her about the shipment then."

"Or we can do it now," Mazie said. "She doesn't live far from here, and I've been meaning to talk to her about it anyway."

I looked at Gary. He sighed.

"Might as well." He glanced up, caught our waitress's eye, and motioned with his hand. "Just let me get those dinners to go."

• • •

Fifteen minutes later we pulled up in front of Londra's house, a small gray, white, and pink bungalow situated on the street directly behind the museum. Mazie hadn't been kidding when she said Londra lived close. I was certain she could see the museum parking lot from her back window. Probably one of the reasons she utilized it as a parking space, since her driveway was extremely narrow. It would have been hard to maneuver that Caddy into it.

As Mazie exited the car, she glanced toward the dark front porch and frowned. "That's odd," she said. "She always leaves the porch light on. Always."

We quickened our steps and hurried up onto the porch. As I reached toward the bell Mazie shook her head. "It's broken," she said. She raised her hand and rapped sharply on the front door. "Londra? Are you home?"

No answer. Gary stepped forward, tried the knob. The door swung silently inward, and we walked into a darkened foyer. The house was as still as death.

"Londra?" Mazie called again. "Are you here?" She gave Gary and me an anxious look over her shoulder. "This is very strange," she said. "Londra never forgets to lock her door when she goes out. Never."

We moved down the hall, peering this way and that. The living room was empty, ditto the kitchen. A room at the far end of the hall, however, had a thin sliver of light emanating from beneath the door.

"She must be in her study," Mazie murmured. With Gary in the lead, we hurried down the corridor. Gary pushed through the door first and then stopped abruptly when he was about two inches over the threshold. I was right behind him, and I had to veer slightly to the right to avoid slamming right into his back.

"What's wrong—" I began, but a quick glance toward the center of the room told me all I needed to know.

Londra was seated behind a large desk, her head bent rakishly to one side, her tongue protruding from the side of her mouth.

She sure looked dead to me.

Twenty-four

I heard Mazie's voice through the fog that permeated my brain. "What's the matter? Why did you stop?" Then she made a strangled sound in the back of her throat and started to swoon. Gary reached out and caught her in his arms, otherwise she might have fallen to the floor.

"I-I'm all right," she said, passing a hand over her eyes. She cast a tentative glance in the direction of the desk. "Is she . . . is she . . ."

"Looks that way," I said. Gary looked at me over Mazie's shoulder and I knew he thought one of us should verify that Londra was, indeed, beyond help. I steeled myself and inched toward the desk. Londra's right arm lay across the top of the desk while her left hung down at her side. I suppressed a shudder of revulsion and felt the right wrist for a pulse. Her skin was cool to the touch.

After a minute, I let go of her wrist and looked at the other two. "No pulse," I announced. "She's gone."

Mazie let out another strangled sob, put her hand to her mouth. Gary guided her to a chair at the far end of the room, and I saw him pull out his cell, presumably to dial 911.

I turned back to the body and forced myself to look at Londra's face. Aside from the swollen tongue, several angry red splotches covered her skin, and her lips were tinged with a faint blue hue. I stepped to the other side of the desk to view her from another angle, and paused as my shoe stepped on something that gave a loud crunchy sound. Looking down, I saw several peanut shells scattered around the bottom of the chair, and something else. A single sheet of paper lying against the side of the chair. The tips of Londra's lifeless fingers just grazed the top, and I could see there was writing on it. I started to bend down, but Gary ended his call just then and said in a sharp tone, "The 911 operator said not to touch anything. We should wait for the authorities outside."

I cast another look at the paper, then reluctantly turned and followed Gary and Mazie back onto the front porch. We didn't have to wait long. A few minutes later a black-and-white patrol car, lights flashing, came to a screeching halt behind Gary's convertible. Two officers got out and hurried over to us. One appeared to be in his mid-fifties, paunchy and balding. The younger one I recognized from my previous murder scene, and judging from the startled expression on his face, he recognized me as well.

"Officer Riley," I greeted him. I was going to add *Nice to see you* and then thought better of it.

He tipped his cap. "Ms. McMillan. *You* found the body?" He might as well have added *again*.

Gary stepped in front of me. "We all did," he said.

"What were you all doing here?" the older man asked. The nameplate over his badge proclaimed him to be Martin Malone.

"We had some business with Londra," Mazie piped up. "She worked for me at the museum." Her chin jutted out, indicating me and Gary. "Ms. McMillan and Mr. Presser had a few questions about a museum shipment, and since Londra handled it I suggested we come here and ask her to clear things up. We got here and found her porch light off and her door open, and Londra . . ." At that point she choked up and couldn't go on. She reached into her jacket pocket, pulled out a white glove and a roll of breath mints, and lastly a Kleenex. She shoved the glove and mints back into her pocket and then blew loudly into the Kleenex before crumpling it into a ball and leaning heavily on the older officer's arm.

Officer Malone looked quite uncomfortable. It was obvious to me that he hadn't had much experience with seeing women cry or get upset. He looked again at Mazie and patted her shoulder awkwardly. "There, there," he murmured. "I'm sorry for your loss, ma'am." He raised his head and looked at Gary and me. "Where's the body?" he asked abruptly.

"In her den. If you'll follow me." Gary motioned to the officers to follow him. Riley immediately fell into step behind Gary. Malone, with a little sigh, pressed Mazie into my arms before practically falling all over himself to follow the other two.

Mazie dabbed at her eyes with the edge of the Kleenex ball. "What happens now?"

"They've probably already notified Detective Bloodgood," I said. "The coroner's men will come out to examine the body, and then the officers will make a sweep of the crime scene. This house will probably be off-limits for a few days."

No sooner were the words out of my mouth than the coroner's truck pulled up behind the police car, followed by a dark gray sedan. Josh got out of the sedan and hurried toward the house. He stopped dead on the steps when he saw me, and I held up my hand traffic cop style and said, "Before you even ask, we all found the body. Gary, Mazie, and me. We walked into the den together, and Londra was sitting behind the desk. And yes, I did touch the body, just the wrist, to make sure she was beyond help before Gary called 911. And aside from ringing the buzzer and pushing open the front door, which was already partially open, none of us touched anything." I glanced swiftly at Mazie for confirmation, and she nodded.

Josh passed a hand across his eyes. "That's a plus." He glanced around. "You said Gary was with you?"

I inclined my head toward the front door. "He went to show the other officers the body."

"Okay." He paused, then added in a gruff tone, "Stay here," before turning on his heel and disappearing inside the house.

Mazie shuddered. "Like we'd want to go back in there." She gave me an anxious look. "Poor Londra. Her face looked so mottled. What do you think it means?"

I had an idea, but before I could voice an opinion, Officer Malone stuck his head outside the door and motioned to us. "Detective Bloodgood would like you to come in and have a seat in the living room. Please don't touch anything, and he'll be with you shortly."

We went inside and Officer Malone ushered us into the living room. Gary was already seated there, on a brocade-covered sofa. I sat down next to him while Mazie eased herself into a wing chair directly opposite the fireplace.

"This is the fun part," I said, drawing air quotes around the word *fun*. "We'll be questioned about what we were doing here, finding the body, yadda yadda."

Mazie frowned. "Didn't we already answer all that?"

"Yes, but Detective Bloodgood will want more detail." I leaned back against the cushions and closed my eyes. "Believe me, I know."

We lapsed into an uncomfortable silence for about ten minutes and then Josh walked in. "I just have a few questions for you three. I'll try and keep this brief." He hesitated, then seated himself in a wing chair to Mazie's left, facing Gary and me. He pulled out his trusty notebook, flipped a few pages, and then raised his gaze to mine.

"I hope finding dead bodies isn't going to become a habit with you," he said.

I shifted my position on the couch slightly. "I hope not either," I said. "It's no fun, I can tell you that."

"The three of you came here together?"

"We've already answered that question," Mazie piped up, a trifle irritably, I thought. "Ms. McMillan and Mr. Presser had a question about one of the museum shipments that Londra oversaw, and I thought we could just ask her about it and settle the matter quickly."

"I see." He scribbled something in his book and then looked right at me. "What shipment were you questioning?"

"The one with the rare knives," I said. "The one with the Tuareg knife, specifically."

"And why were you questioning it?"

"Because I checked with the manager of the shop who sent them," Gary spoke up, "and he claimed the shipment was complete, and none of the items were missing, as Ms. Madison previously reported."

Josh turned his gaze on Mazie. She cleared her throat. "I told them, Londra was the one in charge of that shipment. She was a very efficient worker. There must be a reasonable explanation for all this. I suggested we speak to her to clear the matter up, but instead we found . . ." She choked up again and could not go on.

Josh leaned forward and said in a softer tone, "Ms. Madison, do you know for certain if Londra was involved with a gentleman by the name of Melvin Feller?"

Mazie turned tear-filled eyes to him. "I can't say for certain," she said softly. "There have been rumors, of course, but why do you ask?"

He didn't answer, just scratched at his head and scribbled some more in his notebook. Abruptly he snapped it shut and looked at us. "You can all go."

I stared at him. "Really? Just like that?"

Gary nudged me as if to say *don't look a gift horse in the mouth.*

"My car is back at the Chinese restaurant," Mazie said. "Could someone drive me there?"

"Are you sure you're up to driving?" Josh asked. "I can have Officer Riley escort you home. You can get your car in the morning."

Mazie gave him a relieved look. "That would be perfect, thank you, Detective."

Josh took her arm and they moved into the hallway, where Officer Riley waited. I took the opportunity to whisper to Gary, "Something's up. He had a gazillion questions for me when Amelia was murdered, and none for any of us about Londra?"

"Well, you weren't arguing with Londra," Gary shot back. "Plus, three of us found the body. He's got no reason to suspect foul play on our part." He paused. "Something was off about her body. Didn't you notice it? The splotchy skin, the lolling tongue." He tapped at his bottom lip with his forefinger and closed his eyes for a moment. His eyes snapped open, and he turned back to me. "Was she allergic to anything?"

I made an impatient gesture with my hand. "How would I know?"

"That was a rhetorical question," Gary replied. "I just remember reading in a book once that the victim died from an allergic reaction, and the description of the body fit Londra to a T. Splotchy skin, lolling tongue, bugged eyes."

"I saw some peanut shells scattered around the floor by the desk," I said. "But if she were allergic to peanuts, why would she eat them?"

"A good question."

Gary and I both whirled around. Josh had entered the room so quietly neither one of us had been aware of his presence. I saw that he held a plastic baggie in one hand, with a sheet of paper inside, and my thoughts turned to the paper I'd seen caught underneath Londra's chair. I gestured toward the baggie with my chin. "What have you got there?"

Josh looked at me for a long moment and then said tightly, "Evidence that appears to clear up both Londra's and Amelia's deaths."

Twenty-five

For a second all I could do was gape at Josh, and then I found my voice. "Both deaths? But how?"

"Of course, nothing's set in stone until the official coroner's report comes in, but . . ." He held the baggie out to me. "His preliminary examination suggests an allergic reaction, just as Gary said. And then we found this underneath her chair."

I took the baggie with the printed note inside. I read it aloud, with Gary hanging over my shoulder:

> I'm sorry for all the trouble I've caused, and I don't want to do this anymore. I killed Amelia. She knew I took the knife out of the shipment and she threatened me with exposure. I just can't live with my guilt any longer, or with having innocent people suspected of something I did.
> Londra Lewis

"Holy cats," Gary ejaculated. "It's a confession."

"It would appear so," said Josh. He looked at me. "As you said, there were several peanut shells scattered about. We'll have to check her medical records, of course, but I'm betting we'll find Ms. Lewis had a severe allergy to peanuts."

"She committed suicide by eating peanuts?" I said. It sounded incredible to me.

Josh nodded. "If her allergy was severe enough, it wouldn't have taken much to put her into anaphylactic shock. Death would have been quick. Her blood pressure would have risen, and her air passage and throat would swell, making breathing difficult. In essence, she choked to death."

I tamped down a shudder. "Wouldn't a gun to the temple be quicker?"

"It'd definitely be messier," put in Gary.

Josh eyed us both for about ten seconds, then blew out a breath. "Believe it or not, I've seen cases like this before. Someone wants to end their life, but they haven't got the guts to hang themselves or shoot themselves, so they either take poison, which can also act fairly quickly, or they subject themselves to something they can be fatally allergic to."

"It just seems a shame," I said. "She certainly didn't seem suicidal when I spoke to her. Plus, she'd sent me a text shortly before her death, that she wanted to talk to me tomorrow. Why would she do that if she intended to kill herself?"

"Yes, I saw your phone number scrawled on one of the file folders." He scratched at his head. "I can't answer that. Maybe she wanted to confess to you, and when she couldn't reach you . . ." His voice trailed off and he shrugged.

I stared at him, my eyes wide. "You mean her death is my fault?"

"Oh, no, no," he said quickly. "It's just that when people are wound so tight like that, you never quite know what might set them off. We have no idea what might have been going on in her head." He motioned toward the door. "The two of you are free to go. I'll let you know once we verify Londra's medical records and get the final coroner's statement.

I looked at Josh. "What do you think? Do you think it's a suicide?"

He ran his hand through his hair. "I prefer to reserve judgment until the final coroner's report is in." He paused and then added, "However, as I said, it would *appear* Amelia's murder is solved."

I noticed the extra emphasis he put on the word *appear*, and I had to agree. If something was rotten in the state of Denmark, then it was doubly—no, make that triply—foul in Fox Hollow. I looked at Josh. "*Vertigo*," I said.

He stared at me. "I'm sorry, do you feel dizzy?"

I waved my hand. "No, no. *Vertigo* is the title of a movie. Alfred Hitchcock, 1958, Jimmy Stewart and Kim Novak. Stewart plays Scottie, a detective with a fear of heights. An old acquaintance of his hires him to follow his wife, played by Kim Novak, whom he believes is going a bit bonkers. Scottie ends up falling in love with Kim's character, but he can't stop her when she apparently commits suicide by falling to her death from a bell tower. Later, he meets a woman, Judy, who's her exact double. To make a long story short, it turns out it's the same woman. Scottie's friend hired Judy to impersonate his wife so he could fake her murder as a suicide. He knew that Scottie couldn't follow her up to the bell tower and stop her from jumping because of his vertigo."

Josh's brows drew together, making a slight ridge in the center of his forehead. "O-kay. And you thought of this movie because . . . ?"

"Because Londra's murder just seems too pat, too convenient. It could have been staged, just like the character Kim Novak played in *Vertigo*."

Josh stroked at his chin, his eyes slitted. "Like I said before, I'm reserving judgment until the final coroner's report is in. You might have something there, though." His lips twitched upward. "I guess I'll have to watch this *Vertigo*. Sounds like an interesting movie. I imagine Scottie and Judy end up living happily ever after?"

I barked out a laugh. "It's Hitchcock, after all! But I won't tell you the ending. I don't want to spoil it for you."

He chuckled. "Thanks." Officer Malone appeared in the den doorway and motioned to Josh. "I've got to go," he said. "You two are free to go."

"Gee, thanks," I murmured at Josh's retreating back. I raised my eyebrow at Gary and he followed me out the front door and onto the porch. I leaned against the railing, crossed my arms over my chest, and said, "Okay, Gary, I know you've got an opinion you're dying to share. What do you think?"

"You're not going to like it." He pursed his lips. "I'm not sure I agree with your theory that Londra's death was staged."

"You think she did it?"

"If she was involved with the Feller guy, then there's a good chance she did take that knife out of the shipment for him. Amelia finds out about it, accuses her of theft—you said that they were going at it in the park pretty good that day, right?" At my nod he went on, "So maybe Amelia threatened to turn her over to the police unless she returned the knife, and maybe she snapped. She got the knife, wrote that note to lure Amelia to the museum, and killed her."

"Nice theory, but it's got more holes than Swiss cheese. For one thing, that note wouldn't have lured Amelia to the museum. The note only said that someone had discovered her secret. Amelia called me and told me to come to the museum."

Gary considered this a moment then said, "Maybe it was a habit of Amelia's to go to the museum on Sundays. Londra would have known that, and she could have left the note where Amelia would find it. She'd have been watching, since she only lives a stone's throw away, and once she saw Amelia go inside, she followed her, waited for her chance, and killed her."

"Maybe," I said, "but I don't think so." I glanced at my watch. "It's after ten. Let's see if Mel Feller's arrived back from his gambling junket yet. If so, we might be able to get some answers out of him before he learns of Londra's death."

"You'd quiz the guy and not tell him what happened to his lady friend?" Gary shook his head. "That's pretty cold, Shell."

I looked at him. "So's murder. And I'm not writing Feller off as a suspect."

• • •

As luck would have it, Melvin Feller was just going up his front porch steps when Gary and I pulled up in front of his house. I was out of the car and running toward him before Gary could even put the car in park. "Mr. Feller," I called out. "Wait. May I speak with you a moment?"

Mel turned at the sound of my voice. His clothes, a tan blazer and matching pants, looked wrinkled and his eyes were bleary-looking and bloodshot. He wiped at his beak of a nose with the back of his hand and said in a whiney tone, "It's getting late and I'm tired. What's so important, Miss . . . ?"

"McMillan. Shell McMillan. I promise we'll be brief. This will only take a moment of your time."

He hesitated, then stepped back and let out a loud sneeze. He wiped his nose again with the back of his hand before looking at me again. "What do you want?"

"I understand that you have a relationship with one of the museum workers, Ms. Londra Lewis."

That blank expression again, and then he passed a hand over his eyes. "Sorry, my brain doesn't work right so late at night." He barked out a short laugh. "It was a bad day at the casino, all around. No winners, except the slot machines and blackjack table." He cleared his throat. "I'm sorry? What was the question?"

"You have a relationship with Ms. Lewis?"

"Londra?" He waved his hand. "Sure, I know her. Why?"

"You more than just know her, don't you?" I persisted. "I've heard from many sources the two of you are quite close."

He shifted his weight from one foot to the other and leaned heavily on

197

the porch rail. "Well, if we are, that's really no one's business, now is it? And why would that interest you?"

"I don't know if you're aware, but a shipment of rare knives was recently received by the museum, and there appears to be some difference of opinion as to whether all of them reached their destination."

His eyes narrowed. "And that would involve me . . . how? It's no concern of mine if the museum got gypped on a shipment. I mean, if they'd voted me to the board, I might care, but since I didn't get on . . ." He lifted his shoulders in a gesture that implied he couldn't care less.

I pressed on, determined. "I understand you're somewhat of an expert on antique knives, and that Londra . . . consulted with you on the subject?"

"I wouldn't call it consulting. She may have asked me one or two general questions about knives." He puffed out his chest. "I am sort of an expert on the subject. It's been a hobby of mine for quite some time."

"Did she ask you about a particular type of knife? A Tuareg knife?"

"She may have. I don't rightly remember. I answer a lot of questions about knives for a lot of people, and I never had to keep track of who asked what question," he snapped, then held up his wrist, tapped at the face of his watch. "If that's all you want, like I said, it's very late and I'm tired. If you need any more information, I'm sure it'll keep until morning?"

Mel's recalcitrant attitude was a sure sign I wasn't going to get any more out of him. I plastered a phony smile across my lips and said, "Of course. Thank you for your time." I turned and started down the steps as Mel fumbled in his pocket for his keys. On the third step, I stopped. "One last thing."

He looked over his shoulder at me, still fishing in his pocket. "What?"

"Was Londra allergic to peanuts?"

There was no mistaking the look of surprise on his face. "Peanuts? She was? Wow, well, that would explain why she never ate peanut butter, I guess. If that's all, I'll say good night." He whipped the key out of his pocket, turned it in the lock, and then disappeared inside, letting the door slam behind him. I stared at the closed door for a minute, then turned and walked swiftly toward Gary's parked car. He'd had to do a U-turn to find an open parking spot. He shot me a look as I opened the passenger door and got inside.

"You should have waited for me," he chided. "I might have been able to get more out of him."

"I doubt it." I tapped my chin with my nail. "He didn't know if Londra was allergic to peanuts."

Gary turned the key in the ignition and then turned his head to look at me. "What?"

I drummed my fingers on the armrest. "He didn't know if she was allergic to peanuts. Don't you think he would have, if they'd really been in a relationship?"

Gary shrugged. "Maybe not. I've dated women and not known every single thing about them."

"But they were supposed to be in a serious relationship. Londra stole knives out of a shipment, ostensibly for him. You'd surely think he'd know."

"Maybe he does—did. Maybe he was lying."

"No, I don't think so. He looked genuinely surprised when I told him."

Gary shifted his weight from one foot to the other. "It's not that unusual. You can't tell me Pat knew *everything* about you. The fact you like half-and-half instead of milk in your coffee, and when you drink tea you always wind the teabag string around your finger while it's steeping."

"There's another possibility. Maybe Londra wasn't the woman Mel was dating."

"If not Londra, then who—*ow!*" he cried as my nails dug into his forearm. "Don't *do* that."

"Cut the engine," I hissed. "Don't put your lights on."

"For pity's sakes, why? Don't you want to go home?"

"I'd rather see who this is first."

I inclined my head toward the darkened street. A car had just turned the corner, heading toward us. What was unusual was, it's headlights were off. I grabbed Gary's arm and pushed him down in the seat. I slid down too, and we both peeped over the top of the dashboard, watching as the car made a sharp turn and pulled into the driveway of the darkened house next to Mel Feller's. A few seconds later a horn blasted once, then Mel came banging out of his back door. He hurried over to the car, opened the passenger door, and got in. The driver put the car into reverse, backed out of the drive, and took off like a rocket down the street.

Gary turned the key in the ignition. "Want to follow 'em?" he asked.

I shook my head. "No. They're driving too fast. Could you see what color that sedan was?"

"Not really, but if I had to guess, I'd say maybe . . . dark red."

"When they shot out of the drive, I got a glimpse of the person in the driver's seat—just an impression, but I thought it was a light-haired female."

Gary shook his head. "I didn't notice, sorry." He leaned over to look deeply into my eyes. "I know that look. Your wheels are spinning. You think you know who Feller's nocturnal visitor was?"

"I'm pretty sure I do," I said slowly. "I'm pretty sure that was Mayor Carolyn Hart."

"The mayor?" Gary let out a low whistle. "You've got to be wrong. What would she be doing with Feller?"

"The mayor is an honorary museum board member," I said slowly. "Maybe the museum woman Mel was involved with wasn't Londra. Maybe it was Mayor Hart."

Gary's jaw dropped. "Really? You think the mayor would be running around with that guy?"

"Honestly? I'm not sure what to think."

Gary started up the car and eased away from the curb. "Know what? I think we both need to get back to your place, eat this food, and get a good night's sleep. Maybe in the morning, when we're both fresh, we can put some of this in perspective."

We rode the rest of the way back to my house in silence. Londra might have been responsible for Amelia's death, but somehow, I didn't think so. I had the feeling she'd been an innocent pawn in a very dangerous game, like Kim Novak's character of Judy in *Vertigo*, only Londra had paid with her life. But proving it?

That was another matter entirely.

Twenty-six

The next day I decided that in light of Londra's confession, phony though I thought it was, it at least took the heat off me and I should get back to making arrangements for the grand reopening of Urban Tails. I left Gary sleeping, fed the cats, and drove down to the store shortly before nine. Once inside, I paused and looked around. I could feel Aunt Tillie's presence, smiling at me, encouraging me in this new venture. I knew that wherever she was, she was extremely proud.

First thing I did was measure the area behind the counter. Sure enough, it was just as I suspected. The Poe bust would fit, but there would be little room for anything else, including me. The section over by the cat toys, though, was perfect. A table would fit in between the cat wands and the birdseed, and Edgar and the Raven would be visible enough to welcome both old and new customers. I made a note to ask Gary to help me repack the bust when I got home.

I made some more supplier calls. One was to a parrot breeder that my aunt had used. He was delighted to have Urban Tails's business again, and promised to meet with me early next week to review what I'd need. Next I called the exotic fish supplier and made arrangements to have several different types of fish delivered within the next two weeks. I ordered a larger number of goldfish, figuring they were the more universally appealing. I could always add or subtract as I got more used to my customer base. Which reminded me, I'd also have to see about updating the store's website. Aunt Tillie had created one, but it wasn't exactly what I'd call state-of-the-art. Since I was what one would refer to as technologically challenged, I'd probably have to hire someone to spruce it up a bit, maybe add a section for online sales. I made a mental note to ask Gary. My ex-costar was far more savvy about websites and such things than I.

I'd just finished placing an order for dog and cat food through another of Tillie's trusted suppliers and was just about to call the birdseed supplier when I heard a tap-tap at the door. The sign—*Closed. Reopening Soon*—was still taped there. Couldn't anyone in this town read?

"We're not open yet, sorry," I called loudly. I went back through my ledger but the tapping persisted, more insistent this time. With a groan, I shoved myself off the stool and marched to the front door, flung it open—and then let out a gasp as I saw Josh standing there. I tried not to notice how handsome he looked in a green blazer, khaki pants, and a tan-and-white-striped shirt. The smile he offered me was wide and genuine, and for a moment I was reminded of the day we'd met in the park, when none of the ugliness of Amelia's murder had interfered.

"Good morning, Shell. I stopped by your house, but Gary said you'd come here."

Ah, so Gary had read the note I'd left him. That was encouraging. "Yes, I figured since I was eliminated as a suspect, I could finally start planning the grand reopening." I paused and stepped aside as he came into the store. "I am eliminated, right?"

He nodded. "I never really seriously considered you a suspect."

I raised a brow. "You could have fooled me."

He chuckled. "I just thought I'd drop by to let you know that we got the final coroner's report. Londra died from anaphylactic shock resulting from an allergic reaction to peanuts."

I nodded. "Does that mean you're going to close both cases? Write up Londra's death as a suicide and brand her Amelia's murderer?"

"The evidence makes it *appear* that's what happened," he said. Again, I noticed the extra emphasis he put on the word *appear*.

I looked him right in the eye. "Is that what *you* think happened?"

"I'm not sure. It all seems neat and tidy." Josh leaned his elbow against the counter. "In addition to the peanut shells and half-empty bag we found under the desk, we also found a paper in a file folder on the desk. The amended bill of lading for that knife shipment and the request for refund." Josh reached into his jacket pocket and removed a paper from it. He laid it on the counter and I leaned in for a closer look. There was a long list of items, three of which had circles around them, indicating they were missing. At the bottom was Mazie Madison's signature.

"We compared the handwriting on the suicide note with the note found on Amelia," Josh went on. "They match. Londra probably took the knives to show her boyfriend, Mel Feller, and Amelia must have found out about it somehow. She most likely threatened Londra with theft charges, and Londra felt desperate. She saw an opportunity to solve the problem when you started quizzing, and pissing off, the other board members. Mazie verified that Amelia usually came by the museum on Sunday mornings to look over any board correspondence. Londra knew that, and so she wrote that note to Amelia, figuring Amelia would get in touch with you and tell you to come down, and then she went in and killed her. But the guilt over trying to blame you for the murder as well as Amelia's death finally got to her, and she took her own life."

I had to agree, it certainly seemed neat and tidy. Too neat and tidy.

"What about Mayor Hart?" I asked abruptly.

Josh's brows drew together. "Mayor Hart?"

"She's an honorary board member, as I understand it. Did anyone check on her alibi for the time of Amelia's death?"

Josh stared at me. "Shell, you can't be serious. You think Mayor Hart had something to do with Amelia's death?"

"I'm just wondering if anyone's checked out the possibility that maybe the woman Mel Feller had a relationship with wasn't Londra."

Josh's eyes widened. "You think Mel and the mayor . . . ?" He stared at me, and then started to laugh.

"I don't see where it's so funny," I snapped. "When I questioned Mel last night, it certainly didn't seem to me as if he were in a serious relationship with Londra. He didn't even know she was allergic to peanuts!"

"When you questioned . . . what were you doing interrogating him?" Josh cried.

"Someone had to," I said with a curl of my lip.

Josh started to sputter something, but stopped as his phone rang. He whipped it out of his pocket, glanced at the screen. He gave me a baleful look and said, "I have to take this. Excuse me just a sec." He moved over toward the rack that held the rabbit and gerbil food, and I noticed that he'd left the bill of lading lying on my counter. I picked up my iPhone from the counter, walked over to the piece of paper, and took two quick pictures of it. Why, I had no idea.

Josh returned, sliding his phone back into his jacket pocket. "I'm sorry, that was the station. I have to go." He plucked the paper from the counter, folded it, and slid it into his other pocket. "I'll be in touch."

That was my cue to look adoringly into his eyes and say, "*Oh, Josh, I would love that. Maybe we can get together soon.*" Instead I heard myself saying,

"Have you even questioned Mel Feller about his relationship with Londra yet?"

Josh looked a bit surprised, but he nodded. "I went over there early this morning."

"Was he surprised to learn she was dead?"

"Not really." As my eyes widened he added, "He said that Londra had been having some problems recently. He also admitted that their relationship was fragile and under a strain. He was considering breaking up with her. Quite honestly, he wasn't a bit surprised she committed suicide."

Of course not, I thought, *not when his real girlfriend already tipped him off and probably coached him on what to say.*

"Fine." I didn't even make a move to walk him to the door. "I guess I'll see you around."

He looked deeply into my eyes for a long moment, then gave me a curt nod and said, "Sure. I'll see you."

I watched as the door closed behind him. Then I let out a long sigh, picked up the ledger, and called the birdseed supplier. Sunflower seeds wait for no man.

• • •

"Why did you take photos of this bill of lading?" Gary asked. I'd returned home after finishing with the suppliers to find Gary, dressed in polo shirt and khakis, sitting in the living room, sipping coffee and reading the paper. I'd gotten myself a cup of coffee and filled him in on Josh's visit.

"Honest? I'm not sure. I just have a feeling that all this isn't over yet."

"Because you won't let it be over," Gary hissed back. "Goodness, Shell, I thought that was what you wanted. To get this murder solved and get your name cleared so you could get on with your life, start up your new business and . . ." He glanced significantly toward the doorway. "Maybe have a date or two with the detective when you aren't a murder suspect."

"Yeah, well, I've got a feeling Josh isn't very satisfied with the way this case wrapped up either," I snapped.

"The evidence says otherwise." Gary started to tick off on his fingers. "There's the note, written in her handwriting, confessing to the crime. There' the fact her handwriting is identical to the one on the note Amelia received. There's—"

"Another point I don't understand," I interrupted. "That first note referred to the fact I'd discovered her secret. Just what secret was that, anyway?"

"Maybe Londra was just bluffing. Or maybe she was referring to Amelia's affair with Peabody, intimating that you'd found out."

"I found out well *after* that. And how would Londra know about it?"

"Small town. Big on gossip."

"Maybe." I pushed the heel of my hand through my hair. "The whole thing doesn't make any sense. Plus, I have trouble wrapping my head around the fact she and Mel were involved. I mean, she seemed so nice and Mel was just . . . oh, I don't know, her total opposite. I know opposites are supposed to attract, but in that case . . ." I gave my head a brisk shake. "I can't figure it."

"Yet you have no problem with Feller and the mayor being involved." Gary threw up both hands. "You're impossible, Shell. You just won't let this go."

"I'm sorry, but no, I can't. Everyone said that Londra also hated Amelia because she kept passing her over for a docent position at the museum. Someone who wants to climb the ladder wouldn't endanger her career chances by signing for a shipment and then taking knives she never planned to return, let alone take their own life. It would have been too easy for her to get caught."

"Maybe she thought she'd put the knives back before anyone noticed they were missing. Maybe her plan backfired, and Feller wanted to keep the knives, persuaded her not to return them."

"I doubt that. For one thing, if he loved her, he wouldn't want her to get in trouble, and for another, I still don't think they were a couple."

Gary walked over to me, leaned over, put both hands on my shoulders and gave me a hard shake. "Snap out of it," he said. "I thought you liked that guy?"

"I do," I said miserably.

"You could have fooled me. After all, Shell—"

The rest of his sentence was cut off by a loud *thunk!* from the hallway. I froze. "The bust," I cried. We hurried out, and both of us gasped as we saw Edgar Allan and the Raven, lying on its side on the floor.

"How did that fall?" Gary asked. He pointed to the low table I'd set the bust on. "That was square in the center, I know it was. Good thing it fell on the rug. It doesn't look chipped."

I glanced over at the staircase. Kahlua sat on the top step. She raised her paw, pointed to the back of the bust. I shifted my gaze, saw a blur of white move. "I have an idea," I said.

Purrday peeped around the corner of the bust.

Gary stared, then burst out laughing. "Oh, man. The cat knocked it over? He's pretty strong."

I went over and stood over Purrday, my hands fisted on my hips. "What do you have to say for yourself, young man?" I asked the cat. "What's the fascination with Mr. Poe?"

Purrday let out a loud yowl, then lifted his paw and started clawing at Edgar's neck.

"Purrday," I admonished the cat, stooping to grab him. "Stop that. You'll get scratches on it."

The cat let out another sound, somewhere between a howl and a hiss, that had me backing off. Then he lifted his paw and smacked Edgar full across the neck. The bust rolled a few inches and stopped right at my feet.

"Bad boy!" I said, shaking my finger at Purrday.

"Ow-orr," said Kahlua from her perch on the top step. She seemed to be enjoying her brother's plight. Of course she was. She'd given him up, hadn't she?

Purrday merely swished his tail, hopped up on the table, and sat straight, his blue eye trained on me. "Merow," he yowled.

"Say, look here." Gary had dropped to his knees next to the bust. "Purrday did break old Edgar after all."

I followed Gary's pointing finger and saw a portion of Edgar's neck had separated from the rest of the bust. I kneeled as well to examine the damage. Curiously, the cracks were straight lines.

"It's not broken," I said. "It looks as if whoever made the bust put a hidden compartment in it."

"Clever," said Gary. "Like a hiding place for valuables. And it seems as if your cat's taken full advantage of it." He pointed to the cavity and I could see the tail end of Purrday's catnip mouse protruding. Gary reached inside the cavity and pulled out the mouse, two soft balls, and the wooden button.

Purrday jumped off the table and walked over to Gary, his tail erect. He lifted one paw and pointed to the hand that held the button. "Merow."

Gary dropped the button in front of the cat. "Picking the button over the mouse? That's a switch."

"Not really. The button might still have my aunt's scent on it," I said. I looked at Purrday. "You still miss Aunt Tillie, don't you? I do too. I bet she'd agree with me on this case, too." I rolled my eyes heavenward. "Aunt Matilda, if you agree with me, give me a sign."

"Oh, geez." Gary started to laugh, then stopped abruptly as Purrday started to push the button in my direction. From where we were standing, the initial carved into it looked more like an M than a W.

"M," I said triumphantly, bending down to take the button out of Purrday's claws. "It seems to be the initial du jour of this case. M stands for murder . . . mayor . . . museum . . ."

"Matilda," said Gary practically as he pushed the compartment back into place and set the bust back on the table. "Your aunt had double-duty initials. MW. Matilda Washburn. It's a practical button, just like your aunt was a practical woman."

"Exactly the reason why she would have agreed with me," I said, bending down to give Purrday a pat on the head, and his button back. "Take this and stop hitting poor Poe." My head was swimming with information. I couldn't help but feel all the pieces of this jigsaw puzzle were there, I just had to put them into place. But where to start?

I turned to Gary. "Did you get that fax from the specialty shop yet?"

"Nope. Why?"

"Can you contact them and ask them to fax over both bills of lading—the original marked complete as well as the amended?"

"Sure," he said in a puzzled tone, "but why?"

"Just do it, please. I've got a hunch."

He shook his head and started back toward the den again. I sat down on one of the stools, my thoughts whirling. It was just a hunch, but a good one, I thought. And if I was right . . .

I flicked my iPhone back into call mode and scrolled down to Secondhand Sue's number. A few minutes later I had the assistant manager, Iris, on the line.

"Hi, Ms. McMillan. Don't worry, Sue's holding that table for you."

"Great. I'll be down in a day or two to pay for it, and then I need it delivered to Urban Tails. By the way, is Sue there? Could I speak with her?"

"She went to the city on a buying trip for a few days. Can I take a message, or help you?"

I explained what I wanted. Iris didn't know offhand, but she promised to have Sue get back to me as soon as she could. I had to be content with that and rang off. I leaned against the kitchen counter, tapping my iPhone against my chin. The pieces were falling into place now.

Gary came back a few minutes later. "Okay, those papers should be here within the hour. Care to share your brainstorm slash epiphany with me?"

"Not yet. Still too many ifs."

He studied me closely. "But you're onto something, aren't you?"

"Maybe. I can't be positive until I see that first bill of lading." I pushed the heel of my hand through my hair and took a long breath. I had a feeling I knew who the real murderer was.

But I had no idea in hell how to prove it.

Twenty-seven

While Gary worked on a leak in the sink in the upstairs bathroom (hey, I didn't force him—he offered), I called the newspaper office and inquired about the price of placing an ad. As it turned out, there wasn't a heck of a lot of difference between a quarter-page ad and a half, but there was a substantial jump between a half and a full-page one. Seventy-two hours' notice was required if you didn't have your own artwork, forty-eight if you did. I thought I could handle that.

With Gary still busy being Mr. Handyman, I got in my convertible and drove over to Sweet Perks. Olivia, Rita, and Ron were huddled at a table in the back when I entered. Olivia waved to me, and I got a mocha latte from Rita's niece and then made my way over to the table. Rita jumped up almost immediately to give me a hug.

"Oh, Shell! It's so terrible, isn't it? To think Londra would kill Amelia and then herself, why, I just can't believe it."

"Neither can I," I said. Rita released me from her grip. I set my latte—which, thankfully, had not spilled—down on the table and settled myself next to Olivia. "But as Josh says, the evidence *appears* to point that way."

"*Appears?* It's not a done deal?"

I froze at the voice behind me and turned slowly to face Quentin Watson. I arched a brow at him. "Are you following me?"

"And good morning to you, too." He bowed to the others at the table and then turned his attention back to me. "Am I to understand the investigation into Ms. Lewis's death is still ongoing? I thought, what with the suicide slash dying confession, both cases were pretty much wrapped up."

"It would *appear* so," I replied.

Quentin frowned. "Why do you keep saying it like that?"

I shrugged. "No particular reason. As you know, I'm not a detective or a trained investigator, I just played one on TV. If you have questions, I suggest you contact Detective Bloodgood."

His lip quirked. "I should think you'd be happy with the outcome, Shell. Your name's cleared, and now you can reopen your aunt's store."

I shrugged and turned away, but the newsman wasn't about to be put off so easily. He pulled a chair over from the empty table across from ours, pushed it next to mine, and straddled it. "Listen," he said, his finger jabbing the air, "you owe me. I tipped you in that direction, didn't I?"

"As I recall, you were pushing me to interrogate Melvin Feller."

"And you did, didn't you? How'd that go?"

"About as well as I expected it would." I took a sip of my latte and looked at him over the rim of the paper cup. "I got a definite sense that the Fox Hollow gossip chain might have slipped up."

"Meaning?"

"Meaning I'm not buying Londra and Melvin as a couple of star-crossed lovers."

Quentin's brow furrowed, giving him the appearance of an angry beaver. He tapped at his chin with his forefinger. "You think Londra was, what? A cover for his real affair?"

"Maybe. I don't know anything for certain."

He leaned a bit closer. "I hear she committed suicide by peanuts."

"Yeah, and that's another thing. Melvin had no clue she was allergic. I would think if they were as close as everyone thought, he'd have had a clue." And then, because I just couldn't resist it, I added, "Off the record, I don't think Josh entirely bought it either."

Quentin pounced on my words, just as I knew he would. "Are you trying to tell me," he said, his tone grating, "that the authorities don't believe Londra Lewis killed either herself or Amelia Witherspoon? That the murderer is still at large?"

His tone had risen. I saw several heads at nearby tables turn in our direction, and was surprised to see the museum board at one of them: Mazie Madison, Ginnifer Rubin, Andy McHardy, Larry Peabody, Garrett Knute . . . and, yes, Mayor Carolyn Hart. All their eyes were popping, especially the mayor's.

I dropped my own voice and said to him, "This is hardly the place to discuss this. I'm sure once Josh Bloodgood has all the facts straight, he'll be glad to make a statement."

Quentin, however, wasn't accepting my dismissal with good grace. "What facts?" he asked. "Is there something the police found at the murder scene that hasn't been made public yet?"

I forced a light laugh. "You know very well the police never reveal everything to the public."

Josh chose that moment to walk in the front door of Sweet Perks. He had on black slacks and a black jacket, a white dress shirt, and a black-and-white-striped tie. His hair was slightly damp, as if just from the shower, and his eyes were flat and cold as they scanned the room, then warmed slightly as his gaze rested on me. He moved toward us and I thought Quentin Watson might leave, but he only scooted farther down in the chair, his gaze firmly fixed on Josh.

"Detective Bloodgood," he said before Josh could greet us. "What's all this about an ongoing investigation? I thought Londra's unfortunate suicide resolved Amelia's murder?"

Josh's lips thinned. "Don't worry, Watson, the case is almost closed. Just a few loose threads to tie together."

"What's to tie together?" His voice started to rise again. "What, a signed confession isn't enough these days? Are you planning on holding a séance, calling up Londra's spirit to get a formal confession?"

Mazie left her seat and walked swiftly toward us. The expression on her face was stony, to say the least. "Mr. Watson," she said, in a tone that I'd heard last from my third-grade teacher, "if you can't speak well of the dead, please do not speak of them at all. Crishell and Detective Bloodgood are right. This isn't the place to talk about this."

Quentin didn't seem intimidated by Mazie's manner in the least, but he did push back his chair and stand up, albeit somewhat reluctantly. He looked Mazie straight in the eye, which was easy for him to do, seeing as they were both the same height. "It's a sad day, madam," he said, "when the police cannot even close a simple case of murder. The lead detective here"—he indicated Josh with a sweep of his arm—"says there are still loose ends to tie up. I ask you, how can there be loose ends when there is a confession, a note, irrefutable evidence?"

Mazie's gaze slid to Josh. "Is that true, Detective? I mean, I thought the case was closed."

"Not yet, ma'am. There are still a few details. But I expect it'll be marked closed within twenty-four hours."

"That long? It should already be closed," spat Quentin.

Mazie reached out and touched Josh's arm. "Please understand,

Detective. This has all been greatly upsetting to us on the board. The museum was her whole life. They're just acclimating themselves to what happened and now you say it's not resolved?"

Josh nodded curtly. "There are a few issues that have to be dealt with."

Mazie frowned. "Are you saying there's a chance that Londra didn't murder Amelia? That she was an innocent victim?"

"I really can't comment on anything right now, Ms. Madison. All I can tell you is I expect to have everything resolved shortly."

Mazie's eyes flashed, and for a moment I thought she was going to argue further, but then she shrugged. "If you say so, Detective," she said. She turned on her heel and walked back to her table. She sat down and immediately everyone at the table leaned in their heads and converged on her.

I turned my attention away from them and back to Josh. "Want to sit with us?"

He shook his head. "No, thanks. I'm on my way to the next town to consult with the lieutenant there on one of their cases. I meant what I told Mazie, though—this one should be wrapped up very, very soon."

He gave my hand a quick squeeze, then walked away. I looked after him for a long moment, and then realized Quentin Watson was still standing there.

I gave him a thin smile and raised two fingers. "Twenty-four hours," I said.

"I'll be counting the minutes," Quentin sneered, then turned on his heel and walked away.

Olivia leaned toward me. "Cheery soul. What bug got up his butt?"

"He's just annoyed because he thinks he gave me a lead and I know more than I'm telling," I replied.

Olivia studied my face a moment. "Do you? Know more than you're telling?"

I picked up my latte and took another sip. "I guess we'll just have to wait and see," I said mysteriously.

The front door opened again and Mel Feller shuffled in, wearing the same slacks and jacket I'd seen him in yesterday. My, my, it seemed I'd picked the right spot for a bit of surveillance, at least.

Rita leaned over and said, "Look at Mel. He looks as if he hasn't slept for days."

"Late night at the casino," I said dryly. "I still can't picture him and Londra as lovers."

"Well, who then?" demanded Olivia. "What other woman at the museum? Not Dolly Fitch. She's a hundred if she's a day."

I inclined my head toward the museum board's table. "How about the mayor?"

They all looked at me, and then Ron burst out laughing. "Carolyn? And Mel? You're kidding!"

"Actually, I'm not. When Gary and I went by Mel's place the first time yesterday, his neighbor described Mel's 'friend.' The description fit Carolyn Hart."

"The neighbor had to be mistaken," Rita said firmly. "Carolyn Hart wouldn't get within six inches of Mel."

"She might have to."

I sighed. Quentin had returned and was standing behind me again. I glanced over my shoulder. "And why is that?"

"Because, Mel is Amelia's replacement. They voted him in this morning." He grinned as my jaw dropped, and then added, "They also voted to display your aunt's collection, but don't let on you know. You didn't hear it from me."

• • •

After I left Sweet Perks, I ambled over to Secondhand Sue's. I knew Sue wasn't back from New York yet, but Iris was behind the counter.

"Hey, Iris," I said as I approached the counter. "I've got the check for that table."

"Great. Kyle can bring it over next week." She took my check and reached for the receipt pad. "I talked to Sue last night. She said that bust was one of three from the Pierre School of Art in the city. There were three total. The one of Poe that you bought and two others: Shakespeare and Thomas Edison."

"Great. Can I ask another favor? Will you be speaking to Sue today? Can you ask her who bought the other busts?"

"I might be able to tell you that," Iris offered. "Let me check the sales ledger in the back." She vanished through a curtained alcove and returned a minute later bearing a large black ledger, which she set in front of me. "The one of Edison was purchased by the Edison Library in Edison, New Jersey. Appropriate, right? And Shakespeare . . ." She ran her finger down the list of items, flipped a few pages and then said triumphantly, "Here it is. It was bought by the Fox Hollow Museum for their library." She glanced at me. "Does that help?"

"It certainly does. You wouldn't have a copy of the bill of sale for that Shakespeare bust, would you?"

"I'd assume so. Let me check."

She returned in a few minutes and laid a receipt on the table. "Is this what you wanted? Mazie Madison signed for it."

I looked at the signature and then pointed to the M in Madison. "She might have ordered it, but Londra accepted the order. See that little mark?"

Iris squinted at where my finger pointed. "Barely."

"Londra told me that's how she could tell what she signed for and what Mazie signed for—" I broke off as an image appeared in my mind's eye. "Checkmarks," I murmured. "Of course."

Iris looked at me. "Are you okay, Ms. McMillan? You look a little flushed."

"I'm fine," I said, grabbing my purse. "Iris, can you do me a favor? Can you send a copy of that receipt to my fax at home? I think you've got the number."

"Sure, but why—"

But I was already running out the door. Out on the street I paused and called up the Photo app on my iPhone. When I saw what I wanted was there, I squared my shoulders.

I had another stop to make.

• • •

The cats greeted me at the door with loud meows when I got home. I bent over to give each of them a scratch. "What's the matter, kids? Gary not treating you right?"

I followed them into the kitchen and saw the problem right away. Both food bowls were empty. "Figures," I said. I got two cans of Fancy Feast tuna out of the cupboard and spooned it into their bowls. They were slurping away when Gary came in a few minutes later. I took one look at him and cried, "Yow! You look disgusting."

He looked down at his dirty shorts and T-shirt, grimy hands, and said, "Can't do home repair without getting down and dirty."

"Is it fixed?"

"It doesn't leak anymore, if that's what you mean." He moved over to the sink, squirted soap on his hands, and started to wash them. "Say, is that fresh coffee I smell?"

I chuckled. "That's a hint, right?" I picked up the coffee maker and pulled a can of coffee out of the top cabinet. "I guess it's the least I can do."

"It was nothing. Just consider it partial payment for the food and board—mostly the board." He finished washing his hands and reached for a towel to dry them. "What have you been up to?"

"Oh, nothing much." I put the coffee on and pulled out a stool to sit on. "I, ah, just ran a few errands. Fended off Quentin Watson at Sweet Perks."

"Yeah, Olivia told me."

I wiggled my eyebrow. "Olivia calls you at home, eh? Something you want to tell me?"

He waved his hand. "She was really calling you. I just answered the phone. She thought you'd be home already." He gave me an expectant look.

I felt a bit guilty not sharing my findings with Gary, but the truth of it was, I still wasn't entirely certain I was right. My theory was just that right now—a theory, even though I had an idea on how to find out if it was correct or not. "I told you I had some errands to run," I said lightly. "What's up?"

"There's a theater in town that shows old films. She wanted to invite us to a Jimmy Stewart double feature tonight. It's two of your favorites, *Vertigo* and *The Man Who Knew Too Much.*"

I smiled faintly at the *Vertigo* reference. And while I loved Jimmy Stewart dearly, I had other plans for tonight. I didn't want Gary tagging along, though, so I just gave a big smile and said, "Great. What time?"

"Starts at eight. I said we'd pick her up at quarter of. We can go somewhere for a late supper afterward. Okay?"

"Like I said, sounds great," I said, even though I knew darn well I wouldn't be joining him or Olivia tonight.

No, with any degree of luck, right around the time they'd be watching Jimmy Stewart rescue Kim Novak from drowning, I'd be breaking into the museum, trying to get the last bit of evidence that would close the case once and for all.

The murder weapon.

Twenty-eight

"So, how do I look, kids? Like a second-story man—or should I say woman?"

I paraded before the cats in my bedroom dressed in black jeans, socks, sneakers, and black turtleneck. I even had black gloves I planned to put on later. A short black jacket over all, and then I wound my blonde hair into a tight bun on top of my head and pulled a black cap over it to complete the look.

Kahlua looked me up and down, then made a mewling sound and dove under the bed. Purrday studied me a minute, then hopped off the bed and wound himself around my ankles, getting a smattering of white fur on my jeans.

"No, no, Purce," I said, brushing at the hair. "Can't have any white showing. I've got to blend into the shadows, remember?"

Purrday let out a loud meow as if to say *now you're going a bit too far, human.*

I wiggled my finger at the cat. "It's a good thing that I broke into the British Embassy in Episode 111 of *Spy Anyone.* I'll need those skills tonight."

Purrday cocked his head at me and let out a soft sound that sounded almost like a bleat—or a whine. Like he was trying to persuade me to give up this cockamamie idea, call Josh, and let the authorities handle it.

"I would, but what if I'm wrong? I don't want to look foolish in front of Josh. I've done that enough already. I don't want to involve Gary or Olivia either. After all, if I'm wrong, and I get caught—well, I'll be in a bit of hot water. But if I can find the murder weapon that will prove Londra's innocence and bring her and Amelia's murderer to justice, taking this little risk will be worth it."

Purrday's eye flashed, and his tail did a rapid thump-thump-thump against the comforter.

"I know I've got all these other pieces of evidence, but they could be cleverly explained away, and our murderer is nothing if not clever. The actual murder weapon, though, would be tough to challenge." I gave my jacket a tug and Purrday a swift pat on the head. "Wish me luck, Purrday. You too, Kahlua."

Purrday threw back his head. "Me-oooooow!" he warbled. From the depths underneath my bed, I heard a similar wail from my Siamese.

It sounded more like a warning than a good luck wish. But I was determined to see this through.

• • •

The museum was dark when I pulled into the parking lot. I parked my convertible at the farthest end—not far from where Londra's Cadillac still sat—pulled on my black gloves, and exited the car. I tiptoed stealthily through the lot, making sure to keep to the edges by the shrubbery. I melded into the shadows around the building and glided to the rear service entrance, where I removed my credit card from my back pocket. A pick and a tension wrench would probably have worked much better, but I didn't have time to order them off the internet and I didn't want to go into the local hardware store to purchase them. I'd have to settle for the poor man's method and hope it worked like it had on my show.

I knelt and slid the long end of my AmEx Prepaid Card in between the doorframe and the locking side of the door, just as I'd seen on the YouTube instructional video I'd watched earlier to refresh my memory. I angled the card downward, making sure it was perpendicular to the door. Then, saying a quick prayer the door didn't have a dead bolt set, I slowly but firmly pulled the card toward me while turning the door handle. I held my breath until I heard a sharp click, and then I gave the door handle a twist. It swung inward, and I sent up a quick thank-you as I shoved my AmEx back into my pocket and entered the darkened museum.

I waited a few seconds, letting my eyes adjust, and then pulled out the pencil flashlight I'd brought and switched it on. The tiny beam of light cut through the inky black—not a whole lot, but enough that I could see where I was going. I squared my shoulders and headed straight down the corridor, to the library where I'd found Amelia's body. The door was closed, and I said another quick prayer that it wasn't locked. I didn't think I could get lucky enough to actually pick two locks in one evening. I twisted the knob and the door opened silently. I shone my light around, finally settling it on the object of my search: the bust of William Shakespeare Amelia's body had been stretched beneath.

I walked over to the bust and shone my flashlight on it, paying particular attention to the neck area. Of course, my theory wasn't a hundred percent. There was a chance that I could be wrong, but I fervently hoped not. With my limited light, though, it was hard to see, and for a minute I considered going for the light switch. I ran my fingers along Shakespeare's collarbone. Drat. Nothing.

"Oh, come on," I grumbled. "If you were all made at the same school, it stands to reason you might all have a secret cavity—my theory depends on it." I pressed down a little harder, thinking that if Purrday were here, he'd have found it for me. And then my fingers hit a slightly raised portion of marble. I bit back an excited cry and set the flashlight on the stool, positioning it so the light shone on the spot where my fingers lay. I pressed down hard, as I'd seen Purrday do with Edgar Allan, and the small section of marble moved, revealing a small cavity like the one in my own bust. I reached into my pocket for the baggie I'd brought as my fingers touched something hard and sharp inside the cavity. Carefully, very carefully, I pulled out the object wedged in there and held it up.

In the pale light from the flashlight, the Tuareg knife appeared more sinister than ever. Streaks of red covered the jagged edges of the blade. It had to be Amelia's blood. I held the knife very carefully by the end of the handle and dropped it into the baggie. I reached for the flashlight at the same instant I heard a soft click and the lights in the room went on, illuminating me in their glare.

"It seems we both had the same activity in mind for tonight. I'll take that, Crishell," said Mazie Madison. She was dressed almost identically to me, except her sneakers were white. She pointed with the toe of said sneaker. "Drop it right here," she said, leveling the revolver she held at my chest.

The blood pounded in my ears as I stared into Mazie's eyes, eyes that looked a little bit wild and a lot crazy. Slowly, I set the baggie containing the knife down and kicked it toward her. It skidded across the polished floor. Mazie thrust out her foot and stopped it, then bent down to pick it up.

Eyes still glittering, she faced me. "Great minds think alike. Once I heard that conversation this morning, I knew I had to get rid of this once and for all. I see you had the same thought."

"I wasn't sure what I'd find," I said. "I wasn't positive Shakespeare had a hidden cavity like my Poe bust, but once I confirmed they came from the same maker, I thought the chances were pretty good."

She waved the gun at me, indicating a nearby chair. I sank into it. "Hands where I can see them," she barked. I placed both on top of the desk, and she gave a satisfied nod. "I am curious, though. How on earth did you ever figure it out?" Another high-pitched laugh tittered out of her. "If I do say so myself, I'm a pretty darn good actress. Maybe as good as you, or better."

That I had to agree with. "You certainly are," I said. "And to tell you the truth, up until a little bit ago I wasn't entirely certain if it was you or Mayor Hart."

"Carolyn?" She wrinkled her nose. "Why on earth—? Oh, never mind." She waved her hand. "What convinced you?"

"Mel Feller's neighbor. I took your picture with my iPhone at Sweet Perks this morning and I went over there to see if she could identify you as the lady friend she told me about. She made a positive identification."

"So." Mazie's lips twisted into a sneer. "You figured out that I was the woman from the museum Mel was having the affair with."

"Londra respected you a great deal," I said. "So much so that she was willing to let the rumors circulate about her and Mel to protect you. You were angry with Amelia, weren't you, for not supporting your nomination to have him put on the museum board."

"Oh, you bet I was," Mazie said with feeling. "I was plenty pissed over it. But if you think that's the reason I killed her, you're dead wrong."

"No, you killed Amelia because she threatened to reveal that you stole those knives to give to Mel. She figured it out the same way I did, I'm sure."

"Yeah? And what way was that?"

I leaned a bit forward in the chair. "That day I visited you at the museum after Amelia's murder, I spoke a bit with Londra. She told me that she did most of the signing, and she could sign your name as well as you could. She also told me her little secret about putting a small checkmark inside the M in Madison so she could tell what papers she'd signed and what ones you signed. I compared both bills of lading. They were both signed by you. Londra's distinctive checkmark was missing. That meant that Londra didn't unpack the shipment originally, as you'd said. You did."

Mazie's lips thinned. "I made the mistake of leaving the file on my desk. Amelia found it when she was snooping around, as she usually did on a Sunday, and she realized almost immediately what I'd done. She knew that habit of Londra's too. She threatened to have me charged with theft if I didn't get the knives back from Mel and return them. When I said I didn't care what happened to me as long as Mel was safe, she said that she could send him to prison as well." Mazie had the nerve to look affronted at the idea that Amelia would target Melvin Feller. "Apparently when he'd worked for Garrett, years ago, there was an incident with the museum funds, and Amelia had that evidence too. She used it to threaten Garrett as well. It was one thing for her to threaten me, but to threaten Mel . . . and then you came to town. Amelia was certain you would be against her, especially if you found out about her affair with your aunt's first love. She made sure the poster display was voted down, and when you started to raise such a stink about it, well . . ." She shrugged and smiled. "It was as if the universe was showing me a way out of my troubles. I wrote that note to Amelia, knowing how paranoid she was—and guilt-ridden, believe it or not. I knew she'd call you, and once she did, I surprised her in the office and slit her throat. Oh, the look on her face when she saw it was me! I thought that note and leaving the photo of the *Friday* poster in her hand was a nice touch to put the heat on you for a while."

I lifted my chin. "I arrived at the museum quicker than you anticipated, though."

Mazie's lips slashed into a thin line. "True. I had to get out fast, so I shoved the knife into the bust. I knew about the cavity, because Sue showed it to me before I bought the bust. I had an idea it might come in handy someday. I figured I'd have plenty of time to get the knife and dispose of it once all the hoopla about Amelia's death died down. Until today."

"And once Londra figured out you were responsible for Amelia's death, you decided to kill her, make it look like a suicide and frame her for Amelia's murder."

"It was like killing two birds with one stone, really. I knew she was allergic to peanuts, so I told her I wanted to talk. I was going to make restitution on the knives, turn myself in. Little fool believed me. She'd been going to call you, tip you off, so I had to act fast. I had a needle filled with peanut oil, I jabbed her in the back of the neck. Then I wrote the note and

221

sprinkled some shells around so it would be obvious she'd taken her own life. I knew the handwriting on the notes would match. What I didn't count on," she added with a baleful glare at me, "was you smelling a rat and complicating things by sticking your nose in. Really, Shell, you have no one to blame for your current predicament except yourself. If you'd just minded your own business, everything was tied up neat and tidy. Everyone would have been happy."

"And an innocent woman would be forever accused of a crime she didn't commit," I said. "How could you do that to someone you'd worked with for years, who was so loyal to you?"

"It wasn't easy," she admitted. "Neither was framing you. Believe it or not, I like you, Shell. But I couldn't let either Mel or myself go to prison. It's survival of the fittest."

Man, not only was she crazy, she was the worst type of crazy. A person who appeared totally sane on the outside. I decided to try a little more voice of reason. "Think about it, Mazie. Detective Bloodgood has the same concerns I had. It would be only a matter of time before you were exposed."

"By then, I would be far away from here," Mazie said. "I was planning to resign from the board next week. I'd already tapped Carolyn to take my place permanently, and the board was in full agreement."

"And Mel? How does he feel about you committing murder for him?"

She stood straight at that. "He doesn't know," she said in a choked tone. "And he can never know. He thought I bought the knife as a gift for him, and I didn't have the heart to take it back. I don't want him to think badly of me. That's why, unfortunately, you must die, Crishell. I am sorry. But without you to fuel the fires, interest in these deaths will wane."

I stared at her. She really believed that! "You're forgetting my friends. Gary and Olivia will know my death was no accident. Josh is already suspicious . . ."

"But not of me. You haven't shared your findings with your friends yet, have you?" She gave me a knowing glance. "Of course not. You're the type that likes to have all their ducks in a row before they commit. Isn't that what ruined your last relationship with that director? Oh, yes," she said at my startled look, "I read gossip magazines. No one would ever suspect me, not in a million years, once I destroy that file . . . and silence Mel's nosy neighbor, you know. Just in case."

Oh, Lord. She was all primed to commit more murders. How could she even think that would go unnoticed in such a small town? Olivia's assessment of her had been right: she was a coiled spring, ready to snap.

"Mazie," I said. "Don't do this."

"I was here, at the museum, going over some paperwork when I heard a sound. I grabbed the gun that we keep on hand and raced in here, to see you over the bust—trying to steal it—and I shot you in self-defense," she babbled, waving the gun in the air. "No court in the land would convict me, especially when I turn on the waterworks. My God, I killed Shell Marlowe! I didn't mean to! I'll be racked with guilt for days, weeks, I'll have to leave to get over it . . . and I can do it too."

"You'll never get away with this. You'll never make it stick."

She stared at me, and then barked out a laugh. "Why, Shell. Of course I will. Look at what I've gotten away with already. I'm an excellent actress, you know I am."

It all sounded crazy, but the deuce of it was, the woman was diabolical, and she *was* a damn good actress. Heck, she'd had me fooled up until a few hours ago. I had questioned the evidence, thought for sure I had to be wrong . . . now I was sorry, damn sorry, that I'd never shared my suspicions with Gary or with Josh.

She raised the gun and I shut my eyes, waiting for the shot. My heart was heavy with many regrets. I'd never see my mother again. I'd never get a chance to reopen the store I loved. I'd never see Gary or Olivia or Ron or Rita again. But most of all, I'd never get a chance to tell Josh how I felt . . .

"Drop the gun, Mazie. Right now."

My eyes flew open at the sound of another voice. Mazie whirled, and I saw my chance. I sprang up from behind the desk and grabbed the arm that held the gun, twisted it backward, and slammed it hard against the desk. Mazie let out a strangled cry, and the gun fell from her hand. I gave it a swift kick with my sneaker at the same instant I flung Mazie away from me. The gun slid across the floor and came to a dead stop at Josh's feet.

The moments that followed were a total blur—lights, sirens, men in blue uniforms swarming into the room. One man slipping his arm around my waist, catching me just as I thought for sure I'd crumple to the ground.

"Want to tell me just what the hell you thought you were doing?" Josh growled.

I threw myself against his chest and held on . . . tight. "Am I ever glad to see you, Detective Bloodgood," I gasped.

And then I dropped like a stone at his feet.

Twenty-nine

"The phone is ringing off the hook. You know, I think you've gotten more publicity over this than in ten years on our show."

It was the next morning. After my fainting spell, Josh had taken me straight to the emergency room, where I was released about two hours later into Gary and Olivia's waiting arms. They'd taken me straight home and put me to bed, but now I was up and feeling good, albeit a tad groggy, presumably from the medicine I'd gotten last night to help me sleep. Gary and Olivia both insisted on waiting on me, and truthfully, I wasn't in a mood to refuse it. I lay stretched out on the couch, a blanket over me, Purrday curled up comfortably at my feet.

"I doubt that," I said, reaching for the cup of java Olivia had brought in for me, along with the Spanish omelet Gary prepared. At first I hadn't thought I could eat a bite, but—what do you know—almost being killed made me ravenous. I pushed the tray out of the way, momentarily dislodging Purrday from his post sprawled across my ankles, and reached for the paper Gary held out to me:

Museum Director Arrested for Double Murder.
Actress Finds Murder Weapon, is Almost a Victim Herself

I scanned the article quickly, then shook my head. "Was Quentin Watson outside the emergency room when I was telling Josh what happened?"

"I think he bribed one of the nurses to recount it, actually." Olivia chuckled. "That man will do anything for a story."

I leaned back against the pillows. "You know, Josh never told me how he knew to go to the museum."

Gary picked up the paper I'd dropped and lay it on the coffee table before settling into one of the wing chairs. "For that, you should thank the Fox Hollow theater team—and Purrday." At my inquiring look, he went on, "Olivia and I went to the movie, but the film broke halfway through and they couldn't fix it. We decided to come back here, and it was a good thing we did."

"Purrday went wild when he saw us," Olivia said. She reached behind her and lifted up a garbage pail. "He'd managed to shred all those faxes you got from the store, showing the discrepancies in the bills of lading. Then he knocked the bust over again, and Gary found your phone hidden in the cavity."

I turned my gaze full on the cat and shook my finger at him. "Purrday! You stole my phone! Bad cat!"

"No, good cat, because when I turned it on we saw the picture you'd taken of Mazie, and there was a text from Mrs. Miller saying that she'd thought it over and she *would* swear in court that Mazie Madison was the woman she'd seen Feller hanging around with," Gary said. "It didn't take much to figure out what your earlier errand had been. I called Josh, who had pretty much reached the same conclusions, and when his sister told him what you asked about the busts, he called out the troops and got over to the museum. Just in time too, I might add."

"I have to take some of the responsibility," I admitted. "I honestly didn't think that Mazie would make a run for the murder weapon that fast. I figured she was biding her time till all the furor died down. I guess overhearing that conversation with Quentin this morning at Sweet Perks made her think she'd better get her rear in gear and get rid of the most damning evidence: the murder weapon. In my defense, though, I was still a bit torn between her and Mayor Hart as the killer. After all, the mayor did go to the museum a lot. She would have had the same opportunities as Mazie."

"Except the mayor really had no motive, and once we figured out Mazie was Mel's secret lover, all the pieces fell into place," Gary said.

The doorbell rang. Olivia jumped up at once and vanished into the foyer, returning a few minutes later with Josh. He had on jeans and a crisp white shirt, and a bouquet of beautiful flowers clasped in one hand.

"I think I'll make some more coffee," sang out Olivia. She gave Gary a swift poke in the ribs. "I need some help."

"You do?" At her look, he nodded and gave me a wide grin. "Oh, yeah. You do. We'll be back soon, Shell, but don't worry, not too soon."

They vanished into the kitchen and I motioned for Josh to sit down. "Pay them no mind," I said. "They're just a little tired."

Josh set the flowers on the coffee table. "And how are you feeling?"

"A little bit foolish, but otherwise fine."

He crossed his arms over his chest and gave me a stern look. "That certainly was foolish of you, to go off like that without notifying anyone."

"I know, but I wasn't thinking. Once I found out about the busts, and Mrs. Miller made that ID, I knew where the murder weapon had to be, and the only thing I could think of was getting to it before the killer had a chance to get rid of it." I shot him a sheepish grin. "Next time I'll be more careful."

Both his eyebrows rose. "Next time? Don't tell me you're thinking of joining the detective squad now?"

"Oh, heck no," I said quickly. "I've got lots to keep me busy. See!" I flipped through the paper until I came to the advertisement section. I pointed to the half-page ad at the top:

Grand Reopening. Urban Tails Pet Shop.
Let Us Cater to All Your Pet Needs.

Josh's eyes twinkled. "So it's definite."

I nodded. "I found the original artwork for the very first sign in my aunt's files, so I put it in right before my little break-in. I figured one way or the other, I'd waited long enough. I've even hired live entertainment. One of the acts is a fortune-telling parrot."

Josh burst out laughing. "That's different."

I beamed. "I can't wait. It's going to be a gala, all-day affair. I think after all this, it's just what the doctor ordered."

Josh rubbed at his chin. "I can see I'm going to have to take the day off. No doubt Sue will want to go, and she'll need me to mind Secondhand Sue's."

"No doubt. I do hope you'll find time to stop by, though. There will be human entertainment too, and raffles, and prizes, and refreshments . . ."

He held up his hand. "You don't have to sell me on the idea. I'll definitely find time to stop by. I always did like that store." He paused. "Your friend Gary. Will he be helping you with the business?"

"Gary?" I rolled my eyes. "Lord, no. Gary behind a counter? That would surely be a recipe for disaster. He'd probably give the entire store away, when he wasn't regaling customers with stories about show business, that is. He did volunteer to help me with the technical end, redoing the store's website, though. And interviewing clerks."

"Okay then. Sounds like you've got everything well under control." Josh rose. "I should go and let you get your rest. I just wanted to stop by and make sure you were all right."

Purrday and Kahlua both looked up at Josh. "Merow," they said in unison.

Josh wiggled one eyebrow. "I see you're in good hands here. And I don't mean Gary's."

Purrday and Kahlua both jumped up on the couch, one on either side of me. I chuckled. "I think you mean I'm in good paws. I definitely agree."

Josh turned toward the door, abruptly whirled back to face me. "I hear the theater got that film of *Vertigo* fixed, so if you're up to it tomorrow night, maybe we could take it in, get a light supper afterward?"

I smiled at him. "That sounds nice."

"Good." He hesitated, then leaned over, brushed my cheek lightly with his lips. "I'll call you tomorrow. Take care, Shell."

I couldn't contain the goofy grin that stretched from ear to ear long after Josh had shut the door behind him. Kahlua snuggled into my hip, closed both eyes. A few minutes later I heard her light snoring. I glanced over at Purrday, who was watching me intently with his good eye.

"What do you think, Purrday?" I asked the cat. "It's a date, right? Blink if you think it's a date."

Purrday blinked his good eye.

"Aha, I knew it."

Then he blinked again.

"What?"

And yet again.

I shook my finger at him. "You're messing with my head, aren't you?"

He lifted his chin. "Merow."

Gary came back into the room and looked around. "Where's the good detective?"

"He left, but we're going to that Jimmy Stewart double feature tomorrow night."

Gary flopped onto the love seat. "Olivia and I may join you." As I turned to give him a death stare, he sank back into the cushions. "Or maybe not."

I chuckled. "Not that I haven't enjoyed your little visit, but when were you planning on heading back to LA? I'm sure Max is missing you."

"I did promise to help you out, remember? Redesign your store website, interview potential employees."

"I know, and I appreciate it, but I guess I feel guilty. I feel like I'm keeping you from going back."

He was silent for several seconds, then he stretched his long legs out in front of him and laced his hands behind his neck. "Well, that's the thing. LA is going to have to miss me a while longer, I'm afraid."

I narrowed my eyes at him. "I'm sorry? What did you say?"

"I was going to wait until you were a little more recovered to tell you this, but I've enjoyed my stay here so much, I've decided to extend it a bit."

My eyes narrowed. "A bit?"

"Okay, for a while. Olivia has offered to help me find an apartment in town."

I swung my feet off the couch and stared at him. "You're kidding! Why on earth would you want to stay in Fox Hollow?"

"Why, to help you, of course."

"I don't need that much help. I just need a running start."

Gary scratched at his head. "Okay, you got me. I got to thinking you have the right idea about a quieter life. I'm thinking of starting my own business."

"Your own business?" Well, it could be worse. He could have wanted to work in my pet store. "Doing what exactly? Web designing? Plumbing?"

"Not exactly." He stood up and fanned his hands. "How does Gary Presser, PI sound?"

I shook my head. "Awful."

"Ah, you'll get used to it. It's only a thought. I haven't made a final decision yet." He leaned over and chucked me under the chin. "No matter what, though, just think of it, Shell. You and me together again. The bad guys don't stand a chance."

He meandered back in the direction of the kitchen. I looked at the cats. Kahlua was still sleeping. That cat could probably sleep through Armageddon. Purrday, however, was giving me his undivided attention. We'd see who got extra treats tonight.

"Well, fabulous. I've got to get Urban Tails up and running, Gary's sticking around to do God knows what, and I have a date with Josh. Looks like things are back to what passes for normal in my life. What do you say to that, Purrday?"

Purrday stared back at me for nearly a full second.

Then he closed his good eye in a slow, deliberate wink. Once.

Acknowledgments

I owe a ton of thanks to my fabulous agent, Josh Getzler, and his assistant, Jon Cobb, for always putting up with all my questions and concerns, many at six a.m.!. Thanks also to Bill Harris and the people at Beyond the Page, for breathing new life into Shell and company. Thanks also to furbabies Rocco and Maxx, and to the real Mel Feller and Londra Lewis for lending their names to characters in this story (neither are like those characters, they're nice people!). A shout-out to my mentor and friend, Carole Nelson Douglas, and to all the readers of Rocco's blog, Cats, Books and . . . More Cats, and to all the wonderful authors who have guested on the blog over the years. Last but not least, a shout-out to all my fans and to everyone who has bought and read my books. A writer cannot survive without readers, and I thank each and every one of you from the bottom of my heart.

About the Author

While Toni LoTempio does not commit—or solve—murders in real life, she has no trouble doing it on paper. Her lifelong love of mysteries began early on when she was introduced to her first Nancy Drew mystery at age ten—*The Secret in the Old Attic*. She and her cat pen the Urban Tails Pet Shop Mysteries, the Nick and Nora mystery series, and the new Cat Rescue series. Catch up with them at Rocco's blog, catsbooksmorecats.blogspot.com, or her website, tclotempio.net.